RAT RUN

Her Majesty's Secret Service agent Garrett, investigating a series of suicides by scientific researchers, discovers the parameters of a cataclysmic terrorist strike. The fanatical André Dur puts his unholy scenario into operation over the geological fault called the 'Rat Run', where nuclear submarines stalk each other in the dark depths. Helplessly the world looks on as the minutes tick away. Garrett's desperate mission is to neutralise Dur's deadly countdown — the ultimate ecological disaster, Chernobyl on the high seas.

FREDERICK NOLAN

RAT RUN

Complete and Unabridged

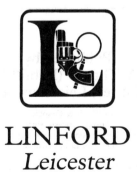

LINFORD
Leicester

First published in Great Britain

First Linford Edition
published 2008

British Library CIP Data

Nolan, Frederick W., *1931 –*
    Rat Run.—Large print ed.—
    Linford mystery library
    1. Suspense fiction
    2. Large type books
    I. Title
    823.9′14 [F]

    ISBN 978–1–84782–372–4

Gloucestershire County Council	

This is for Emma and Jody,
without whom
it would have been finished
some weeks earlier.

1

The telephone rang at 2 a.m.

Charles Garrett picked it up on the second ring, but Jessica was already awake. She shook her head, as much as to say, I knew this was too good to last.

'Charles?' It was the unmistakable voice of Nicholas Bleke. 'Is that you?'

'It's me.'

'Where the hell have you been? I've been trying to reach you all day.'

'I'm on vacation,' Garrett reminded him.

'Not any more. We've got an Alpha Black alert. Get down to Ben Gurion as fast as you can. I've got a private plane on standby, waiting to fly you to RAF Akrotiri in Cyprus. You'll be briefed on arrival.'

'What's happened?'

'Don't you even read the damned newspapers?' Bleke snapped, impatiently. 'We've got a hijack on our hands. British

Airways Tristar. The plane has landed at Larnaca.'

'Do we know who the hijackers are?'

'They call themselves Sons of Saddam. That's all we know.'

'I'll get moving,' Garrett said, and hung up. Jessica was watching him, immobile, silent. She knew who he had been talking to, of course. Who else?

'That man,' she said, a world of meaning in the two small words. 'I suppose this means the holiday is over?'

He told her what Bleke had just told him.

'I take back what I was thinking,' she said crisply. 'Get packed. I'll drive you down to Tel Aviv.'

2

Thursday, 6 April. The first faint pink fingers of sunlight were lightening the snowy peaks of the Troodos mountains when the hijackers broke radio silence.

'Tower, this is Emad. Come in please.'

The bleary-eyed radio operator looked at the wall clock. 6.57 a.m. Jesus, he thought, here we go again. He gestured to one of the policemen, who shook the foreign minister awake. The little man looked startled for a moment. He came across to the radio console, rubbing his eyes.

'This is Akis Stefanidos. We hear you.'

'Will you now do as you promised and refuel the plane?'

'We have no ground staff on duty this early in the morning,' Stefanidos said. Someone brought him a cup of coffee. He gulped it down gratefully, signalled for more.

'We have to refuel immediately. I don't

want to remind you that the plane is planted with high explosives.'

'Will any hostages be freed?'

'No passengers will be released.'

'We will try to arrange the refuelling. In the meantime, do you want us to send you food? Breakfast for the passengers? You will allow a small van to approach the aircraft?'

'Not yet. We will tell you when.'

Stefanidos turned to the group of advisers who had been watching him: Chris Tzianos, head of airport security, Colonel Nikolaos Kokotos from the Ministry of Defence, and Group Captain Robert Parker, security liaison officer from the Royal Air Force base at Akrotiri, one of the two major British bases on Cyprus. The other was the signals intelligence post at Dhekelia, a few miles north of the airport.

None of the group was looking at Stefanidos; they were all awaiting the reaction of the man who had arrived by private jet from Tel Aviv during the night to assume control of the hijack operation. The tall, powerfully built man dressed in a tan windbreaker, a navy-blue cotton polo-necked sweater, blue jeans and Nike running shoes told them his name was Charles Garrett, and that he was empowered on the highest level to act in any way he saw fit to ensure the safety of the Tristar and the passengers aboard it. He did not elaborate further.

Immediately on arrival he had been briefed on the situation by Foreign Minister Stefanidos. The Tristar — BA 032 from Manila and Kuala Lumpur — had been hijacked two hours after leaving Bombay. The terrorists, who called themselves Sons of Saddam, might be Iraqi or pro-Iraqi. The Ministry of Defence officer, Colonel Kokotos, said they had names for three of the hijackers — the leader, Emad Al-Din, Hassan Namar, and Sayeed Al-Nawar. The pilot, Captain Hector McLean, at forty-nine a BA veteran, had been told that plastic explosive had been stowed in the luggage hold.

The hijackers had intended to put down at Beirut, Garrett was told, but Lebanese air traffic control had shut

5

down its radar and direction-finding equipment, blacking out the entire airport so that the pilot had no choice but to fly on. With only an hour's fuel left, their Mayday call had been answered by Akrotiri. The plane had touched down at 22.28 local time and been directed to a parking slot on the northwest angle of the apron runway, eight hundred yards from the terminal building. From photographs taken during the landing, Kokotos said, it appeared the hijackers were armed with Walther MP-K 9mm sub-machine guns and Browning High Power 9mm Parabellum automatic pistols.

Garrett's next priority was to talk to the RAF officer who had been sent over from Akrotiri to liaise with the negotiating team. Group Captain Parker was in his early fifties, a strongly built man of medium height with the solid neck, arms and legs of a weightlifter.

'We haven't got a lot of time, Group Captain,' Garrett told him. 'First things first: I was told there'd be an SAS assault team on standby at the base. Is there?'

'Twelve men. Fully equipped.'

'Get them over here,' Garrett said. 'We may need some hardware ourselves.'

'No problem', Parker said, briskly. 'What do you have in mind?'

'I don't know. We'd better be ready for anything. Tell them to let us have three or four high-power limpet microphones, thermal imagers — what are you using these days?'

'Barr and Stroud IR18 Mark Two,' Parker replied. 'I'll get some Steadyscopes as well, shall I?'

The Steadyscope is a hand-held gyro-stabilized sight designed to be used in place of conventional binoculars, giving the user a steady picture unaffected by hand tremor or vehicle movement.

'Good idea,' Garrett said. 'We'd better have some night viewers as well. Can do?'

'We've got night vision adapters for the Steadyscopes,' Parker said, as he headed for the phone. 'Anything else?'

'Yes,' Garrett said. 'What I want most of all is some of those American smoke ball grenades, the ones made by Accuracy Systems in Arizona. Can you lay your hands on a supply?'

Parker frowned, but no explanation was forthcoming. 'I expect so,' he said with a shrug. 'How many do you think you'll need?'

'Get ten,' Garrett said. 'And don't stop to pick daisies.'

Parker nodded and hurried away. Garrett turned to the head of airport security, a tall slender man of about forty, with jet-black hair and eyes like black olives.

'Body armour,' he said. 'What have you got?'

'Anything you need,' Tzianos said. 'Vests, helmets, high-velocity shields . . . '

'How many fire tenders?'

'Fire tenders?'

'I want two brought around behind the terminal building. Full equipment for twelve firemen: uniforms, helmets, everything.'

Tzianos nodded. 'Okay, no problem.'

'Good,' Garrett said. 'All we have to do now is wait for our sleeping beauties to wake up.' He looked at the clock. 5.14 a.m. Parker was just putting the phone down.

'They'll have the stuff you want over here in fifteen minutes,' he said.

'Good,' Garrett said. 'One more thing: is there a freezer in here anywhere?'

Parker looked puzzled. 'What do you want a freezer for?'

'To make some ice cubes,' Garrett replied. 'I'll explain later. Is Dhekelia zeroed in?'

'Affirmative,' Parker said. 'They'll satellite-pickup anything the hijackers broadcast, anything anyone sends them.' His expression betrayed his thoughts. What the hell is he doing, thinking about ice cubes at a time like this? Garrett grinned.

'Right,' he said. 'Somebody get word to the local radio station. A complete news blackout. They'll be listening in on the plane. I don't want them to have any idea what's happening or how much publicity they're getting.'

The hijack was already world news, of course. Representatives of the Press and TV, herded away from the airport, were waiting for news in Larnaca. As yet the hijackers had made no demands. No one knew why they had taken the plane.

9

Everything was going to be managed very carefully, Garrett decided; it wasn't his job to provide journalists with copy.

'I'll arrange that.' The speaker was Stefanidos. 'Leave it to me.'

'Tower, this is Captain McLean.' The sudden crackle of the pilot's voice startled everyone. The air in the control tower became electric with tension. Garrett looked at the clock: 8.17. He leaned forward, listening intently. It was not difficult to detect the tremor in McLean's voice.

'Go ahead, Captain,' the controller said.

'I have to inform you that the hijackers are starting to threaten the passengers. They say that unless the plane is refuelled within the hour, there will be a punishment.'

'I will report it at once, Captain.' The controller looked at Garrett. Garrett pointed at the foreign minister, who went over to the console.

'Tango Juliet hijackers, this is Stefanidos. We are making every effort to comply with your request. We will do our very best.'

'One hour and no more,' came the flat reply. It was the voice of Emad Al-Din. 'It is our intention to destinate Libya, the concerned country. Cyprus has one hour interval to refuel this plane and top up engine lubricants also. Otherwise we will read that Cyprus has decided to be a party against us.'

'I repeat, we will do our best to accommodate you,' Stefanidos said, his tone urgent. 'You must understand that we have only limited facilities here at Larnaca. It will take time for these supplies to be tankered over from the military airfield.'

'We call upon our brothers in the struggle against British and American aggression to assist us. To the world outside, we say, free our brothers imprisoned without trial, their rights usurped by the puppets of American and British imperialism. All we ask is that Cyprus government behaves as an independent country, and prevent a slow massacre taking place here on your island.'

'We understand,' Stefanidos said. 'Now

I will read you an official statement prepared by the government of Cyprus. 'Threats will not help your cause and will work against our efforts to help you. We hope you will reconsider your attitude and release the passengers and we can assure you that every assistance will be given.' '

'We hear your message,' they heard Emad snarl. 'Now you hear ours. If these tanks are not one hundred per cent full by 10 a.m., we are going to begin to kill the passengers. One every fifteen minutes. Is that understood?'

'You mean one hour and thirty-three minutes from now, correct?'

'You heard us. There will be no further dialogue.'

Stefanidos stepped away from the microphone; the controller checked to make sure the switches were in the 'off' position, then nodded to Garrett.

'What's your estimate, Mr Stefanidos?' he asked. 'How long do you think we can stall them?'

The older man shook his head. 'I cannot say,' he said wearily.

'Then we don't have a choice,' Garrett said. He turned to Group Captain Parker. 'Go to green. Get the SAS squad kitted out in the firemen's uniforms. I want them on those fire tenders and ready to move when I give the word.'

Parker nodded and hurried away. Garrett turned to Colonel Kokotos, the officer representing the Ministry of Defence. 'Colonel, how many men do you have here at the airport?'

'Two officers, ten men.'

'Kit them all out. Body armour, small arms. I want them on full alert when I come back in.'

'What are you planning to do?' Kokotos asked, a worried frown on his face.

'I'm going to get those people off,' Garrett said. 'That's why I want your men out there on the tarmac. They've got to get them out of harm's way the minute their feet touch the ground.'

'You plan to storm the plane?'

'If all else fails, yes.'

'This is madness!' Kokotos snapped. 'There are explosives on board! What if these men blow up the plane?'

'I'll have made a mistake,' Garrett said.

'Madness,' Kokotos said again. He looked at the others as if seeking their agreement. 'Madness. I protest most strongly.'

'I note your protest, Colonel,' Garrett told him, turning away. 'Somebody get me a white coat of some kind. I'll take the food out to the plane now. How many people on board?'

'Fifteen crew, a hundred and seventy-two passengers. And seven Sons of Saddam.'

'Armed with Browning automatic pistols and Walther submachine guns, right? And explosives?'

'They probably smuggled explosives aboard at Manila, but we can't be sure. What we can be sure of is that they took whatever they thought they might need aboard with them.'

'Seven of them, you said.'

'That's right. We've got names for three. The others are just *rifa'at* — bullets, as they call them.'

'All right,' Garrett said. He shrugged

into the body armour jacket. It weighed about four pounds, and would stop a .357 Magnum bullet or a 9mm Parabellum at three metres. He waved the helmet away: the hijackers would be alerted immediately if they saw a supposedly innocuous ground service technician wearing one.

'What about a weapon?' Kokotos asked him.

'I'm armed,' Garrett replied, patting the shoulder holster beneath his left arm. In it was his favourite weapon, the conversion of the 9mm combat version Smith & Wesson M39 pistol manufactured by Armament Systems and Procedures of Appleton, Wisconsin, a seven-shot automatic fitted with a Guttersnipe sight that was the best weapon he knew for high reliability and good first-shot accuracy.

He went down the stairs to the tarmac level, where a white service van stood outside the doors, engine running. As he appeared a young policeman got out and held the door open for him.

'Everything you'll need is in there,' Tzianos told him.

'Including my 'ice-cubes'?'

15

'Straight from the freezer,' the young man grinned. 'Good luck.'

Garrett lifted a hand and moved off from the terminal building toward the plane, parked about half a mile away. It was already hot; the noon temperature had been in the eighties for days. A whirl of white birds circled the salt lake on the south side of the airport. He turned west across the wide, empty apron. Surfers and sailboats speckled the glistering blue sea beyond the beach fringing the western edge of the airport.

The Tristar loomed huge above him. He stopped the van and got out. The forward exit door on the port side of the plane had been opened. He saw the figure of a man moving in the shadowy interior. He was about thirty, with dark hair and a beard, short and powerful-looking. He switched on the loud-hailer.

'Tango Juliet hijackers, I have your food and other requirements here,' he called. His voice sounded harsh and unfriendly in the stillness. Seabirds rose squalling over the lake. 'Do you want me to bring up the passenger stairs?'

16

'No stairs!' the man above him shouted. 'No stairs near! We use the hoists only!'

'Understood,' Garrett said. 'Have I your permission to connect the power line?' There was no reply. He stood in the flat sunlight, waiting.

'What is power line?' Al-Din hissed to the pilot.

'Electricity,' McLean told him. 'You'll need it to operate the food hoists. It'll also mean we can put the lights and the air-conditioning on, heat food, start the refrigerators up without having to use the generators.'

'Good, good!' Al-Din nodded. 'Tell him go ahead!'

Garrett lugged the heavy cable into place and jammed it into the female socket in the belly of the plane. For the moment, at least, he was completely concealed from the hijackers. He took out the six small blocks of ice he had put in the rear of the van and stowed two in each of the huge wheel bays above his head. He crept along beneath the fuselage to the front wheel and placed the last two ice blocks inside the nacelle above it. When this was done he emerged into full view, walked to where the pilot could see him, then gave a thumbs-up signal.

The pilot waved acknowledgement, and Garrett knew he would be relaying to the imprisoned passengers the good news that they had power. It would take an hour or two to get the stale air out of the cabins and cool them down, but probably conditions were so bad inside the plane that anything would be an improvement.

Garrett walked back to the van and looked up. The man he had seen earlier was standing on the sill of the doorway, a submachine gun pointing down at him. MP-K Walther 9mm, Garrett observed automatically.

'Which one are you?' he shouted. 'Sayeed or Emad?'

'I am Sayeed!' the man called down.

'Okay, Sayeed, how do you want to do this?'

'Mineral water and ice first. You have it?'

'Bottled water. Ice in plastic bags.'

'Very well. Get started.'

Garrett walked over to where the hoist feeder vehicle stood. It worked on a principle not unlike a forklift truck. He piled the boxes from the rear of the van on to the loader base and got into the driving seat, operating the controls to send the lift up to the hatch that one of the terrorists had opened on the port side behind the wing. He could see the two men unloading the boxes quite clearly. So, in that case, could the watchers in the control tower. The battery of catadioptrics and telephotos up there would already have taken several dozen pictures of them.

'How are things in there?' he called up. 'Do you need any medical supplies of any kind?'

'We will tell you what we need!' came the sharp reply. 'Get on with what you came to do!'

Garrett did as he was ordered. The main thing right now was not to rock the boat. One by one, the boxes went aboard, hauled inside by unseen hands. It was getting warmer. The strengthening sun bounced heat off the flat concrete surface of the tarmac. Perspiration soaked through his white overall and the heavy body armour beneath it.

'That's all the water and ice!' he shouted. 'You want the food next?'

The man with the gun made an impatient hurry-up gesture. Garrett stacked the neat clingfilmed trays into cartons and ran them up on the hoist. He watched them being taken aboard then repeated the performance. Finally he came to the last stack.

'This is the last of it!' he shouted. He watched the boxes being taken aboard. The hatch closed. Nobody spoke. He got out of the hoist truck and returned to the front of the plane. Sayeed was standing in the doorway, ten feet above his head.

'It is well,' Sayeed told him. He made a gesture with the barrel of the gun. 'Return to the terminal!'

Garrett waved a hand, got into the van and drove it back the way he had come. Once inside the terminal building and out of sight of the hijackers, he ran up the stairs to the control room, throwing aside the white overall. Someone stuck a cold drink in his hand. It tasted like Paradise in a can.

'Everyone ready?' he said.

'What have you done out there?' Stefanidos asked him. His face was chalky white with fatigue.

'An old mercenary's trick, Minister,' Garrett said. 'You remember I wanted a freezer?'

'You said something about ice cubes.'

'What you do is you pull the pin on a grenade, put it in a small plastic box that holds the lever in position, fill it with water, then freeze it. You plant the ice block somewhere it will melt. When it melts, the trigger flips off and the grenade explodes.'

'Grenades?' Stefanidos whispered. 'But . . .'

'Smoke grenades, Minister,' Garrett told him reassuringly. 'I want them to think the plane is on fire. We'll tell them they have to evacuate.'

'And you think they will do it?'

'We're about to find out,' Garrett said. He went over to the microphone console.

'Tango Juliet, this is the chief engineer, Larnaca airport.'

'Go ahead, chief.'

McLean sounded tired, but his voice was firm. Garrett wondered how the co-pilot, Peter Duncan, and engineer Steve Mayer were coping. They'd soon be finding out.

'Captain, did you experience any overheating or any other malfunction of the air-conditioning systems en route?'

'Negative.'

'Everything operating okay now?'

'Affirmative. Why do you ask?'

'Your first sector was Manila-Kuala Lumpur, yes?'

'Correct.'

'K-U-L telexed us that one of your generators may be sparking. Keep an eye open.'

'Roger, chief. Thank you.'

Garrett switched off and went back over to the window that looked out across the apron. The big plane sat like a dinosaur on the shimmering concrete. The silence in the control tower was palpable. The quartz clock clacked the seconds away. Half an hour passed. Forty minutes.

'Look!' Tzianos shouted.

Everyone rushed toward the window. Thick smoke was coiling from the belly and the nose of the plane.

'All right, controller!' Garrett snapped. 'Tell them they're on fire! Colonel, let's go!'

He ran down the stairs and out to the rear of the terminal, where the two fire tenders were parked out of sight of the plane. The commander of the SAS unit was standing beside the nearest machine. He straightened up when he saw Garrett coming out of the terminal building.

'Major John Oliver, SAS, sir!' he said, snapping a tense salute. 'Are we go?'

'We're go!' Garrett confirmed.

'How do you want to hit them?'

'The minute we get out there, I want stairs wheeled up against that open door. You'll be the fire chief, telling them the plane's on fire, they've got to evacuate. We go in through the port entrance. Your people get everyone out of first class and move through the plane at the same time. Stun grenades, whatever you need to use.'

'What about the ones with the pilot and his crew?'

'That's our job,' Garrett said. 'So let's make sure we don't fuck up.'

'Gotcha,' the young soldier said, and banged the driver on the shoulder. 'Let's go, Steve!'

The driver hit the siren and moved out across the apron, circling the plane, which was already half hidden in a dense spiral of heavy black smoke. The M329 grenades were filled with a composition called Magdex, which could ignite any combustible material on which it fell. There was a good chance one or more of the tyres were smouldering. Pray God it didn't develop into a real fire, Garrett thought, as he snapped on the breathing mask and shifted his shoulder holster to a more comfortable position. The first fire tender stopped below the nose of the Tristar. Oliver jumped up on the hood, a loud-hailer in his hand.

'Tango Juliet hijackers, you are on fire!' he bellowed. 'You must evacuate the plane immediately! Evacuate immediately!'

The second fire tender had come to a stop to the rear of the starboard wing, only intermittently visible through the rolling smoke. Garrett could hear the officer's voice blatting through his loud-hailer.

'Tango Juliet hijackers, we are bringing up passenger stairways!' Oliver shouted. 'Open all emergency exits and utilize all escape hatches at once!' His men were lugging foam spreaders off the fire tender. *Go for it, you bastards*, he willed them. *Go for it.* The grenades would burn only for three or four minutes. He could already detect a thinning of the heavy coils of screening smoke. He ran beneath the plane; there was no sign of flame, thank God. He took two more smoke grenades from his pocket and ripped out the safety pins, jamming one in the port wheel arch and the other in the starboard. Huge fresh billows of black smoke swirled upward around the fuselage of the plane. The air-conditioning system was sucking it into the interior. He could hear muffled shouts of fear. In the darkening interior, coughing, retching people would be convinced that the plane was burning.

As Garrett ran back toward the front of the plane he saw one of the 'firemen' driving a mobile stairway unit up to the forward port passenger door. Almost at once it opened, and a man came out, retching, coughing, staggering against the rail and reeling down the steps. Now Garrett could hear people screaming inside the plane. The atmosphere of chaos was convincingly authentic. Almost simultaneously, emergency chutes billowed down from the sides of the plane, and Garrett saw cabin staff hustling passengers into them and sending them sliding down to the tarmac, some of them sprawling awkwardly as they landed.

He switched on the walkie-talkie. 'Colonel Kokotos, this is Garrett. Get your people out here! *Now!*'

Two armoured personnel carriers slid out from the rear of the terminal, making a long curving run to the rear of the plane where they would be hidden by the turning smoke. Garrett saw teams of soldiers running toward the foot of the emergency chutes.

'Head count!' he shouted to one of Kokotos' men. 'I want to know when everyone is out of there!'

The soldier waved an acknowledgement, and ran toward the fire tender, shouting orders. Two men jumped down and followed him, running after the passengers being herded away from the plane toward the terminal building by stewardesses. More passengers streamed in their wake, and more still were coming down the chutes and stumbling down the stairs. Garrett saw a blue uniform, another. If the cabin staff were coming down, it meant the passengers must all be off.

Major Oliver came running. They went up the stairway and turned into the first class cabin. Behind them, Oliver's men surged in through the doorway and disappeared into the smoke-filled body of the plane. The flat sharp crack of stun grenades sounded like small cannon. Oliver and Garrett were alone now. The first class cabin was full of smoke that turned lazily in the still air. As the two men moved toward the cockpit, Al-Nawar came out, his arm locked around the neck of the pilot, his Browning automatic laid against McLean's forehead.

'Get back!' he screamed.

'You've got two minutes!' Garrett shouted back at him, his voice distorted by the gas-mask amplifier. 'The wing is on fire! Look for yourself!'

'Out, out!' Sayeed screeched. 'Or I kill him now!'

Garrett held up both his hands; he and Oliver retreated toward the open doorway and backed out on to the stairway. Coughing and retching, his eyes streaming, Sayeed Al-Nawar came closer, pushing McLean in front of him. Sweat was streaming off both of them.

'Go down, down, down!' Sayeed screeched at Garrett, gesturing with the gun. He was at the doorway now. He pushed McLean outside, stepped over the coaming.

'Look!' Garrett shouted, pointing vaguely toward the rear of the plane. 'The plane is going to blow up! Look!'

Involuntarily, Sayeed turned his head and that was all the advantage Garrett needed. His hand moved like a striking snake, the extended fingers driving into Sayeed's unprotected eyes, blinding him. He reeled back against the body of the plane, firing the gun in reflex agony. As the slug whispered past, Garrett shot him through the forehead; the man folded backwards over the side of the stairway and somersaulted down to the tarmac.

'Get out of here!' Garrett yelled at McLean, shoving him down the stairway. As the pilot stumbled and half fell down the steps, Garrett and Major Oliver ducked back into the smoke-filled cabin. Somewhere at the back of the plane they heard the staccato voice of automatic weapons. In the murky gloom of swirling smoke, they saw the cockpit door opening. They slid quickly behind the galley curtains as the co-pilot and the engineer emerged, handkerchiefs tied over their mouths. Then another man, similarly masked, appeared behind them. It was the leader of the hijack team, Emad Al-Din.

In his right hand was a Browning 9mm

automatic, which was laid against the back of Peter Duncan's neck. In his left was a small plastic box not unlike a TV remote control unit. Seeing no one, he took the gun away from Duncan's neck and straightened up, shoving the co-pilot toward the exit with his left hand, the control unit still clenched in his fist. Duncan staggered forward involuntarily, putting a two-foot gap between himself and the terrorist.

The half-second opportunity was enough for Garrett and Oliver. They moved in unison through the coiling smoke, Garrett to the right, Oliver to the left, firing simultaneously at point-blank range. Two bullets hit the terrorist, one above the right eye, the other almost in the centre of his forehead. Emad Al-Din folded sideways to the floor, his last expression one of astonishment. Even as the man was falling, Oliver had grabbed the co-pilot's arm and spun him around and away from the firing line, while Garrett hurled Mayer to safety behind a row of seats. Almost in the same movement, Oliver kicked the Browning away from Emad Al-Din's outstretched right hand and Garrett snatched up the plastic detonator box, ripping out the battery.

The flat stutter of Walther submachine guns, the harder stammer of Uzis in the passenger cabins, the shouts and curses had stopped. The acrid whiff of cordite and the softer stink of grenade smoke drifted toward them, sucked out through the open door. Sensing, rather than seeing movement, Garrett threw himself on to the fallen form of Steve Mayer, saw Oliver do the same with Duncan, squashing him against the wall behind the big first class seats. They were not a moment too soon.

Two of the terrorists appeared out of the smoke like wraiths, moving crablike, back to back, one covering the direction from which they had just come, the other the first class cabin they were now entering. The smoke was thinning now, spiralling out through the open doorway, and the terrorist in the lead saw the dead body of Al-Din lying near the door. He spoke sharply; the two of them inched forward warily, like some strange four-legged, four-armed mutation, the Walthers moving in a steady arc. Crouched tensely behind the row of seats on the port side, Garrett looked across at Oliver. He made a hand signal and Oliver nodded. A rolling dive across the cabin might give them a chance to pick off the two hijackers.

Garrett took a deep, deep breath. He was just about to move when Oliver's men came out of the smoke. The two Arabs heard the movement and wheeled, but they were always going to be too late. The vicious, fast *brraaaaaap* of automatic weapon fire ripped the air, and the two men wilted and collapsed face-down.

'Hold, hold, hold!' Oliver shouted, as the weapons swung towards them. One of the SAS men made a signal, and Oliver moved after him, running back down the aisle into the rear passenger cabin. As Garrett helped Steve Mayer up, he heard a ragged cheer. Across the cabin, Peter Duncan was sitting with his head between his knees, coughing and wheezing. After a few more moments, Oliver came back from the rear of the plane. He was smiling.

'All done,' he said.

'Any casualties?'

'A couple of my men have flesh wounds, nothing serious.'

'What about the passengers?' Duncan asked.

'All safe,' Oliver assured him. 'It's over.'

'And the fire?' Mayer said, looking first at Garrett and then at Oliver as if they were alien beings. 'Have they put it out?'

'No fire,' Garrett told him. 'Just smoke grenades.'

'Jesus,' Duncan said. 'Are you all right, Steve?'

'Who, me?' Mayer said. He had collapsed into a seat, looking around the cabin as though this was the first time he had ever been on a plane.

'I just saw it,' he said, shaking his head. 'I just saw it happen with my own eyes and I still don't believe it. Who the hell are you people, anyway?'

Garrett grinned wearily. 'I'm Laurel,' he said. 'And he's Hardy.'

'You never saw us,' Oliver told him. 'You don't know what we look like. You can't remember anything about us. Got it?'

Eyes wide, Peter Duncan nodded his understanding.

'Good,' Garrett said. 'Come on, Major. I'll buy you a beer.'

'Damned right you will,' Oliver said.

3

Charles Garrett checked the time: twenty-two minutes past ten. Nicholas Bleke was scrupulous about punctuality. A ten-thirty appointment meant just that. Not ten twenty-nine. And especially not ten thirty-one. He took the elevator from the lobby to the third floor; there were no stairs at the front of Lonsdale House. Flush, blank oak doors faced the otherwise empty hall opposite the elevators on the third floor. Garrett inserted his keycard into a slot in the wall and waited for the buzzer that signalled clearance.

The security lock clacked open, admitting him to a parqueted hallway with a semicircular desk at the far side. An athletic-looking security man took Garrett's thumb-print on the desktop scanner and waited for the bleep. He knew perfectly well who Garrett was; but no exceptions to the security check were permitted.

'Thank you, sir,' he said. 'Go in, please.'

Garrett went through the swing door into a brightly lit inner foyer; the soft whirr of electronic machinery could be heard. Three doors faced him: one to his left, one to his right, and one straight ahead. The left-hand doorway led to the south aisle, which housed Administration, Finance and the library. The right-hand corridor led to the north aisle, on which were Registry, Computers, and the five divisional offices, amongst them his own. Garrett went through the door straight ahead of him. It led into a grey-carpeted corridor with double doors at its far end. There he pushed the buzzer beside the heavy oak doors, standing in the centre of a square set into the carpeting so that the CCTV camera could log his entry.

Once again he heard electronic locks moving. He entered an office decorated in muted greys and browns, with nylon net curtains which, while admitting abundant light, made it impossible to see into the building from outside.

On the right-hand wall were two doors:

between them stood a modern L-shaped desk unit with a PC console. Behind it sat Elizabeth James, Bleke's executive assistant. When Bleke became director of this organization in 1985, Liz had come over with him from K-7, the counter-espionage division of DI5.

She looked up as Garrett came in. She was an attractive woman of perhaps forty-five. Today she was wearing a tailored black Austin Reed suit and a white, shirt-style blouse. Her blonde hair was greying, but attractively styled, her skin smooth and unlined. She wore a minimum of makeup; Bleke disliked too much powder and paint, as he referred to it.

'Hello, Liz,' he said. 'Am I on time?'

'As always,' she smiled. 'He's waiting for you. Would you like some coffee?'

'Why not? Black — '

'With one sugar, I know. I'll bring it in.'

He knocked and went into Bleke's office. It always looked exactly the same. Liz James said the Old Man could tell immediately if someone had moved one of his precious files three centimetres from where he'd left it the night before.

'Good morning, Charles,' Bleke said. 'Come and sit down.'

Garrett sat down in one of the two leather chairs that stood in front of Bleke's desk, taking the chair on the right, as he always did, and waited. Bleke had a file on the desk in front of him. The diagonal red stripe told Garrett it was highly restricted.

'Ah,' Bleke said. 'Coffee.'

Liz James put a tray on the desk. On it were a silver coffee-pot, sugar basin and milk jug, two china cups and saucers, and a plate of biscuits. Bleke had a box sent round weekly from Fortnum's; his sweet tooth was one of the few things he indulged.

As Liz poured the coffee, Garrett looked around Bleke's office.

To the left of the bookcase behind Bleke was a door that led into a briefing room, austere and functional except for a harmonium which stood in the far corner. A long time ago, Bleke had discovered that playing Bach aided his mental processes; the old harmonium had followed him from office to office ever since. There was a standing joke at Lonsdale House: ten thousand pounds reward for the man who located Bleke's music teacher — and killed him before he taught anyone else.

'You've seen these, of course?' he said, jerking a thumb at the pile of newspapers stacked on the right-hand side of his desk. The topmost was a recent issue of one of the noisier tabloids, the headline set in huge capitals that screamed TRAIL OF DEATH: ANOTHER MYSTERY.

'Hard not to,' Garrett smiled.

'They're baying at the minister's heels.' Bleke said. 'Told him he was a damned fool to release the news so soon.'

'He could hardly sit on it much longer.'

'Suppose not,' Bleke said, as if reluctant to admit it. He slid a dossier across the desk. 'Take a look at this.'

Garrett leafed through it quickly. It was a Special Branch report into the bizarre suicide of Ronald Morris, a consultant executive of the giant Hayling-Brittain Avionics and Defence Systems company. Morris had fixed wires to an electric timer and then fastened them to the metal part of his dentures. He had wound a clothes line around his feet and hands and then switched on the power, electrocuting himself instantly. Garrett laid down the dossier.

'Hardly surprising the newspapers started up that Trail of Death business again,' he observed.

'Tcha!' Bleke said, expressing his opinion of newspapers in one contemptuous sound. He was a short, stockily built man with a large head and grey-white hair cut very close to the scalp. His eyes were shrewd and alert, his mouth firm, his jawline resolute. He might have been a high-ranking naval officer, the governor of a public school, the senior consultant in a major hospital; there was about him an air that inspired respect, invited confidences.

'I haven't followed the case too closely,' Garrett admitted. 'I seem to recall reading there had been a lot of mysterious deaths, every one of them a defence worker, some of them involved in classified projects. Is that right?'

'Twenty, altogether,' Bleke told him. 'It

seemed to be stretching happenstance a considerable distance too far. The Minister ordered an internal inquiry. I've got a copy for you. It takes the position that there's no evidence of any sinister links between the deaths. The Minister himself assures me that most of the men were never involved with anything more secret than a catering memo.'

'Most?' Garrett observed.

'Exactly,' Bleke nodded. 'Like you, I am familiar with the nuances of mandarin-speak. That was why I decided to get Special Branch to do a deep dig on the Morris case.'

Special Branch is the executive arm of the security services, none of which has so much as even powers of arrest. An élite force within each regional police force, the main duty of Special Branch is defined as 'the preservation of the Queen's Peace'. For that purpose SB gathers information about threats to public order, espionage, terrorism, sabotage and subversion, and is empowered to act as armed personal protection for persons at risk.

41

'And?'

'They haven't come up with anything, either,' Bleke said angrily. 'And I am not best pleased about it.'

'Maybe there isn't anything to come up with.'

'I'd accept that if Ronald Morris were not involved.'

Garrett looked at Bleke inquiringly.

'Ron Morris was a friend of mine,' Bleke said slowly. 'I'd known him and his wife Dorothy for, oh, damn near forty years. Attended their sons' christenings. Fine man, fine woman.'

'I'm sorry,' Garrett said.

'Not looking for sympathy,' Bleke told him abruptly. 'Looking for a motive.'

'You said the ministry has conducted an investigation. And Special Branch,' Garrett pointed out.

'Yes, yes,' Bleke said, impatiently. He got up and walked across to the window and stared out. Garrett concealed a smile. The Old Man hated to say 'please'. He would go to the most convoluted lengths to avoid appearing to ask anyone — even someone he knew well, like Garrett — for a favour. He invariably phrased such requests obliquely, and Garrett bet himself this time would be no exception.

'I've just got a feeling about this thing,' Bleke began. 'What's needed here is someone who could poke about without upsetting the ministry and Special Branch.'

Someone like me, you mean, Garrett thought. 'I understand your concern, sir,' he said. 'But a series of suicides and accidental deaths, connected or otherwise, is hardly our line of country . . . '

'I know that!' Bleke growled exasperatedly. 'I don't want a crusade, dammit! Just poke around a bit, see what you can come up with.'

Garrett shrugged. 'I've got a lot of paperwork to catch up on,' he said. 'The British Airways security people have asked me to sit in on a conference. After that hijack, they're tightening up their procedures worldwide.'

'I read your report. You took a lot of chances.'

'Hobson's choice,' Garrett said, with a shrug.

'I wasn't criticizing your actions,' Bleke

said gruffly. 'Just making an observation.'

'It was the passengers and crew I was concerned for.'

'You got them out of it, that's the main thing. Sorry about your holiday, though. The way things are shaping in the Middle East, it'll be a long time before anyone can go to Israel for pleasure again.'

'It was no great loss,' Garrett said. 'Although Jessica was looking forward to her week at Eilat.'

'Ah, yes,' Bleke said, leaning back in his chair. 'Dr Goldman. You're still . . . seeing her?'

'Of course.'

'You must bring her to lunch at my club some time.'

Garrett concealed a smile; Bleke's words were a perfect example of what he referred to as the Great British Non-Invitation. The Old Man had no more intention of taking Jessica Goldman to lunch at White's than he had of making love to Benazir Bhutto. Jessica made no secret of the fact that she mistrusted the power Bleke had been given, and she mistrusted even more the way Bleke used Charles Garrett as the extension of that power. She knew how highly Garrett thought of him, but made no effort to conceal her belief that his loyalty was ill-judged. And Bleke knew it.

Garrett looked at the Morris dossier again. He had the highest regard for Bleke's intuition, but he was reluctant to commit his time and energies to something which, on the face of it, Special Branch had handled perfectly capably. He had bigger fish to fry.

In the years since its formation, PACT had achieved a number of significant successes against world terrorists. It had its origins in the days immediately subsequent to the bombing of the Grand Hotel, Brighton, in October 1984, when the IRA nearly succeeded in assassinating Margaret Thatcher and most of her Cabinet ministers. A high-level secret meeting to review the government's security and counter-terrorism capabilities had been called at Chequers, the Prime Minister's official country home near Princes Risborough in Buckinghamshire.

It was a summit meeting, in the truest meaning of the phrase: among those present were the Home Secretary; the Euro-minister responsible for co-ordination with the TREVI group; the directors general of DI5 and DI6, the security services; the co-ordinator of intelligence and security at the Foreign Office; a representative of the Joint Intelligence Chiefs; the Deputy Assistant Commissioner in charge of Special Branch; the Commissioner of Metropolitan Police; the President of the Association of Chief Police Officers; and the Colonel Commandant of the Special Air Services Regiment. TREVI was the central organization of European police and security agencies. The French acronym was an abbreviation for *Terreur, Radicalisme, et Violence Internationale*. To Garrett it always sounded like something Ian Fleming might have dreamed up at his Jamaican hideway, Goldeneye, for one of his James Bond plots.

The result of their weekend deliberations was the establishment of a new executive, designated PACT — Punitive Actions,

Counter-Terrorism.

The following January, a front company called Diversified Corporate Facilities was established, with offices in Lonsdale House, Berkeley Square. Early in February, Bleke, at that time a senior officer in K-7, the counter-espionage arm of DI5, was appointed Chief Executive Officer.

Bleke was given *carte blanche*; the Prime Minister had the highest regard for this dedicated and ruthless spycatcher. Bleke knew exactly how and where to find the officers he wanted. He began by persuading his own executive assistant, Liz James, to 'defect' to the new organization. As executive officers he chose Harry Loeb, the best financial man at Curzon Street House; Arthur Cotton, the top movements and transportation officer at Century House, headquarters of DI6; and Tom Ashley, a computer genius at the Royal Armaments Research and Development Establishment in Chertsey, whose job it would be to set up the links between PACT, the security service network known as R2, and the TREVI computers in West Germany.

The most important of all Bleke's decisions was to select as his head of operations a man he had himself recruited into the Service a decade earlier: Charles Frederick Garrett. Like Bleke, Garrett had a reputation as something of a maverick, which was a decided plus, as was his reputation for ruthlessness.

When Garrett's service record was sent up from Registry, however, Bleke was surprised to discover that Garrett was on secondment to Special Branch, training operatives destined for Ulster.

It took Bleke only a short while to establish that Garrett's being shunted into the backwater of operative training had come about after a collision with Antony Belgrave, then head of DI5's Forward Planning Executive. It wasn't by any means the first time Garrett had been too outspoken for the liking of some mandarin. His clash with Belgrave was a classic illustration of this.

Garrett's wife Diana had been killed by an IRA terrorist in a hostage switch that went badly wrong; on his return from 'compassionate leave' — another euphemism: the big man had lost himself in the wilds of County Galway for nearly four months, trying to drink himself to death on Irish whiskey — Garrett had re-presented himself for duty at Curzon Street House. Belgrave was in a dismissive mood; he told Garrett that, frankly, he did not think he was in good enough psychological condition to go back into the field. Garrett replied — all too publicly — that he wouldn't accept Belgrave's psychological assessment of a decomposing rat. Not only did he hold Belgrave personally responsible for the doublecross that had resulted in the death of his wife, he told him, he also considered him a liar, a knave and a blundering incompetent.

The outraged Belgrave demanded an immediate retraction and apology. Garrett refused to make either. Belgrave took the matter to the Director General, recommending Garrett's dismissal or at very least suspension. The DG carpeted Garrett; their conversation was terse. It ended when the DG asked Garrett how, if the man was as incompetent as he seemed to think, Belgrave had managed to rise to the top of the profession.

'Simple,' Garrett replied harshly. 'Gold sinks. Shit floats.'

Faced with insubordination on this scale, the Director General dithered; after all, Garrett had an outstanding record. He decided instead to put him as far away from Antony Belgrave as possible. That was why Garrett was where he was when Bleke had him seconded to PACT. He had never regretted the decision: for the kind of work PACT was going to do, he needed men who could play rough and dirty. Garrett had proved — in a dozen secret actions against Palestinian and IRA terrorists, more recently in the freeing of the hostages in the Larnaca hijack — that nobody played rougher, or dirtier, when the chips were down.

'I've got you a copy of the secret report that was made to the Home Secretary,' Bleke said. 'It will give you the bare bones of the thing, names, dates, and so on. Let me know if there's anything else you need.'

'I'll check it out,' Garrett said.

'Do that,' Bleke replied. He was deep into another dossier, oblivious to the world, before Garrett even got to the door.

4

Garrett's face was thoughtful as he left Bleke's office. It was not difficult to determine the position the Old Man found himself in as a friend of the Morris family, nor to sympathize with his reaction to the old soldier's shabby suicide. However, while Garrett had the highest regard for Bleke's feelings, he was still reluctant to commit his energies to something like this. His job was counter-terrorism: detecting its perpetrators, infiltrating their organizations, neutralizing their plans.

He came out through the conference room, which opened on its far side to the brightly lit north aisle. Outside each of the offices lining it was a metal slot with a card showing in neat Helvetica type the name and rank of the occupant, and whether or not he or she was on duty. At the end of the corridor was Garrett's office.

When he had first worked here, the

office had been functional and bare: no pictures, no personal touches at all. Now there was a brass-framed colour portrait of Jessica Goldman on the desk, and a couple of oils by a minor Edwardian painter called James Townshend on the wall facing it. Every time he looked at them he would remember Jessica's excitement as she bid for them at Christie's in the Old Brompton Road.

Other than these, however, the office was all business: filing cabinets, a fax machine, an IBM PC. A tall window, screened by the standard nylon net curtains used in all MoD establishments, looked down on Berkeley Square. A pair of louvre doors concealed a small dressing-room and shower. A Krups coffee machine stood on a low table to one side. Garrett filled it and switched on.

While he waited for the coffee, he sat down in the armchair beside the window and reopened the dossier Bleke had given him. When the coffee machine gave the expiring sigh that announced its work was done, he poured a mugful, added sugar, took it back and started to read.

Foreign and Commonwealth office
   Library and Records Department
   Cornwall House Stamford Street
   LONDON SE1 9NS

For the Personal Attention of The Home
Secretary

Minister:

1. You asked me to conduct an investigation, and upon its conclusion submit to you a dossier outlining my findings. We agreed that I should operate within certain stipulated parameters and observe the following terms of reference:

'Examine the circumstances surrounding the deaths of any or all staff and personnel of Hayling-Brittain Avionics and Defence Systems: establish and assess the involvement if any of outside or inimical parties: review the question of the security status of each of the deceased; investigate any information or material which might come to my attention in this connection; consider any evidence there may be for believing that national security has been, or may be endangered; and upon completion of these objectives report thereon to you.'

2. You were good enough to say that, if I needed extra powers, I was to ask for them. I have not felt the need. Every witness whom I wished to interview has come forward, without duress or subpoena. I have had throughout the complete co-operation of the Special Branch, the security services, the coroners and the various police forces which were involved in the initial investigations of these deaths.

3. Below is appended a chronology and brief précis of all the cases which have come to the attention of the police, together with brief comments on each.

Chronology and précis of deaths of defence workers investigated

subsequent to
The Home Secretary's request
as at 15 May 1989

24 March 1985.
Kenneth Bates, 46, computer scientist, Sussex University, Brighton. Car plunged off a bridge into a drydock at Newhaven, Sussex. Verdict: accidental death.

4 April 1985.
Lt. Ernest Rashbrook, 49, head of work study unit, defence expert, Royal Military College of Science, Shrivenham. Disappeared: presumed dead.

6 March 1986.
Geoffrey Wood, radar designer and draftsman, Hayling-Brittain Avionics and Defence Systems. Death in garden shed at home, by means of shotgun in mouth. Verdict: suicide.

11 November 1986.
Derek Darlington, 44, digital communications expert at British Telecom's

Martlesham Heath research centre, and at Hayling-Brittain Avionics and Defence Systems. Fell from a hotel room window while on holiday in Nairobi. Verdict: open.

27 August 1987.
Ajai Mehta, 24, computer software engineer, Hayling-Brittain Avionics and Defence Systems. Chew Valley, Somerset. Found dead, an apparent suicide from gunshot wound, beneath a viaduct of the M25 in Buckinghamshire. Verdict: open.

3 October 1987.
Said Malik, 26, computer analyst, Hayling-Brittain Avionics and Defence Systems, Stanmore. Hanged himself from a tree in West London. Verdict: suicide.

7 December 1987.
Ernest Blackmore, 24, software engineer at the Ministry of Defence experimental station, Gosport, Hants. Valium overdose. Verdict: suicide.

22 January 1988.
Colin Taylor, 29, MoD computer consultant. Found dead in woods near home, shotgun wounds. Verdict: accident.

29 January 1988.
Dr Peter Mumford, 52, computer and MoD tank batteries expert, formerly of Royal Military College of Science, attached to Royal Armaments Research and Development Establishment at Chertsey, Surrey. Found dead in parked car with engine running. Verdict: accident.

14 February 1988.
Ian West, 46, design engineer, Hayling-Brittain Avionics and Defence Systems, Portsmouth. Overdose of drugs. Verdict: suicide.

21 February 1988.
John Lowrie, 46, scientist and senior lecturer in metallurgy at the Royal Military College of Science, Shrivenham. Found dead beneath his car: carbon monoxide poisoning. Verdict: open.

26 February 1988.
Bryan Haven, 43, engineer, Hayling-Brittain Avionics and Defence Systems, Leicester. Found dead in car with hosepipe attached to exhaust. Verdict: suicide.

15 April 1988.
Thomas Wakenshaw, 39, satellite project manager, Exmoor Systems, a subsidiary of Hayling-Brittain Avionics and Defence Systems. Drove 4WD vehicle loaded with petrol cans off Beachy Head. Verdict: suicide.

23 April 1988.
Harold Andrus, 32, systems analyst at Bristol Polytechnic. Found drowned in Volkswagen Scirocco in Manchester Ship Canal at Runcorn, near Liverpool. Verdict: death by misadventure.

13 May 1988.
Edwin Raftery, 22, digital communications expert on defence-related project for Exmoor Systems. Car crashed into motorway central barrier near Poole, Dorset. Verdict: misadventure.

17 June 1988.
Derek Pickles, 60, electronic weapons engineer, Exmoor Systems at Christchurch, Dorset. Heart attack. No inquest.

22 September 1988.
Vernon Ashworth, 33, engineering manager, Hayling-Brittain Avionics and Defence Systems, seconded to British Aerospace. Found in car with hosepipe connected to exhaust. Verdict: suicide.

23 January 1989.
Michael Linaker, 23, laboratory technician with the Atomic Energy Research Establishment at Sizewell, Suffolk. Found dead halfway down a cliff at Hartland Point, Devon. Verdict: suicide.

7 March 1989.
Harold Siggs, 52, digital computer engineer (manager) at Hayling-Brittain Avionics and Defence Systems, Stanmore. Found in car with hosepipe attached to exhaust. Verdict: suicide.

---

4. *Actions*. Pursuant to your instructions, I carried out a stringent and comprehensive inquiry into the circumstances of each of these cases. When I had compiled dossiers on each, I arranged for these, together with the personal dossiers of all the deceased, to be passed to the security services for vetting. Computer analysts at R2, Euston Tower, compiled AKF (All Known Facts) dossiers on each of the men, combining material from the spread of information available in their APD (All Personal Details) and AKA (All Known Associates) files with details of all assignments, postings, even vacations, looking for common denominators. Although there were some areas of commonality, such as work location or even, in some cases, acquaintance, no common denominators of any valid significance were discovered.

5. *Assessment*. It is apparent from the results that the criticisms levelled against the Ministry of Defence by

some sections of the Press, alleging that it has been blind to the implications of so many apparently linked deaths, are unfair and inaccurate. Like the police and the security services, the Ministry's position is that there is no evidence of any sinister links between the deaths, and this view is completely supported by my findings; indeed, among other facts this inquiry has established that the incidence of suicides among defence workers is actually lower than that of the population as a whole.

6. *Conclusions*. After due and diligent study of all the available evidence appertaining to the above cases, including that assembled by the internal inquiry conducted by Lord Bletchlock, chairman of Hayling-Maxwell, I am completely satisfied that:

a) in no instance has there been any involvement by outside parties;
b) in no instance has there been any evidence that national security has been, or may be, endangered;

c) there is not now and never has been any sinister or engineered connection between any of these deaths.

I have therefore terminated the inquiry and returned all staff engaged upon it to their normal duties.
Respectfully submitted,

Julian Haversby

Julian Haversby,
Permanent Under-Secretary.

'Very good, Julian,' Garrett said, rubbing his eyes. On the face of it, the Permanent Under-Secretary's report was comprehensive and conclusive. But it still left a lot of questions unanswered.

There was the fact, apparently not thought significant by Haversby, that a number of the victims appeared to have been working on underwater technology projects. Two deaths by shotgun, two by electrocution, two by drugs, five by carbon monoxide poisoning, the others even more outré. The average UK suicide rate for men was fourteen per hundred thousand of the population. Hayling-Brittain employed about fifty thousand people, at least half of whom, one could suppose, were women. Which put its suicide rate significantly higher, not lower, than the national average.

Garrett picked up the telephone; he needed some specialist help, and he thought he knew just where to get it.

5

When Garrett first got to know him, Tony Dodgson was working as a member of the Serious and Organized Crime Squad from an office on the second floor of the Tottenham Court Road police station. There had been a lot of changes in Dodgson's life since then, and he now held the rank of Deputy Assistant Commissioner, Criminal Intelligence Squad, located on the seventh floor of the faceless City of Westminster block known as New Scotland Yard. It stood almost directly opposite the wartime headquarters of the secret service on Broadway, just off Victoria Street.

Garrett was passed through security and escorted to the seventh floor by a uniformed woman police constable. The layout was open-plan; Dodgson's office was at the far end of the central aisle. In the outer office a dark-haired young civilian secretary was using a word processor. On the desk in front of her was a neat plaque which announced that her name was Joanna McCallum.

'Mr Garrett?' she said. 'DAC Dodgson is expecting you.'

'Thank you,' he said gravely. 'You're new around here, aren't you?'

'If you call six months new, yes,' she said.

'Where were you before this?'

'SO-thirteen,' she said. 'Anti-terrorist squad.'

'Enjoying it here?'

'We may be poor,' she said, 'but we do see life.' The grin was only there for a moment, but the dimples were sensational. When she stood up, the top of her head was about the level of his chin. Good figure, too, Garrett thought: and no wedding ring.

'This way, Mr Garrett,' she said. She opened the door to her left, the one with the frosted-glass panel that was the only concession to privacy Garrett had seen on the entire floor.

'Well, well, looka here,' Dodgson said, getting up as he saw who his visitor was.

'Pat Garrett just rode into town.'

It was an old joke between them. Dodgson loved old Western movies; he had been calling Garrett by the name of the sheriff who killed Billy the Kid in 1881 for so long Garrett hardly noticed it any more.

He was a tall, thin man in his mid-forties, with thinning brown wavy hair that he allowed to grow long at the nape of the neck. He had a long jaw and soulful brown eyes. In spite of the fact that he had spent virtually all of his working life in London, there was still a faint burr of his native Dorset in Dodgson's voice. He was one of the very best cops Charles Garrett had ever worked with.

'Congratulations on your promotion.'

'Couldn't happen to a nicer fellow,' Dodgson grinned. 'What brings you within these hallowed portals?'

'Got a problem,' Garrett told him. 'Thought I'd share it with you.'

'That's uncommonly decent of you,' Dodgson said. 'We never get problems, you know. In fact, I've been sitting here for weeks just hoping someone would come in with one.'

'Then you'll love this,' Garrett said. 'Tell me about the Trail of Death.'

'For Christ's sake, Pat!' Dodgson groaned. 'We've all been over it so many times, I can practically recite the dossiers by heart.'

'Good,' Garrett said, with a smile. 'That'll save time.'

Dodgson sighed a mock-weary sigh. 'What do you want to know?'

'How many of the deaths didn't you like the look of?'

Dodgson didn't answer for a moment. He held Garrett's gaze, his dark eyes thoughtful. 'What makes you think there were any I didn't like the look of?'

Garrett said nothing, waiting. After a few more moments, Dodgson shook his head, a small smile touching the corners of his mouth.

'The trouble with you, Garrett, is you know me too well.'

'Could be,' Garrett said. 'How many?'

'Eight. Maybe ten.'

'Bleke thinks something smells. He

asked me to take a look.'

'Not strictly your line of country, is it?'

'The idea is I'm supposed to take a look and then decide that. Ten out of twenty is a lot of uncertain.'

'I prefer to call it curious.'

'It's just another word. Give me a for-instance.'

Dodgson swung his long legs up on to the desk and took a file out of the right-hand drawer of his desk, opening it so that it lay across his thighs. He put on a pair of steel-rimmed reading glasses and scanned the documents.

'Let's start with the first one,' he said. 'All the way back in March 1985. A man called Kenneth Bates. Forty-six years old. Worked as a computer scientist at Sussex University, Brighton. Married, with a couple of teenaged children. No debts, no apparent problems. Then one day, his car goes off a bridge in Newhaven docks and falls eighty feet into a drydock.'

'So the man had an accident.'

'That's what the local police said. No other vehicle involved, no indication the driver hit anything. No alcohol in the blood, either. The coroner brought in a verdict of accidental death at the inquest. Open and shut.'

'But?'

'His wife claims the car was sabotaged. She says the tyres that were on the car when she saw it were not the ones that belonged to it. She thinks someone changed them.'

'Did anyone check?'

'Of course. Even if the tyres had been changed, we couldn't see how they would have caused the accident. And there was always the possibility she might have changed the tyres herself, after the fact.'

'Why would she have done that?'

'Grief. Wanting to find someone to blame.'

'It's a bit far-fetched.'

'That was our conclusion. We let it go. Only in the context of all the others does it appear . . . well, curious.'

Garrett smiled. 'Curious word, curious. Always makes me think of *Alice in Wonderland*.'

'How I envy you literary types,' Dodgson said. 'All right, pass on Bates.

Let's look at another case.' He turned the pages. 'Lieutenant Ernest Rashbrook, defence expert. Attached, as they say, to the Ministry of Defence.'

'Military intelligence.'

'That's what it usually means. Rashbrook was almost fifty years old. Married, with two grown children. Head of a work study unit at the Royal Military College of Science in Shrivenham. He was the sort you could set your watch by. Then one day four years ago, he disappears off the face of the earth. No one has the remotest idea what has happened to him.'

This time Garrett played devil's advocate. 'People have all sorts of reasons for disappearing,' he offered.

'Happily married, due to go on vacation, daughter-in-law expecting a baby? That's not the profile of a runner, Pat.'

'All right. Conclusion?'

'Possibly foul play. Possibly just a well-planned dropout. Until we find him, either alive or dead, it's moot.'

'Try another.'

'November 1986. Derek Darlington: British Telecom digital communications expert on attachment to Hayling-Brittain. Forty-four years old. Found dead in the grounds of the Serena Hotel in Nairobi. He appeared to have fallen from the window of his room on the sixth floor. Coroner brought in an open verdict.'

'Which could also mean he might have jumped. Or been pushed.'

'Any of the above. You noticed he worked at Martlesham Heath?'

'That's British Telecom's research centre.'

Dodgson nodded. 'Darlington worked on the top floor. You know what they have up there, don't you?'

'R.12,' Garrett said. 'The special investigations division. That's where they make all those cute little listening toys our friends at Century House love to play with. What was Darlington doing in Nairobi?'

'Vacation. He'd been working in Mombasa. The Royal Navy Armilla Patrol is based there.'

'That's the sophisticated ships unit, isn't it? Lynx helicopters, hi-tech weaponry.'

'That's why Darlington was in Mombasa. But it doesn't tell us why he might have jumped out of his hotel window.'

'My old Mum used to say, Men over thirty are either married or singular,' Garrett suggested.

'That's a bit sweeping, isn't it?'

'However.'

'You're right. He was gay.'

'A lot of sailors in Mombasa,' Garrett observed.

'Quite a few elephants as well,' Dodgson retorted. 'As far as we can ascertain he didn't take either into his hotel room.'

'So he killed himself because . . . ?'

Dodgson made an exasperated sound. 'That's what's so frustrating about all these cases, Pat. You keep on getting the feeling that something isn't quite kosher. But you can't find anything to get hold of. It's like trying to put fog into a bucket.'

'I know the feeling. I got it when I read Haverby's report. Go on.'

'Up to now, we've just been talking about, well, maybes. But now we're coming to the really weird ones. Let me tell you about Ajai Mehta.'

'Indian?'

'British, of Indian immigrant parents. He was twenty-four, worked as a computer software engineer at Hayling-Brittain Avionics and Defence Systems in Somerset.'

Mehta had been found dead beneath a viaduct of the M25 in Buckinghamshire, more than a hundred miles from his home at Blagdon, in the Chew Valley, Dodgson went on.

'Shot himself through the mouth with an old Enfield revolver, one of the old No. 2 models that were made by the thousand in 1940. Museum piece. Christ knows where he got ammo for it, never mind the gun itself.'

'You said weird,' Garrett remarked.

'I'm coming to that,' Dodgson said testily. 'His body was found in a ditch alongside a lane that's used by commuters to get to the Chorleywood station car park. Probably several hundred people drive past the place every day. Yet nobody saw anything. The body was found by a man walking a dog. You want to see the pictures?'

Garrett shrugged. Dodgson slid half a dozen ten by eights out of the manila envelope and laid them on the desk. The dead man lay on his back, mouth wide open, eyes staring at nothing. He wore a cheap cotton shirt and a windcheater. His dark trousers were down around his thighs.

'He shot himself with his pants down?' Garrett said.

'That's the way they found him,' Dodgson replied. 'Something else. There was a puncture mark on his right thigh. No trace of anything in the bloodstream, though.'

'He could have detoxified immediately prior to death.'

'Possibly.'

'How long had he been there?'

'Forensic guessed about thirty-six hours. Mehta had gone to work as usual. Behaved quite normally during the day, apparently. He'd arranged to meet a friend that night. Didn't turn up, didn't telephone. She called his parents. When he didn't come home that night, they called the local police.'

'What was he working on?'

'Hayling-Brittain declined to be specific. Some sort of underwater vibration simulator.'

'So he had access to classified material.'

'I'd say almost certainly.'

'Classified enough to get him kidnapped?'

Dodgson shrugged. 'What might look unimportant to you and me might be vital to some other interested party, Pat.'

'Industrial espionage?'

'That's the way my thoughts went wending. But apart from the fact that all these people had access to some kind of classified material, there wasn't any discernible pattern.'

'What's the next one?'

'October third, 1987,' Dodgson said. 'Another first-generation British Indian, East African this time. Said Malik. Twenty-six years old, a computer analyst at Hayling-Brittain Avionics and Defence Systems, Stanmore. He hanged himself from a tree on Ealing Common.'

'Suicide?'

'That was the verdict. The police put up the proposition that Malik was involved in an unhappy relationship with a woman, but we checked it and found out he hadn't seen the woman in question for three years. Not only that, the day he killed himself he had an appointment at the Home Office in Croydon, something to do with getting a visa for his fiancée to come to Britain.'

'What was he working on at Stanmore?'

'Torpedoes.'

'That all you know?'

'That's all they'd tell me. Underwater guidance systems.'

'How many more are there, Tony?'

'Just a few. I'll concentrate on the more bizarre ones. Like John Lowrie.'

On 21 February the preceding year, John Lowrie, a forty-six-year-old senior lecturer in metallurgy at the Royal Military College of Science, Shrivenham, near Swindon, had been to a dinner party with his wife, Amanda, who was a district nurse. They had played bridge. Because her husband had drunk a couple of whiskies, Amanda Lowrie drove their Vauxhall Cavalier back to Canterbury Road. When they got there, Lowrie told her he would put the car away. She went on up to bed, and fell asleep. When she woke up next morning, his side of the bed was unslept in. She went out to the garage and found him lying underneath the car, with the engine still running. At first she thought he had suffered a heart attack: in fact, the cause of death was carbon monoxide poisoning.

'The man had just been given a sizeable rise,' Dodgson added. 'He had tickets for *Mamma Mia* the following week. That doesn't sound like a scenario for suicide, does it?'

'Anything else?'

'Yes. Maybe. I don't know. Take a look at the photographs.'

He opened the brown envelope and slid the scene-of-death pictures out. Garages only came in two types: neat and cluttered. John Lowrie's was of the latter variety, with cardboard boxes and ladders and paint pots and rubber boots and garden implements. His body lay beneath the car, his face close to the exhaust pipe. Garrett frowned.

'How the hell did he get under the car

like that?' he said. 'The top of his head is almost touching the doors.'

'You tell me,' Dodgson replied.

'It almost looks as if he was laid out on the floor first, the car was pushed in over him, and then the doors were closed. How else could he have got into that position?'

'Good question,' Dodgson said. 'The verdict, however, was suicide.'

'How the hell could they . . . ?'

'That's what Amanda Lowrie would like to know,' Dodgson said. There was a small smile playing around the corners of his mouth. 'Is this thing beginning to get to you, Pat?'

Garrett nodded. 'It's like *Alice in Wonderland*, all right. Curiouser and curiouser. How many more have we got?'

'Only three. But they're all beauties.'

In some ways, he said, the death of Tom Wakenshaw, a thirty-nine-year-old satellite project manager with Exmoor Systems, a subsidiary of Hayling-Brittain, was one of the most bizarre deaths of them all. Wakenshaw was working on a secret MoD radar project: something to do with nuclear submarines, about which the company declined to be more informative. One day he got into his brand-new Range Rover, packed it with jerrycans full of petrol, and drove it straight over the white chalk cliffs at Beachy Head.

'You know, Tony, I think I've got as lively an imagination as the next man,' Garrett said reflectively. 'But I'm damned if I can imagine what would make a man turn his car into a petrol bomb and drive it off the top of a cliff.'

'I talked to the chief security officer at Hayling-Brittain myself,' Dodgson said. 'He couldn't offer any explanation. Nobody could. Wakenshaw was very successful, very confident. He'd just pulled off a great coup for the company. He had a very bright future ahead of him.'

'He still drove off the cliff.'

'At the risk of repeating myself, it's bizarre. But as far as we can make out, that's all it is. A man who seems to have every reason to stay alive decides to kill himself. He picks what seems to our eyes to be the most outlandish method he can think of. He doesn't even — I don't say this is significant, but it is unusual — leave a note. His family refuses to believe there isn't something sinister connected with the death. But try as we will, we can't come up with a single thing to support the theory.'

'You have a theory, then?'

'It sounds a bit far-fetched. But we wondered . . . if there was actually someone behind all this, what would he want?'

'Have you mentioned your theory to anyone else?'

'I tried it out on Five. They told me not to waste my time on it. You know how they talk, that damned spookspeak. While it was not unfeasible that the operations of Hayling-Brittain could be of interest to foreign intelligence agencies, they had no intimation of any such interest in the present instances — something like that.'

'Then nobody will complain if I have a poke round.'

Dodgson shrugged. 'All contributions gratefully received,' he said. 'Have you got any idea where you might start?'

'I thought I'd start with Ronald Morris.'

'Why him?'

'He was a personal friend of Bleke's.'

'Ah,' Dodgson said, as if that explained something that had been bothering him.

'What do you mean, *ah*?'

'Couldn't figure out why your people would be interested. That explains it. You know the details, I take it?'

'He electrocuted himself in a particularly ghastly way.'

'Just so,' Dodgson said. 'The funny thing is, the day before, a man named Lawrence Peterson, who worked for Exmoor Systems, died in almost exactly the same way.'

Garrett's attention sharpened. 'I hadn't heard about this.'

'We only just got the dossier from the Surrey police. It happened over a Bank Holiday weekend. The inquest was delayed, and somebody didn't follow through.'

'What happened?'

'It was a Saturday morning. Peterson was planning to work on an Austin Seven he was rebuilding in his garage. His wife worked part-time in a local dress shop. He drove her down to the village at about nine-thirty, and told her he'd pick her up at lunchtime. Went back home, fed the cat, had a cup of coffee, then wired himself up, bypassed the fuse with a paperclip, and tripped the switch with his toe. When he didn't turn up at lunchtime, the wife got a lift home, and found him electrocuted in the garage.'

'I know what the answer is going to be, but I'll ask you anyway: no note?'

'No note, no nothing. His wife is convinced someone killed him. Said he was perfectly all right when he left her. The police pointed out that the garage was locked from the inside and there was no sign of foul play. Made no difference. She won't believe it.'

'Happy marriage?'

'Normal. Nice house in Norbury, three teenage kids, good income, no debts.'

'Coroner's verdict?'

'Open.'

'He had doubts, then?'

'I don't think so. The local police were

quite satisfied no outside parties were involved. Just playing safe.'

'Anything else?'

'Nothing you won't find out for yourself. Do you want some coffee or tea?'

'Another time,' Garrett said, getting up. 'I thought I'd have a day in the country.'

'With Dorothy Morris?'

'Holmes,' Garrett said, 'you amaze me.'

6

'I knew at once that something awful had happened,' Dorothy Morris said. 'I saw that young policeman coming up the path, twisting his helmet in his hands, and I *knew*. I felt so sorry for him. He looked so very young.'

She sat ramrod straight on a chintz-covered sofa, maintaining the fierce control over her emotions that is the way of Army widows.

'They took me to London in a car, and I identified the body.' She made a small grimace; having seen the pictures of Morris's corpse, Garrett could under-stand its cause. 'They gave me whisky. I never drink it, normally. It made me woozy. They told me there would be trouble with the media, that maybe I should go away for a while. I didn't take it in properly. I said I couldn't do that.'

They managed to get her away from the inquest before the reporters could get to her, but it was only a brief respite. She had been home less than half an hour, she said, when the first of the tabloids rang. After that it was non-stop: doorstep visits from the local papers, reporters from the Sunday scandal sheets ambushing her on her way to the shops. A woman came to see her, claiming to be a social worker specializing in grief counselling; it turned out she worked for one of the more garish of the dailies.

'They all wanted to know the same thing,' she said. 'Was I happy with the coroner's open verdict? In other words, did I think Ronald had been murdered?'

'And what did you tell them?'

'I told them I did not care to air my feelings in the tabloid Press,' she said. 'I told them to go away and stop pestering me.' She allowed herself a small smile. 'I wasn't quite as polite as that.'

'But they didn't stop.'

'It made things worse, if anything. Since I hadn't come right out and said I agreed with the verdict, the inference was that I did not. So they went ahead and printed their stories that way.'

'Do you mind talking about it now?'

'No,' she said calmly. 'Not any more.'

Dorothy Morris was perhaps fifty, perhaps five years more; it was hard to tell from her fair skin and well groomed ash-blonde hair. She looked like a very together lady; he wondered how she was really feeling.

'I know you've been asked a dozen times already, Mrs Morris, and I apologize for asking again, but . . . I take it you don't subscribe to the conspiracy theory that the newspapers have been peddling?'

'That nonsense!' she said vehemently. 'They ought to be ashamed, printing such lies!'

'Tell me about your husband,' Garrett suggested. 'When was the last time you saw him?'

'Two nights before . . . he died,' she said. 'We went to the theatre, and had dinner afterwards. With clients.'

'You didn't stay in town?'

She shook her head. 'Ronald was going to the factory at Ashford early the next day. It wouldn't have made sense to drive all the way out from central London when it's only about twenty miles from here.'

'Where did you eat?'

'The Caprice. Ronald likes . . . liked to eat there.'

'Had you met these clients before?'

'No. They were over here with their wives. From Sweden. A junket, Ronald called it.'

'So, you had dinner at the Caprice . . . '

'Then we walked them back to the Ritz, which was where they were all staying.'

'What time did you get back here?'

'It must have been about one when we got in. Ronald left at about seven next morning. He had to go to the factory at Ashford, and then be back in London by four for a meeting. He said it would go on late, so he would use the company flat.'

'Do you know what the meeting was about?'

'I don't think he said. But if he was staying in Grosvenor Square I assume it was something to do with work.'

'How did he seem? Was he preoccupied? Worried about anything?'

'No,' she said, perhaps just a shade too brightly. 'He was his usual self. Quite normal.'

'Your husband was a highly paid executive. I take it he had no money worries, Mrs Morris?'

She smiled forgivingly and shook her head.

'And . . . no one else in his life?'

Her chin came up. 'What are you suggesting?' she said, her voice noticeably cooler.

'I'm not suggesting anything, Mrs Morris,' Garrett said, keeping his own voice neutral. 'I'm just trying to come up with an explanation for the inexplicable: why would a normal, healthy man with no problems and apparently everything to live for, kill himself?'

'We were happy,' she said, the words a litany. 'Happy.'

An old journalistic saw popped unbidden into his mind. 'The bigger the reaction, the closer you are to the truth.' There was something Dorothy Morris was not telling him, something very close and personal she did not want to talk about. Like someone with an open wound, she had flinched at the thought of its being touched.

'I'm sorry,' Garrett said, getting up. 'This is distressing you. I'll come back another time.'

She made a gesture: there was apology in it. He sat down again.

'Suicide is . . . so hurtful,' she said. Her voice was pitched very low, and he had to strain to hear her. 'It's as if you are being punished for something you don't even know you did. The guilt . . . '

She made the helpless gesture again, and he could see the glint of tears she was struggling not to shed.

'There's no reason for you to feel guilty,' he said softly. The words *is there?* hung unspoken in the air.

'I don't know about that,' she sighed. 'I don't know about that at all.' She got up and went across to the french windows, looking up at the tops of the tall oaks at the far side of the beautifully kept garden. He saw her shoulders rise fractionally, then come down again, as if she was making a great effort to control her emotions. When she turned round, she was smiling.

'There's something so . . . comforting about a garden, don't you think?' she said.

'I'm sure you're right.'

She came back to the sofa, sat down.

'You have to understand,' she said. 'Ronald was so deeply involved with his work, it was . . . all-important. He never stopped. Even when he was home for the weekend, he often used to go into his study and work all hours. Sometimes half the night.'

'He had a computer here?'

'That damned computer,' she said, with a rueful smile.

'How long have you lived in Rushlake Green?'

'Fifteen years. The longest we've ever lived anywhere. You know how it is in the Army.'

'Has anyone from Hayling-Brittain been to see you?'

'Lord Bletchlock telephoned. He couldn't get to the funeral. There were more than a hundred people there, you know. Ronald had a great many friends.'

'But no one has been to the house?'

'No. Wait, yes. They sent someone down a few days after . . . it happened. They said Ronald had some papers that had to go back to the office.'

'What kind of papers?'

'I don't know. I took the man into the study and left him there. I assume he took whatever it was he needed.'

'Do you know the name of this man?'

'Halford. Ian Halford. He said he was in charge of security.'

'Did he tell you where he was from?'

'I never asked. I assumed it was Ashford.'

'Did your husband keep a diary, Mrs Morris?'

'Not a 'dear Diary' diary, if that's what you mean,' she smiled. 'That wasn't Ronald's style. But a business diary, yes.'

'Do you have it?'

'It will be in the study. I'll go and get it.'

She went out of the room, gently closing the panelled door with its polished brass hardware behind her. He went across to a high Georgian window looking out over immaculate lawns. The dog looked up hopefully, then put its head down again, its eyes reproachful.

'It's not there,' Dorothy Morris said behind him. He turned round. Standing in the doorway, she wore the faint frown of someone mildly annoyed at not being able to find immediately what she was looking for. 'It was on Ronald's desk, I'm sure. I remember seeing it.'

'Don't worry about it,' Garrett said, reassuringly. 'I'm sure it will turn up. Perhaps you'll give me a call when you find it.'

'Of course,' she said 'But . . . are you leaving?'

'I have to get back to town,' he told her.

'I thought — ' She stopped herself from saying whatever it was she had intended to say. She had clearly expected a lot more questions.

'With your permission, I'd like to ask a colleague of mine to come and see you,' he said. 'Her name is Jessica Goldman.'

'Of course,' Dorothy Morris said. 'You have my number.'

She came with him to the door and said goodbye. She made him feel like a subaltern who has just had tea with the colonel's lady. He got into the Audi and headed for the main road.

★   ★   ★

He called Jessica about six forty.

'You do something to me,' he said. 'And I'll do something to you.'

'That isn't Cole Porter.'

'No, that's Abe Burrows,' he told her. 'Whatcha doin'?'

'Just working up to reading a lovely relaxing monograph on the psychopathology of the serial killer,' she said. 'That's how we high achievers spend our evenings, you know: a warm bath, a glass of white wine, a little light reading.'

'You deserve better. Much, much better.'

'I know. Make me an offer.'

'How about scallops Mornay, followed by English strawberries and fresh double cream?'

'Sold,' Jessica said. 'That screech of

brakes you can hear outside your door is me arriving.'

'Can't resist me, huh?'

'Not you, scallops. Half an hour?'

'I'd better warn you, I put on aftershave.'

Jessica lived in an apartment overlooking Cadogan Square that she was gradually furnishing and redecorating in her own idiosyncratic style. It would take her no more than ten minutes to dress: she was not one of those women who tried on fifteen things before she came to a decision about what to wear. She kept her Renault in the underground car park opposite her apartment. Fifteen minutes more to drive over to his place: half an hour she said, half an hour it would be. He looked at the clock. Get a move on, Garrett.

He washed and dried the scallops, separating off the bright orange roes, then put them all into a pan with a slice of onion, a few peppercorns and a bay leaf, and covered them with a wineglass of water and a half glass of dry white wine. He set the timer for eight minutes and put them on a low heat to poach very slowly. Cook them too fast and they would turn to rubber.

While the scallops and roes were cooking, he melted an ounce of butter in a pan, blended in an ounce of flour, and then added half a pint of milk, whisking it vigorously until it thickened. Setting it aside, he grated an ounce of Gruyère and an ounce of Cheddar. A minute or so later, the timer pinged, and he took the scallops off the heat, pouring maybe a wineglassful of the stock in which they had cooked into the sauce. He kept it boiling gently for about three or four minutes before folding in the grated cheese, and then, finally, two tablespoonsfuls of cream.

He sliced the scallops and laid them in a Pyrex cooking dish and poured the Mornay sauce over them until they were completely covered. On top of this he arranged the poached roes, then grated a little more cheese over them. He set the dish to one side, and turned his attention to the strawberries. They were fat and juicy. He put them in a crystal bowl, squeezed fresh lemon juice over them, and left them to chill on the coldest shelf at the bottom of the fridge. He looked at the clock again and smiled. Twenty-eight minutes: eat your heart out, Gordon Ramsay.

The intercom buzzed. 'Ready or not, here I come,' Jessica said.

He met her at the door with a glass of Chablis. She was wearing a loose-fitting light blue double-breasted cotton jacket with neat revers and gold buttons to the waist over a sleeveless white one-piece Halston day dress. She gave a little *mmmm* of appreciation as he kissed her. She smelled like springtime. Or maybe Nina Ricci.

'You look beautiful,' he said. 'How do you do it?'

'You should see the picture in the attic,' Jessica grinned. She was quite tall, around five feet seven, with the willowy body of a model, dark lustrous eyes and a thin, high-cheekboned face. Her long, black, naturally curled hair tumbled in a proud mane down to her shoulders. She had a full-lipped, mobile mouth that smiled easily. They went in together, arms around each other's waist.

'You want to eat first or make love first?' he said.

'Subtle as ever, Garrett,' she said. 'Do I answer to please you or to please me?'

'How about to please me?'

'Damn,' she said. 'And I'm starving.'

'Okay,' he said, with a mock-nonchalant shrug, 'so the aftershave doesn't work. Let's eat.'

He went into the kitchen and switched on the grill. When it was at full heat he slid the dish with the scallops underneath.

'Five minutes,' he said. 'Another glass of wine?'

'Half,' Jessica said. 'I want to taste those scallops.'

They ate in the dining alcove that overlooked the River Thames. It was a bright, warm, sunny evening and the open windows gave them the feeling of eating al fresco, with all the sounds of London drifting up from the busy streets and the ever-changing river.

'I do like it that you're such a good cook, Charles,' Jessica said. 'It never fails to surprise me. Who taught you?'

'Nobody taught me. It's not difficult. All you have to do is think, Scallops would be nice. Then look in a cookbook to see what you can do with them. Coquilles St Jacques looks pretty difficult. Making a Mornay sauce doesn't. So that's what I cook.'

'I ate too much,' she said. 'Bleah.'

'Want to go for a walk?'

'What a good idea.'

He put on a lightweight jacket and they took the elevator down and walked up Horseguards Avenue and across White-hall. Horse Guards Parade was almost deserted, but there were still a lot of people in St James's Park.

'Are you very busy at the moment?' he asked.

'Not very,' she replied. 'Why?'

'I need your help.'

'Go on.'

'Do you know anything about Hayling-Brittain?'

'Major defence supplier. Chairman Lord Bletchlock?'

'The very one,' he said. 'What else do

you know about them?'

'Only what I read in the papers.'

'Then you've read about the Trail of Death, as they call it.'

'Is there anything to it?'

'I don't know. Bleke has asked me to poke around.'

'Ah,' she said. 'The redoubtable General Bleke.'

'He was talking about giving you lunch at his club.'

'That'll be the day we'll dance all night, as my father used to say.' Jessica smiled to take the sting out of the words. 'The papers think there's something rotten in the state of Hayling-Maxwell. Does this mean Bleke does, too?'

'One of the men who died, Ronald Morris, was a friend of his. I went down to see the widow yesterday. She lives in East Sussex, a pretty little village called Rushlake Green.'

'And?'

'I just sensed something was amiss. She was so self-possessed, so cool and calm, and yet . . . '

'You think she's hiding something?

Something she hasn't told anybody?'

He shrugged. 'I don't know. Yes, maybe.'

'What do you think it is?'

'Skeleton in the closet. Another woman, perhaps. Something. I wondered . . .'

'Oh-oh,' Jessica said. 'Are you going to say what I think you're going to say?'

'I could put in a formal request for assistance from your department,' he said. 'But there's no guarantee I'd get you. And it's you I want.'

Jessica was a staff psychotherapeutic counsellor at Kelvin House, the Ministry of Defence Central Medical Establishment in London's Cleveland Street.

'Why has it got to be me?'

'Because you happen to be very good at what you do,' he said. 'And because I trust your judgement implicitly.'

'You are a bastard, Garrett,' she said, without heat. 'How could I refuse you after a pretty speech like that?'

'I think she needs to talk to someone, Jess,' he told her. 'But she won't — I don't think she'll unburden herself to a man. Not the nature of the animal, if you

101

know what I mean. Stiff upper lip and all that. But another woman . . . '

They turned right along the Mall and walked under Admiralty Arch and out into the noisy hubbub of traffic and tourists around Trafalgar Square. A crewcut youth in jeans and a Union Jack T-shirt was taking a shower in one of the fountains, egged on by a noisy scrum of supporters with cans of lager in their hands.

'London by night is a wonderful sight,' Garrett muttered, turning right into Whitehall.

'Don't be such an old grouch,' Jessica grinned. 'You were young once.'

'I was never that young.' They passed the old Whitehall Theatre and crossed over near the Cenotaph. 'Well?' he said.

'Well, what?'

'Will you talk to Dorothy Morris?'

'If you want me to,' Jessica said. 'First, tell me something. How did the husband die?'

'He electrocuted himself. Very messily.' He told her about some of the cases, Bates skidding into the drydock, Wakenshaw driving his Range Rover off the cliffs at Beachy Head. 'Out of the deaths we know about, there were eight suicide verdicts. The UK suicide rate is one in seven and a half thousand. Even if we only count those eight, Hayling-Maxwell's suicide rate is double the national average. If all the deaths were taken into account, it would be nearly seven times the norm.'

Jessica shook her head. 'Twenty-two people out of twenty-five thousand is less than one tenth of one per cent. Eight is one thirtieth. You can't draw meaningful conclusions from such a small sample. It could be nothing more than coincidence.'

'That's why I'm concentrating on Morris for the moment. I've got a hunch there's more to it, but what that more is, I haven't the faintest idea.'

'Has anyone looked into the medical histories of these people? You know, of course, that at least two-thirds of those who commit suicide are — clinically, at least — mentally ill.'

'It occurred. Quite apart from the probability that Hayling-Brittain would tend to go to some lengths to avoid employing people who were mentally ill, the medical backgrounds of all the subjects were checked, and in no instance was there any history of mental disturbance. That's why I want you to try to find out whether Dorothy Morris is hiding anything, and if so what it is.'

'I'll try,' Jessica said. They turned back into Whitehall Court. 'Just tell me one more thing. Was there a note?'

'It's in the dossier. I'll show it to you later.'

'Later?'

'Abe Burrows,' he said. 'Don't tell me you've forgotten.'

Jessica smiled, bright mischief dancing in her eyes. 'No,' she said, standing on tiptoe to kiss him on the mouth. 'But I was beginning to think you had.'

7

The headquarters of Hayling-Brittain Avionics and Defence Systems was an enormous 1930s-style redbrick complex that stood on four and a half acres of open ground, screened from the main road by high walls behind which grew even higher shrubbery, a few miles outside Amersham, Buckinghamshire, about twenty-five miles from London. Garrett pulled the Audi Quattro to a stop at the gate and gave his name to the security guard.

When his appointment was confirmed, the guard asked him to sign in, giving his name and time of arrival. That done, Garrett was given a plastic clip-on tag with the word VISITOR on it and directed to drive to the visitors' parking facility alongside the main building. A sign pointed the way to Reception. He entered a large, semicircular foyer with a domed glass roof that reminded him of one of those palm houses in municipal parks. On a huge circular dais at its centre stood what looked like a full-size Cruise missile. Garrett found himself wondering how the workers at Hayling-Brittain felt about being daily reminded that they made weapons that could end all life on earth. Maybe, like Scarlett O'Hara, they just resolutely decided not to think about it today.

To one side of the hall in which he found himself was a desk where he was again required to sign in. An elevator took him up to the eighth floor to the Muzak accompaniment of Paul McCartney's lugubrious 'Yesterday'; he emerged into an environment markedly different from the one below.

Facing him was a small reception area, with simulated leather armchairs and a glass-topped table on which lay half a dozen of the snootier illustrated magazines. A large *Monstera Borsigiana* grew in a wooden tub beside one of the chairs. The floors were carpeted; not the practical, unglamorous carpet tiling of lower levels, but deep, expensive wool in a pleasing brown tone that perfectly complemented the pale beige hessian on the walls. The room smelled faintly of air freshener. And money, Garrett thought. Discreet, big company money.

He waited. Bletchlock's timekeeping was appalling: he was always late for appointments, requiring punctuality in others but observing none himself. His schedules were constantly interrupted by an open-door style of leadership that inevitably led to unscheduled conferences, and by answering personally every telephone call directed to him. He was famed for a saying that went something along the lines of his company being a democratic institution, but that the man who had the gold made all the rules. Twenty minutes went by on leaden feet.

After fifteen more, a young woman came through the glass door to Garrett's right. She wore a tailored suit that was as unobtrusively expensive as the décor and did absolutely nothing to conceal a showgirl figure. Her eyes were bright blue.

'Mr Garrett?' she said, with a dazzling

smile. 'Lord Bletchlock will see you now. Follow me, please.'

She turned and led the way down a short corridor with a glass roof that let in the bright sunshine. It was a pleasure to watch her walk. She opened a door and stood aside.

'This way,' she said. He caught a trace of Arpège as he passed her. Facing him was a man he recognized immediately from photographs: well above medium height, wide-shouldered and even wider around the middle, Arnold Bletchlock would have been an imposing figure in almost any gathering. Here in his own lair he was almost intimidating, the famous eyebrows like two black caterpillars, the large head thrown back, a huge hand outstretched in welcome. He looked, Garrett decided, like a cross between Robert Mitchum and Leonid Brezhnev.

'Mr Garrett, Mr Garrett,' Bletchlock said enthusiastically, his voice just softer than a sonic boom. 'Come and sit down, sit down.'

Garrett let himself be ushered to a comfortable modern leather-upholstered upright chair in front of the enormous Victorian desk. Bletchlock sat in his own hugely padded executive driving seat. It came as no surprise at all to Garrett that he had to look up at him.

'Something to drink?' Bletchlock boomed. 'Coffee, tea?'

'Thank you, no,' Garrett said. 'I don't want to take any more of your time than necessary.'

'Glad to hear it,' Bletchlock rumbled. 'I'm getting sick and tired of this whole damned business. Thought you people had asked us everything you wanted to know, anyway.'

'I didn't come to ask you questions, Lord Bletchlock. I've got a slightly different brief.'

Bletchlock frowned. 'I don't understand. I was under the impression that you'd been sent up here by the ministry to ask me some questions.'

'For the purposes of this exercise, I suggest we keep it that way,' Garrett replied. 'However, I'm not exactly from the ministry.'

The caterpillar eyebrows drew together

in a frown. Bletchlock leaned forward and fastened his eyes on Garrett. 'If you're not from the ministry, you've got about four seconds to tell me who the hell sent you,' the big man growled.

Garrett smiled. 'I've read about you, Lord Bletchlock,' he said. 'The profile in *Newsweek*, the authorized biography and all the other things. I'm quite prepared to believe you're as tough and ruthless as they say you are. Don't let's get off on the wrong foot by your feeling you have to prove it.'

Bletchlock's head came up, like a buffalo scenting a prowling lioness. Garrett thought he detected the vestiges of a smile at the corners of the full lips, but it was hard to tell. Anybody who made the kind of millions the man born Walter Horn in East Prussia six and a half decades ago had made, had not done so by giving away his innermost feelings.

'Ever thought of working in the private sector, Garrett?' Bletchlock asked. 'I think I could use a man like you.'

Garrett shook his head. 'I hear you have a high turnover in executives.'

'That's a calumny,' the big man rumbled. 'If a man is pulling his weight in my organization, he has a job for as long as he wants it. A job considerably higher paid than in other sections of our industry, I might add. But only as long as he delivers.'

' 'If at first you don't succeed, you're fired'?'

'Nothing of the sort,' Bletchlock snapped. 'I believe in complete delegation. I give a man a job and tell him to go and do it. If he does it well, I reward him well. If he makes a muck of it, I replace him. Simple as that.'

Garrett let that one pass. One of the stories told about Bletchlock was that when he learned ten of his senior managers' company cars were uneconomic to run and needed replacing, instead of authorizing the purchase, Bletchlock ran a check on whether the managers were necessary. He found that six out of the ten were not, and abolished their jobs. He claimed there was a ninety per cent drop in requests for company cars over the next twelve months.

'You're chairman of a number of multinational companies, Lord Bletchlock,' Garrett said. 'How much do you involve yourself with the day-to-day running of Hayling-Brittain?'

Bletchlock got up and walked over to the window. 'I know the big picture. I rely on my divisional CEOs to keep me informed as to details. As I said, complete delegation.'

'What about security? Are you happy with the way it's handled?'

Bletchlock frowned. 'Security? We've got a very good man in charge of that. A former police commander.'

'Ian Halford.'

'You know him?'

'I've heard about him. They say he's something of a hard man.'

'He does the job and he does it well. I don't ask questions about his methods. I judge my executives on results.'

'And you rate him highly?'

'One of the best,' Bletchlock said firmly. 'Why?'

'Because I need unrestricted access to all your facilities and all your personnel. I want to be able to go into computer installations, weapons-testing facilities, research laboratories. I want to be able to talk to anyone I want to talk to, see anything I want to see, and I want to start immediately.'

The big man smiled, shaking his head. 'Is that all?' he said sarcastically.

'I don't know. Perhaps not. But it will do to start with.'

Bletchlock frowned, pursing his thick lips. 'I doubt there are more than two dozen people in the country who have sufficiently high security clearance to be given the kind of access you are asking for.'

'You're probably right,' Garrett said. 'Do you think the people who sent me don't know that?'

'Ah,' Bletchlock said thoughtfully. 'It would appear, then, that this investigation is moving on to a higher plane than before.'

'You could say that.'

'You'll have my complete co-operation, of course,' Bletchlock told him. 'But I have to warn you that my head of security may not concur with your request.'

'I'll try and talk him round,' Garrett said. He watched as the big man picked up the intercom, buzzed his secretary, and told her to ask Mr Halford to come to his office. So her name was Elaine, Garrett mused. Captains of industry had all the luck.

'He'll be along directly,' Bletchlock said. 'I'm going to have a glass of champagne. Join me.'

It wasn't an invitation. I suppose they get used to people doing whatever they're told, Garrett thought. Well, maybe he needed a victory, even one as small as that. It wasn't worth arguing, and anyway, it looked like a decent wine: Krug, from the shape of the bottle. As Bletchlock took two long-stemmed glass flutes from a cupboard and filled them, Garrett took a moment to look around the office.

It had obviously been furnished without any thought of expense. Leather, oak, brass; the tycoon's office as the bridge of a ship, the tycoon as captain?

The big picture windows, shaded by Luxaflex blinds, looked out over a landscaped garden with an ornamental pond that stretched as far as the perimeter road encircling the entire complex. The layout was more like that of a luxury apartment than an office. On the flat roof above them was a helicopter landing pad; a private Lear jet was on twenty-four-hour standby at London's Heathrow airport. Somewhere on one of the world's oceans was his luxury yacht. Today Tokyo, tomorrow Rio, the day after that Sydney. The style was the man and vice versa. It ought to be enviable, Garrett thought as he sipped his champagne, but somehow it wasn't.

'Ah,' Bletchlock said. 'There you are, Ian. I'd like you to meet Charles Garrett from, ah, the Ministry of Defence. Garrett, this is my head of security, Ian Halford.'

Halford was big, but not in the same way that Bletchlock was. His grip was solid and uncompromising, the shake-hands-as-if-you-mean-it variety.

'Garrett,' he said, his voice a slightly hoarse rumble. He was a solidly built, expensively dressed man, about six feet tall, and not by any means handsome; his face was full and slightly puffy, as if he'd done some sparring. A short, snub nose, eyes dangerously close to piggy, and hair combed to divert attention from the onset of baldness. A lot of vanity, Garrett decided.

'Mr Garrett is conducting a further investigation into the death of Ronald Morris,' Bletchlock told Halford.

'For God's sake!' Halford snapped impatiently. 'Don't you people ever give up? You've already had seven different kinds of policeman poking their noses through our files. I personally conducted an investigation of the most searching kind. What else do we have to do to convince you there's no connection between all these deaths?'

'Let me look into them,' Garrett said.

Halford frowned at Bletchlock. 'What does he mean?' he said.

'Mr Garrett has asked for a pass authorizing him to go anywhere he wants to go and see anything he wants to see. I'd like your input on that.'

Halford looked at Garrett again,

eyebrows slightly raised, as if he hadn't really seen him properly the first time.

'Do you have any particular reason for requesting such a pass, Mr Garrett?' he asked.

'Yes, I do,' Garrett said. They both waited; when no elucidation followed he saw another frown crease Halford's forehead. The security chief again glanced at Bletchlock for guidance. Getting no help there, he shook his head.

'You obviously misunderstood the question,' he said. 'I want to know why you need a go-anywhere pass.'

'I understood the question perfectly,' Garrett told him. 'But I'm afraid I can't discuss my reasons.'

Halford shrugged. 'Then whistle for your pass.'

Garrett smiled. Bletchlock made an apologetic sound, somewhere between a cough and clearing his throat.

'Mr Garrett's authorization comes, ah, from the very top, Ian,' Bletchlock said. 'The very top.'

'I see,' Halford said, changing gear smoothly. 'Well, I'm sure we won't have any problems. You tell me where you want to go, Mr Garrett, who you want to see. I'll arrange clearance. That way, if you do run into any difficulty, I'll be right there to iron it out.'

'I don't seem to be getting through to you, Mr Halford,' Garrett said. 'You won't be there holding my hand and neither will anybody else. Your job is to see to it that the doors are open. Have you got any problems with that?'

Halford looked mad clear through. He glanced at his superior, his big fists curling and uncurling. Garrett watched Bletchlock, who was sitting with his hands folded across his belly like some benign Buddha. Nothing showed on the craggy face or in the obsidian eyes. He was watching Halford, waiting to see how he would cope. Or not. In Bletchlock's book, losing your nerve was like losing your virginity: you only did it once.

Halford saw that, and shrugged. 'You'll forgive me, Mr Garrett, but my job is to formulate and direct the security policy of this organization. That's why no matter where the authorization comes from, I'm averse to issuing the kind of clearance you're asking for. Nothing personal, you understand. It's just that we have so many sensitive research areas where we prefer — ah, how shall I put it? — we prefer to avoid external incursions.'

'Very commendable,' Garrett said, unimpressed by Halford's fence-mending. 'Do I get my pass now?'

'Of course,' Halford said, making his tone genial. 'It's . . . I'm sure we can cope. When and where do you want to begin?'

'Now,' Garrett told him. 'I'll let you know where.'

The dismissive tone made Halford's puffy face set with anger. 'Is that all, sir?' he said to Bletchlock.

'I think so,' Bletchlock growled. 'Get on to it, Ian, will you?'

Halford nodded and went out without shaking hands with Garrett or saying goodbye.

'You've hurt his feelings,' Bletchlock observed.

'I'll cry tomorrow,' Garrett said, unfeelingly. 'Is there any more of that champagne? It's a shame to let it go to waste.'

Bletchlock went across to his drinks cabinet and lifted the bottle out of the insulated plastic cooler he had put it into. He poured more wine for Garrett, then filled his own glass. The fizz made a surprisingly loud sound in the sound-proofed silence of the air-conditioned suite. Garrett sipped the wine, aware Bletchlock was watching him the way he might have watched a poker player whose hole card he was trying to figure out.

'Did you know Ronald Morris, Lord Bletchlock?' Garrett asked, abruptly.

'You mean personally? Not very well. Why do you ask?'

'He was an assistant marketing direc-tor. What exactly does that entail?'

'You probably know we employ a great many ex-ministry and ex-military people,' Bletchlock said. 'It's mainly, of course, for their contacts. Bowler-hat a top soldier, who takes his place? His former assistant. So who better to sell our products to him? His old boss — he's already got a head start on anyone else.'

'And what sort of products was Morris selling, do you know?'

'Underwater electronic equipment. Halford would be able to tell you exactly what.'

'Not important at this stage,' Garrett said offhandedly. 'You know how he killed himself?'

'We conducted our own investigation,' Bletchlock reminded him. 'Halford was very thorough. I read his report three times.' He shook his head sadly.

'Did Halford send people to the homes of any of the dead men?'

'I don't know. But I doubt it. Why should he?'

'Mightn't they have had classified material at their homes, papers or plans they were working on?'

Bletchlock shook his head. 'No one is allowed to remove classified material from any installation. There are no exceptions — not even myself.'

'Who's your head of personnel?'

'His name is Daniel Hampson. Do you want to see him?'

'Maybe later,' Garrett said. The door

opened and Bletchlock's secretary came in. Elaine the fair, Elaine the lovable, Elaine the lily maid of Astolat. She wore no wedding ring. She looked as if she ought to be starring in the mini-series of a Barbara Taylor Bradford novel.

'This just came up from Security,' she reported. 'Ian — Mr Halford told me you were waiting for it.'

She handed Bletchlock a sheet of paper in a glassine folder and went out, closing the door noiselessly behind her. Bletchlock took his reading glasses out of his shirt pocket and put them on, nodding as he went through the document.

'That would seem to cover most eventualities,' he said. He picked up a fountain-pen and dashed a signature across the bottom of the page, blotting it with an old-fashioned wooden rocker blotter. He handed it across the desk to Garrett 'There's a photo booth in the reception area downstairs,' Bletchlock said. 'Take it to the desk. They'll reduce this to ID size and heat-seal it. Anything else you need?'

'Not right now,' Garrett said. He picked up the glassine envelope. 'Where's Halford, by the way?'

'Probably in his office, sticking pins in an effigy of you,' Bletchlock said, his shoulders moving with silent mirth. 'He's not a good loser.'

'Tell him if he doesn't want a 'Z' on his forehead, he shouldn't cross swords with Zorro,' Garrett replied.

Bletchlock's shoulders twitched some more, and Garrett heard a sound like a snake wriggling in a wastepaper basket. He realized Bletchlock was laughing. The two men shook hands and Garrett started for the door. As he opened it, Bletchlock's voice stopped him.

'Give some thought to what I said,' Bletchlock said. 'We can always use good men here at Hayling-Brittain.'

Garrett didn't bother to reply. On his way to the elevator, he stopped at Elaine's desk. She looked up.

'Tell me something,' he said. 'Do complete strangers rush up to you in the street and press bouquets of flowers on you?'

'All the time,' she smiled, the full lips parting to reveal perfect teeth.

'Then I don't suppose there's any point in asking you to have dinner with me.'

'Sorry,' she said, still smiling her adorable smile. 'I only fuck the first team.'

8

His name was André Dur. The son of a Malaysian woman and an English diplomat, educated at private schools in Singapore and Switzerland, he looked every inch an Englishman. At thirty-two years of age, he was tall and slim, with dark blond hair and brilliantly blue, almost violet eyes. His clothes, which he bought off the rack, fitted him as though they had been made in Savile Row. He looked as if he might be a City high-flyer or some other successful product of the enterprise culture. But he was none of these things; any more than he was a freelance photographer, as it said in the forged passport he was carrying.

At the beginning of June, the project which he had been preparing for the best part of five years was almost ready. The team was assembled, the weapon almost complete. It was time now for the final reconnaissance. For that, André decided, he needed another identity.

Obtaining the papers necessary to set up a false identity was ordinarily not too difficult, providing one had time, because the British have no privacy laws protecting the records of their births, marriages and deaths, and it is a matter of moments to choose an appropriate birth certificate, pay the appropriate fee, and proceed from there. In this instance, however, he had neither the time nor the inclination to set up an elaborate 'legend' — he automatically used the security services jargon for a manufactured identity — so he flew to London at the beginning of June and as Robert Taylor — the name on the passport — checked into one of the luxury apartments in Down Street operated by the Athenaeum Hotel. It was not self-indulgence; far fewer questions are asked of the rich than of the poor. In addition, André had stayed there before: by simply refraining from using the hotel's facilities, he remained almost completely anonymous.

Almost immediately he began his search for a likely pigeon. Every night he went into the Café Royal in Regent Street, and sat at the bar listening to the pianist go through his enormous repertoire of show songs. After eight, the early evening crowd moved on and the place was relatively quiet, with just a few tourists nursing their drinks and enjoying the music. From about ten forty-five onward, the after-theatre crowd crammed in; often actors and actresses working in the nearby theatres would come in and sing a number from their show at the piano.

André found his pigeon on the third evening, an American tourist he'd spoken to briefly the night before. The man's name was Charles Ballard, and he was from Oklahoma City. Travelling alone, staying at the Hilton, en route to Paris and then Rome, he was not expected back in the States for another two weeks. Perfect.

'Oklahoma City,' André said. 'That's on Route Sixty-Six.'

'Used to be,' Ballard told him. 'Twenty years ago.'

'I wish you hadn't told me that,' André

said. 'My name's Taylor, by the way. Robert Taylor.'

'Like the movie star, huh? You live here in London?' he asked André.

'That's right. I have an apartment in Chelsea.'

'Hey, I hear that's a swinging place.'

'Used to be, Charlie. Twenty years ago.'

They laughed, and André bought drinks. Ballard was on a business trip; something to do with the construction industry.

'Have another of those,' André said. 'What was it?'

'That's mighty generous of you, Bob. Jack Daniel's on the rocks.'

They took their drinks across to a table and André listened patiently to the American's harmless prattle until the theatre crowd started coming in.

'You know, Charlie, this place is a little noisy for my taste tonight,' André said impatiently. 'How do you feel about moving on?'

'Sure,' Ballard said. He was already a little drunk. So much the better. 'What have you got in mind?'

'There's an American bar I know near here. They serve quite a decent champagne.'

'Champagne? What's the occasion?'

'Paying you back for Lend-Lease,' André said.

'I'll drink to that!' Ballard chortled. He was easy to amuse.

They went out of the Café Royal and crossed over Piccadilly, cutting through to Jermyn Street. Jules Bar was on the south side, just along from the Duke of York Hotel. It was dark inside, in the American style, with a padded leather bar behind which an impressive array of bottles was displayed in tiers. André ordered a bottle of the house champagne and made sure Ballard drank most of it; the American became increasingly expansive as he drank.

'Work hard, play hard, that's my motto,' Ballard said, expansively. He was a short man, a little overweight, probably not yet fifty years old, although he looked more. 'Hey, waddya say we get s'more of that champagne?'

They stayed in the bar until around

eleven; Ballard never stopped talking, about his lovely wife Carol, his business, his beautiful home in Nichols Hills, his three cars, his timeshare apartment in St Croix.

'I hate to break this up, Charlie,' André said. 'But I've got an early start tomorrow. You're at the Hilton, aren't you? Why don't I give you a lift back there? It's on my way home.'

'Hey, would you mind doing that, Bob?' Ballard said. ''ass great.'

André had parked the car outside Boss & Co., the gunsmiths in Dover Street, just opposite the Arts Club; it took them only five minutes to walk there. Charlie Ballard made the usual American mistake of going round to the right-hand side to get in. He realized what he had done and went round to the other side, chuckling to himself.

'Bad enough you drive on the wrong side o' the road,' he said, getting clumsily in. 'You guys drive on the wrong side of the goddamn car as well.'

'Let me help you with that seat belt,' André offered. He had the hypodermic in his left hand as he reached across with his right. Without warning he clamped a hand like a steel claw across the man's face, pinning him against the headrest. In the same movement, he slid the needle into Ballard's flabby thigh. Ballard's eyes bulged; he arched his back and flailed with his one free arm, trying to break André's grip, but he was too drunk and out of condition. The drug — an intravenous anaesthetic called propofol — took only a minute to do the rest of the job; Ballard's body went slack and his head lolled.

André smiled. He fastened a seat-belt around the flaccid body, racked the seat back so that it looked as if his passenger was dozing, and moved off.

Twenty minutes later the big Rover was speeding through south London, heading for the motorway spur that runs due south and almost arrow-straight to Gatwick airport and Crawley. From there, André took a minor road towards Colgate, swinging off on to a single-track lane before he reached the village. He knew exactly where he was going. When he saw the lay-by he had located on an earlier reconnaissance, he pulled off the road.

He leaned over and unfastened the seat-belt, then reached into Ballard's inside pocket, taking out his billfold. It contained a wad of dollars and English pounds, a driver's licence, and half a dozen credit cards. André took out the American Express card; that'll do nicely, he thought, with a grin. He removed the driver's licence and replaced Ballard's billfold. Another pocket yielded an American passport and a folder containing an American Airlines ticket. He pocketed the passport and replaced the other papers. By now, the American was making the inarticulate sounds of someone coming out of an anaesthetic. It was time to finish it. André got out of the car and walked around to the passenger side, wedging the door wide open.

'Come on, Charlie,' he said, helping the American out of the car. 'Let me give you a hand.'

He draped the semi-conscious American's arm around his shoulder and half-walked, half-dragged him into the dark and silent woods. Their feet made hardly any sound on the ancient leaf mould. About fifty yards in, they came to a gully with steep sloping sides covered in high bracken, weeds and brambles.

'Wha . . . ?' All at once, Charlie Ballard straightened up, pushing away from the man beside him. 'Wha's goin' on?' he slurred belligerently. 'Wha' — where the hell is this?'

'This is where we say goodbye, Charlie,' André said. He put the silenced .22 calibre Swiss P210-5 SIG pistol hard against the base of Ballard's skull just below the occipital bulge, and pulled the trigger. The first requirement of any silencer is that the bullet fly subsonic, otherwise the silencing effect is minimal. The SIG .22's muzzle velocity of 335 metres a second actually slightly exceeded the speed of sound but not enough to do more than make the soft splat of the explosion slightly harder. Ballard fell forward on to his knees, then face-down on the ground.

Grunting with effort, André rolled the

body down into the gully. It thrashed noisily through the bracken and came to a stop twenty feet below. André followed, ensuring by torchlight that the body was completely concealed. When he was satisfied, he put a second bullet into Ballard's head above the right ear, then scrambled out of the gully. He walked unhurriedly back to the car, checked that there was still no one around, then drove away. When he got back to London he ditched the Rover — stolen in Bristol three days earlier — went back to his apartment, and slept without dreaming for eight hours.

Next morning, he went to the Hertz office in Russell Square; using Ballard's driving licence, and Amex card, he rented a Mercedes 190. He drove out of London and headed north up the M1 motorway toward Birmingham and turned on to the M6. Something less than four hours later he left the motorway at Junction 32, following the signs for Blackpool till he saw a turning marked A585 Fleetwood. The road meandered through pleasantly rural countryside, swinging west to pick up the west bank of the River Wyre at the point where it makes its sharp turn toward the north and its estuary in Morecambe Bay.

The town of Fleetwood is little more than a genteel extension of Blackpool, its raucous seaside resort neighbour to the south. The streets were Sunday morning deserted, the drab shops closed.

At the seafront there were promenade gardens, a lighthouse and a short pier, amusement arcades and cafés, and the usual unlovely clutter of seaside concessions, trashy souvenirs and postcards. A car ferry alongside the dock dwarfed everything near it; Fleetwood, the largest fishing port on the west coast of England, is the terminus of the ferry to the Isle of Man, sixty miles to the west.

André parked the Mercedes outside the Tramways Café and Grill on North Albert Street. Around the corner was the lighthouse. It was a long way from the sea, rendered obsolescent by civic development, now just a place for elderly holidaymakers to rest their legs on sunny benches facing the sea. From a nearby shop he bought a cheap street map and a copy of the local paper, the *Fleetwood Gazette*. Small ads told you more about a town than Chamber of Commerce brochures. He got into the car and looked at the map. The harbour was on the west bank of the Wyre, about half a mile out of town.

He drove until he saw a sign: West Side Wyre Dock. He turned into a narrow road lined with old warehouses. There was a long left-hand bend, and then he saw the entrance to the dock on his right.

He stopped the car and got out. The old quay made a dog-leg out toward the open water. Clumps of couch grass, weeds and dandelions grew in the concrete edging. A notice-board displayed a document dated two years earlier, warning of hazards in the Irish Sea. Everything looked shoddy and neglected.

The tide was out, so only the tops of the masts of fishing boats moored alongside the quay showed above ground level.

He saw a man coming along the quay toward him. He wore a shabby blue jacket, collarless shirt, baggy pants and cracked, worn-out shoes; on his head at a rakish angle he wore a mariner's peaked cap with a tarnished badge.

'How do,' he said, showing tobacco-stained teeth. He had rheumy blue eyes and a grizzled four-day stubble.

'Tell me, do they still fish from here?' André said.

'Oh, aye,' was the reply.

'And are these the biggest trawlers operating out of here?' André jerked a thumb at the boats tied up along the quayside.

'Nah.' The old man took off his cap and scratched his greasy, unkempt iron-grey hair. 'Nah. Big ones are in the East Dock.'

'That's over there?'

'Right.'

'They go out every day?'

The man looked faintly surprised. 'Course,' he nodded.

'How many boats?'

A shrug. 'Forty. Sixty. It depends.'

'Where do they fish, around the Isle of Man?'

'Aye. Rockall, sometimes.'

'What are the biggest trawlers operating out of Fleetwood these days?'

'Hundred, hundred and twenty-footers.'

'How many crew on one of those?'

'Five, six. Skipper, bosun, cook and a couple of deckies. These days cooks are often deckies too.'

'Deckie — that's a deckhand?'

'Aye,' the man said. 'You a fish merchant, or what?'

André shook his head. 'I'm writing a book,' he said. 'Need some background.'

'Book about what?'

'Tell me something,' André said. 'Where do all the trawlermen go for a beer when they come in?'

'Fleetwood Arms,' the old man said. 'Over there.'

On the far side of the road beyond the storm-fenced container park stood a Victorian redbrick building with a slate roof and white-painted sash windows. It was by far the best-maintained building in the area.

'I feel like a drink,' André said. 'Will you join me?'

138

'Danny Ackerley,' the old man said, extending a grimy hand. 'Ex-skipper the *Baby Boy*, Fleetwood.'

'Glad to meet you, Danny,' André said. He did not volunteer his own name. Danny Ackerley did not appear to notice. Or care.

'Nice car,' he said, pricing the Mercedes. 'Get in, I'll give you a lift.'

'Got me push,' the man said. 'Go ahead. I'll meet you there.'

He scuttled across to a building on the main quay, wheeled out a beaten-up old bicycle with no mudguards, and pedalled off toward the main road. André coasted across in the car and pulled up outside. The old man was waiting for him, a wide grin showing his wasted teeth.

Inside, the wide oak bar was shaped in a half-U, with floor tiles that gave the place the impression of being set on a giant chessboard. There were long leatherette-covered benches along the wall; half partitioned booths, small tables with cast-iron legs, stools. There were only about twenty people in the place, most of them at the bar. Danny got out a packet of Rizla cigarette papers, a packet of Old Holborn tobacco and a little machine for rolling the cigarette.

'What'll you have, Danny?'

'Pint of Boddington's,' the old man said, briskly. André ordered the beer, settling for a half pint of draught Guiness for himself. He took the drinks back to the table and started asking questions.

After thirty minutes and two more pints of beer, he knew all he wanted to know; but he stayed listening for another hour, as Danny Ackerley reminisced about the good old days, when boats from here had gone as far north as Iceland. It wasn't hard to imagine being on the heaving deck of one of those cockleshell trawlers in a North Atlantic Force Ten, swinging the nets aboard — 'bags', the old man called them — swollen with cod, icy water cascading down, as the huge waves smashed over the bows of the boat and came down the decks like a runaway train, and God help the man who went overboard, or the poor bastard who was too near to a steel cable when it sheared.

'Take yer 'ead off neater than the

guillotine,' Danny said. 'Lose a couple of fingers without even realizin' it'd 'appened. Lose a man overboard, never even know 'e was gone.'

André nodded and smiled, only half-listening now. In among the ramblings, he had picked up snippets of information that might be useful: the fact that it took about six hours for the fleet to get out to the fishing grounds around the Isle of Man, that they went out line astern down the channel to the estuary, the kind of equipment they carried these days, the shore-based facilities available to them in case of trouble. You never knew what you might need to know.

'Let me get you one more,' André said. 'Then I have to make a move.'

He set up another pint, then picked up his camera bag. The old man looked crestfallen.

'I'll give you me phone number,' he said. 'You want anything, you can call me.'

'Good idea,' André said. 'Write it down.'

The old man scrawled his name and address on a piece of paper, and they shook hands.

'I'll just see you out,' Ackerley said. As they left, André noticed some of the men at the bar watching covertly. He could almost read their thoughts: Danny found himself a soft touch — the old bugger. He unlocked the car and put the camera bag on the passenger seat.

'You going straight back to London?'

'I want to stop off at the East Dock, take some photos.'

'You want me to come with you? Show you around?'

'I can manage. You go back and finish your pint.'

'Good idea,' Danny Ackerley said. He took his cap off and scratched his head. 'Listen, you couldn't let me have a few quid, could you? The old pension doesn't go far these days.'

André had been ready for this. He took all the change out of his pocket and put it in the old man's grubby hand. It wasn't a lot of money, maybe three or four pounds, but no doubt it felt like more.

'That's the best I can do for you right now, Danny,' he said. 'But I'll see you right.' The stupid phrases these people used.

'Aye, right,' Danny Ackerley said. 'Good luck, now.'

He turned and went back into the pub as if a drought had just been announced. André grinned and drove to the larger East Side Dock. A sign at the entrance directed all visitors to report to the gatehouse; he drove straight past it. The guard inside watched him go by without making any move to stop him. The Mercedes, André thought; it opened more than just the more obvious doors.

The East Dock, he noted, was a rectangular basin with a narrow channel exiting to the river; a long, low, two-storey building on the jetty obviously housed the port radar facilities, the coastguard, perhaps a couple of customs officers. They would present no problem. He walked along the quayside examining the boats. The trawlers here were exactly what he had hoped they would be, sturdy, solid vessels with deep steel hulls, Kelvin Hughes or Raytheon radar and direction-finding equipment, sophisticated ship-to-shore radios.

He clambered down a ladder on to the deck of one of the larger boats, a hundred-footer with powerful lifting gear, registered at Beaumaris, in Anglesey. She had a bright blue hull, a boxlike midships crew-room and galley painted sand brown, and a neat sheltered bridge reached by a four-step companionway. He tried the door; it was locked, but it was a simple Yale pin-tumbler that would present no problem to a man who knew how to use a pick and a tension tool. He peered in through the window. The radio and radar equipment, although clearly well used, was comprehensive; the brass ship's telegraph was brightly polished.

'Hey, you, what you doing down there?'

He looked up; a mop-haired young fellow in rubber boots, dirty jeans and a thick wool sweater was standing at the top of the ladder, his hands on his hips and a belligerent look on his face.

'Inshore Fishermen's Association,' André said, putting a snap in the words. 'This your boat?'

'Nah,' the man said, his hostility evaporating. 'Harry Jackson's.'

'Danny Ackerley told me I'd find him here. Any idea where he is?'

André saw him fitting it all together: the sharp tone, the new Mercedes, the non-local accent. It smelled like officialdom, and he wanted nothing to do with it.

'Search me, mate,' he said, turning away.

As he watched the fisherman shambling off, André allowed himself a thin smile. The British were great respecters of authority. They also rarely asked for identification. They didn't like to give offence. He climbed up the ladder to the quay and wandered around the dock for perhaps another half-hour taking photographs. As he finished, he noticed that one of the Fleetwood trawlers was called *Cando*.

'You and me both,' he said. He got back into the Mercedes and drove out of the dock, well pleased with his day's work. Easy, he thought. Easier than mugging a blind man.

9

Jessica Goldman had no vanity about her work or the way she did it. She did not consider herself by any means accomplished enough yet, although she knew she was good at what she did. In most instances, the men and women sent to the Central Medical Establishment at Kelvin House by the security services were field operatives taxed beyond endurance by the nature of the work they were required to do. Stress was endemic, unavoidable, in intelligence work, where people were trained to be suspicious, to read the worst motives into the simplest of actions; it was enormously difficult to shake off these attitudes at the end of a working day.

New recruits to the service were given no cover story to help them keep secret the nature of what they did. Told only to say they worked for the Ministry of Defence and that their work was classified, they often found it difficult to talk to people. Older operatives fell into the habit of silence, and became unable to communicate at all. Others were affected not so much by the work as the kind of decisions it entailed.

Sometimes the damage was nothing worse than the trauma of an operative unable to cope with making the decision to open a file on someone, which meant listening in on phone taps, reading personal letters, making an assessment that could ruin that person's life. Another time, the patient might be someone who was solving his problems with booze or drugs, or perhaps a cryptanalyst stretched a long way past her limit by endless hours crouched in front of a computer console trying to get inside the mind of a cryptologist with a mind just as devious as her own. In such cases the prognosis was often good. Treatment revolved around restoring self-worth, reminding the patient of past successes, and emphasizing the value of the work.

But then there were the other kind. Burn-outs, they called them, zombies, Dracula's daughters. They might send you a man who had been forced to hide in a cupboard while a friend was being kneecapped in the next room. It might be a woman operative who had been compelled to watch a film of her husband making love to another man. Sometimes, not often, it was an agent who had just been out in the cold too long, nerves shot to pieces by the unremitting tension of maintaining his legend in an unchangingly hostile environment like Northern Ireland, Iraq, Iran. Not often, because very few of them ever got back safe.

With the burn-outs, Jessica did what she could. There were no miracle cures when it came to the mind; psychology was an inexact science at best, and in most cases it was never likely to be more than a palliative. Her dislike of psychobabble and her preference for behavioural therapy was typical of her: it was direct and simple. It involved a tacit agreement between the patient and the therapist: I have a problem, as another might have a bad tooth. You solve the problem, as a dentist might repair or remove the tooth, without regard to the subtleties of relationship. She had no illusions about psychotherapy: she saw her endeavours as a sort of psychic aspirin. It was not a cure, but it alleviated the condition. Like aspirin, the fact that nobody knew how it worked was less important than the fact that it did.

There was a technique to it, of course, but the skilful therapist concealed it from the patient. This, Jessica decided, would be doubly true in the case of Dorothy Morris, because Jessica was imposing herself upon the situation, rather than the woman coming to seek her help. So how Jessica looked, what she wore, how she conducted herself and what questions she asked would be of primary importance when she met Dorothy Morris for the first time. If the first impression was disagreeable a molehill of reticence would become a mountain of hostility. Ask one wrong question, and failure would follow.

She decided to wear a Donald Campbell paisley print suit and low-heeled shoes. She tied her hair back with almost Victorian severity and wore no makeup, trying for a neat, unfussy, but feminine look. If she had read the woman's character correctly from her dossier and from what Charles had told her, the tone would be about right. That done, Jessica got her Renault out of the underground car park in Cadogan Square and drove down to Rushlake Green.

'You are punctual,' Dorothy Morris said, smiling as she opened the door.

'What a lovely house,' Jessica said. 'And such a pretty spot! Why do I know the name Heathfield so well?'

'It's traditionally the place one first hears the cuckoo each spring,' Dorothy Morris said. 'Do come in, please. I made some coffee. Would you like a cup?'

'Thank you,' Jessica said. 'Just milk, please. No sugar.'

She was shown into the library, on the left of the spacious entrance hall. It was a very English room, with chintz-covered chairs, and floral curtains framing tall Georgian windows. The general atmosphere was one of charming clutter — a pile of magazines on a coffee table, a collection of thimbles, books stacked haphazardly on the oak shelves, photographs in silver frames on top of the small grand piano. The ceilings were twelve feet or more high, with curved cornices that gave the room an airy feel.

Dorothy Morris came back, carrying a silver tray with a silver coffee-pot and milk jug, Spode cups and saucers, and a small dish containing the kind of cookies the Swiss call *bretzeli*. A golden retriever followed her in and lay down on the hearthrug in front of the fireplace.

'I was just admiring your family pictures,' Jessica said. 'Are those your sons?'

'This is Paul and his wife, Sally,' Dorothy Morris said, picking up a wedding photograph in a silver frame. 'They have a house in Putney. White Lodge — it's on the Richmond Road.'

She poured some coffee and handed a cup to Jessica.

'And your other son?'

'David? He was married last year. His wife's name is Ailsa. She's from New Zealand. They live in East Grinstead.'

'Have you had many visitors since your

husband . . . passed on?'

'Not really. My husband . . . wasn't keen on entertaining. Said he got enough of that while he was travelling.'

'What do you do with yourself all day?'

'Oh, there's always plenty to do,' Dorothy Morris smiled. 'The garden, keeping the house clean. Then there's Edgar. He and I take long walks together, don't we, old boy?'

The retriever looked up, wagged its tail, and put its head down on its front paws again.

'You haven't talked to anyone? Your daughters-in-law, perhaps . . . ?'

Dorothy Morris shook her head. 'They have small children,' she said with a small frown. 'I can't expect them to take on my problems as well.'

Jessica remembered that Garrett had said she was an Army wife. Stiff upper lip and all that. One bore one's own sorrows, one kept one's chin up, one soldiered on. And then one day, Jessica thought grimly, one had a nervous breakdown.

'You remember the man who came to see you, Charles Garrett?'

'Yes, of course.'

'He asked me to ask you whether you ever found your husband's diary.'

'No,' the older woman said. 'I looked everywhere. I can't imagine what happened to it. Is it very important?'

'He didn't say,' Jessica said.

'I searched . . . I don't know how long I was in Ronald's study. Ages. It seemed like ages.'

Jessica nodded her understanding. It often happened. The widow found herself sitting in her husband's chair for hours. Touching his books. Burying her face in his jacket. Weeping softly for all that never was, and listening to the sad silence of the gone.

'You must miss him terribly.'

Dorothy Morris's chin came up; she straightened up in her chair.

'It's . . . sometimes. But I . . . cope.'

'Friends who have gone through the same kind of bereavement tell me that they're fine during the day,' Jessica said softly, 'but that the nights seem endless. Do you find that?'

Dorothy Morris nodded. 'I sometimes

don't even know what day it is,' she said. 'I potter about in the garden, take Edgar for a walk, do some shopping. But after dark . . . watching TV until there's nothing left to watch, falling asleep in the armchair and waking up stiff and cold at three in the morning and realizing . . . '

'That you're alone.'

'Yes. And . . . thinking about — everything.'

'You mean your husband's death?'

'No,' Dorothy Morris said.

'What, then?'

'What he did. Why he . . . did it.'

'It must be hard to come to terms with that. To understand it.'

'Oh, I understand it,' Dorothy Morris said, and there was a strength in her words that had not been there before.

'You mean . . . you know why he killed himself?' Jessica asked, her voice barely more than a whisper.

Dorothy Morris shook her head. Then she took a long, deep breath. 'Yes,' she said, almost fiercely. 'Yes.'

★ ★ ★

It had been a week now, and Garrett was damned near ready to quit. He had retraced every single step taken by the investigators who had preceded him, checked every statement, reread every interview from every interested party, and reviewed every available piece of physical evidence concerning the death of Ronald Morris. He was no further forward now than he had been the day he started. Thinking it might help, he had spread his net wider, opening dossiers on the cases about which Tony Dodgson had expressed uneasiness. He had travelled all over the country, talking to mothers and wives, daughters and sons, friends and lovers of the dead men. Apart from the vague suspicions of a distraught West Indian woman in Notting Hill who was convinced that Ajai Mehta had been murdered, and the equally unspecific convictions of Amanda Lowrie and Cynthia Peterson that there was something sinister about the deaths of their husbands, he ended up right back where he had begun.

The telephone rang. Garrett had no

secretary; the select few people who had his personal number at Lonsdale House had no need of screening. He picked up the receiver.

'Today's clearance is Waverley,' Jessica said, giving the code, changed daily, which confirmed the call was secure and not being made under duress.

'Where are you?'

'I'm at my place. I have Dorothy Morris with me. She wants to tell you something.'

'Put her on.'

'You won't want it on the phone,' Jessica said.

'Give me fifteen minutes,' Garrett said, and bolted out of his office. He grabbed a taxi that was coming around the north side of Berkeley Square, and told the driver to see if he could break the world record to Cadogan Square. The driver was an old hand, and they made good time; he gave him a tenner and sprinted up the steps to Jessica's door. She opened it almost before he had taken his hand off the bell.

'Inside,' she said. 'Gently, Charles.'

He nodded. Jessica led the way in. Dorothy Morris was sitting on a chair by the window looking out across the square. She looked unbearably sad.

'Hello, Mrs Morris,' he said. 'You remember me?'

'Of course,' she said. 'I'm sorry . . . to put you to so much trouble.'

'No apologies are necessary. I understand you have something to tell me.'

'Jessica tells me . . . you'll be discreet,' she said.

'You can trust him, Dorothy,' Jessica said. 'I do.'

Dorothy Morris nodded. 'I don't know where to start.' She looked up pleadingly at Jessica, who went across and sat beside her, taking her hands.

'I thought we agreed that what happened wasn't your fault, Dorothy,' she said. 'You can't go on punishing yourself.'

'I know,' Dorothy Morris sighed. 'I know.'

'Let me ask you a question, Mrs Morris,' Garrett said gently. 'Is what you're going to tell me about your husband?'

She made a visible effort to collect herself. Then the chin came up proudly, the back straightened. 'Yes, it's about Ronald. About how he died.'

'Go on.'

'He . . . was being blackmailed.'

'How do you know?'

'He told me. He had an affair.'

'And the woman was blackmailing him?'

'No, a man. A man got in touch with Ronald at his office. He said he had photographs . . . with the — woman. He told Ronald that if he didn't do what he was told, he would be finished.'

'What was the man's name?'

She shook her head. Did that mean she didn't know or wouldn't say? He let it go for the moment. The thing was not to push too hard too soon.

'This man. What did he want — money?'

'No. Things from Ronald's work. Components.'

Garrett leaned forward, his voice urgent. 'Components of what?'

'I don't know, Mr Garrett. I don't know.'

'Charles,' Jessica said, her voice so soft as to be almost inaudible. It was a warning. He made a conscious effort to speak more softly.

'Do you know the name of the woman?'

'He . . . never told me.'

Once more that momentary hesitation. What did it mean? 'And you never saw the photographs?'

She shook her head again, her eyes fixed on the square below. Garrett looked at Jessica Goldman. She raised her shoulders in an infinitesimal shrug.

'When did he tell you all this?'

'Just a . . . just a few days before he . . . died. He said he had no choice, he had to do what they said.'

'The man told your husband he had to obtain components of some kind. From Hayling-Brittain. Is that right?'

She nodded, not speaking.

'But you don't know what they were, or even for that matter whether he gave them to the man?'

'He told me he'd written it in his diary.'

'The one you couldn't find.'

'He said it was in code, but if I showed it to the right people they wouldn't have any trouble reading it.'

'You're quite sure he never mentioned any names at all? Think now, Mrs Morris.'

'I'm sure I would have remembered.'

'Nothing about the woman? Who she was, where she lived, anything?'

Dorothy Morris wrapped her arms around her body, rocking from side to side, shaking her head, tears suddenly streaming down her face. Jessica's expression changed to one of alarm. She went across and knelt beside the distraught woman, patting her hands.

'It's all right, Dorothy,' she said reassuringly. 'There won't be any more questions. It's all right.'

'I should have known,' the woman sobbed. 'I should have known. But he never said anything. Never ever anything.'

'Some men aren't able to,' Jessica told her softly. 'They just never learn how.'

She looked up at Garrett. The movement of her head was unequivocal: leave us alone for a while. He got up and went into the kitchen, put on the kettle and waited. He got cups and saucers out of the cupboard and put them on a tray, and then put some milk into the little matching jug. He made enough noise for Jessica to know what he was doing. After a few more minutes she came to the kitchen door.

'A little obvious,' she observed, 'but supportive. Bring it in.'

He carried the tray into the sitting-room. Dorothy Morris looked at him and tried for a smile that didn't quite make it. He poured the tea, gave her a cup and sat down in a chair near the window. There was a silence that nobody seemed anxious to break.

'I lied to you,' Dorothy Morris said abruptly. 'I lied to both of you.'

Garrett turned sharply; Jessica's eyes killed the words he was forming before they were born. Dorothy Morris looked at him and then at Jessica.

'It wasn't a woman,' she blurted out. 'It was a boy.'

★   ★   ★

Three hours later, Garrett took a taxi back to Lonsdale House and got the Quattro out of the underground car park. It took him only about forty minutes to drive out to the Hayling-Brittain complex in Amersham, where he presented his ID to the security guard and asked to see the chief of product development, Eric Mackenzie. The guard took a long look at the plastic tag, then pressed the button that operated the mechanism for raising the striped pole barrier. As Garrett drove past, he saw the man pick up the telephone. Enemy at the gates. But who was he calling?

He parked the Audi and walked across the quadrangle in the centre of the complex, where workers sat in fine weather to eat their lunch. He followed the road that ran between the administration building and the assembly shops, and went into the three-storey engineering building.

Eric Mackenzie's office was on the top floor, a small untidy room with a drawing board in one corner; it was cluttered with blueprints and exploded diagrams. Mackenzie was a short, thickset Scot with sandy hair and a ruddy complexion. He looked at the special ID and handed it back.

'Aye,' he said, unimpressed. 'What can I do for ye?'

'I need the answers to a couple of questions.'

Mackenzie nodded, as if Garrett's words confirmed his worst expectations. 'What with the newspapers and you people,' he said, 'it's a wonder we ever get any damned work done at all.'

'I won't keep you long,' Garrett said. 'I just want to run half a dozen names past you.'

'Oh, aye?' Mackenzie said warily. 'For instance?'

'A defence expert named Ernest Rashbrook. Military intelligence, working at Shrivenham on a secret underwater project.'

'Never heard of him.'

'Derek Darlington. BT digicom expert, working for HB on attachment. Something to do with the Royal Navy in Mombasa.'

Mackenzie shook his head. 'Sorry.'

'Ajai Mehta? Said Malik?'

'I know the names. Malik worked at Stanmore. He's the one who hanged himself, isn't he?'

'Do you know what they were working on?'

Mackenzie shook his head, lips pressed together.

'What about John Lowrie?'

'Don't know the name,' the Scot replied.

'Tom Wakenshaw?'

'Aye, I knew Tom,' Mackenzie said. 'He worked for Exmoor.'

'On radar projects.'

'That I couldn't tell you.'

'What about Ronald Morris? Lawrence Peterson?'

'Look, Mr Garrett, this is a big company. If you want information on its employees, you should go and talk to Daniel Hampson in Personnel. He's got files on all of us.'

'I might do that,' Garrett said. 'But I'm asking you for a different reason. You see, all the people I've mentioned have something in common.'

'Oh, aye?'

'Secret underwater technology,' Garrett said. 'My bet is, something very special, very secret and very new. Am I right?'

'I've no idea,' Mackenzie said.

'You mean Hayling-Brittain isn't developing anything like that right now?'

Mackenzie made an impatient sound. 'Man, man, there's probably fifty or sixty projects being developed at any given moment,' he said. 'Who knows which one they might have been working on?'

'You know what I think?' Garrett said. 'I think you're being deliberately obtuse.'

'Ah,' the Scot said. 'Brilliant. Ye don't just ask questions, ye answer them as well. Ye'll hardly be needin' me, then.' He turned away as if to leave. Garrett laid a hand on his shoulder.

'Tell me something before you dash off,' he said. 'Why am I so popular everywhere I go at Hayling-Brittain?'

'Och, man, ye can't be that stupid!' Mackenzie said. 'Let me by, I've work to do.'

'Answer the question, Jock.'

Mackenzie glared at him. 'Don't call

165

me Jock, I hate that.'

'I won't do it again. But answer the question.'

Mackenzie's head came up. He took a deep breath and then let it out with an exasperated sound.

'Laddie,' he said slowly. 'Ye don't work here. Ye're just passing through. So you've no idea of the . . . pressures that can be brought to bear on people.'

'Halford?' Garrett said, softly. 'Is it Halford?'

'Word goes around, laddie. Someone askin' about that — what do they call it? — the Trail of Death, isn't exactly inconspicuous around here.'

'Are people that frightened of him?'

'I don't know who ye're talkin' about, of course,' Mackenzie said. 'But the answer is, yes, they are.'

'But why? Why doesn't someone go over his head, talk to Bletchlock or someone at the top?'

Mackenzie shook his head sadly. 'I was hoping ye were smarter than that, laddie. Yon wee mannie doesn't work that way.'

'Which way does he work?'

'Laddie, I told you, I don't know who ye're talking about.'

'Let me see if I can guess,' Garrett said. 'You don't have to say anything, just nod your head if I'm right. He puts the black on someone: me, say. The word goes out: something along the lines of 'Show him everything but tell him nothing.' Anybody who steps out of line finds himself in deep shit. How am I doing so far?'

Mackenzie nodded, still wary-eyed.

'But how does he make it stick?'

'Think it through, laddie,' Mackenzie suggested drily.

'The ministry?' Garrett guessed.

Mackenzie shook his head.

'Five?' Garrett breathed. 'The security service?'

Mackenzie nodded again, a faint smile touching his lips.

'A negative security report,' Garrett said. 'Of course. He files a negative security report with DI5. It's Catch-22. The blacklist doesn't officially exist, so you can't be on it. If you're not on it, how can you be taken off it? Once a man is labelled a security risk, there's no way he can get off the list. There's no appeal to the DI5 computer. And if in addition Halford files a 'With Prejudice' report, the poor bastard will probably never be able to find work again.'

'Amazing thing, the human brain,' Mackenzie observed. 'Once you start using it.'

'So we've got an interesting situation here, Eric,' Garrett said. 'It would appear this ID card they gave me with so much ceremony isn't worth doggy-doo.'

'I'd say at that you were overvaluin' it.'

'You're right,' Garrett said. 'So I won't waste any more of your time.'

Mackenzie regarded him levelly for a long moment. 'Ye're going to butt heads with Halford, up on the fifth floor, is that it?'

'You sound as if you'd advise against it.'

'I don't know you laddie,' Mackenzie said. 'I know Halford. He's got brass balls.'

'I'll keep that in mind,' Garrett grinned. 'In case I ever need to pawn anything.'

He went back across the garden, took the elevator to the fifth floor and went through the swing doors into the open plan offices. One or two people looked up curiously as he made his way to Halford's office, but that was all. As he neared it, the door opened and Halford stood waiting for him.

'Garrett,' he said. 'I heard you were here.'

That answered the gatekeeper question. 'I wanted to ask you a few things,' Garrett said. 'It'll only take a moment.'

'Come in. Sit down.'

No luxury here; no carpets, no drinks cabinet, no antique desk. Halford's office was functional and unadorned. A desk, a comfortable chair, a memory bank phone, a PC terminal. A couple of shell chairs for visitors. The windows looked out over the visitors' car park. Take me as I am or leave me be.

'What can I do for you?' Halford asked.

'As head of security, how close an interest do you take in the private lives of Hayling-Brittain employees?' Garrett began.

'I think the word I'd use would be

'benevolent',' Halford replied. 'Everyone working at H-B is positively vetted by the security service. Everybody signs the Official Secrets Act as a matter of course. I presume, although I don't know it for a fact, that DI5 has dossiers on most, if not all of us.'

'So if someone was, say, being black-mailed, you might not necessarily know about it?'

Halford's surprise showed momentarily, then was quickly concealed. He shook his head. 'Not unless he or she came to me and told me about it. We don't keep our people under surveillance.'

'You think anyone could get anything out of a Hayling-Brittain plant? Secret documents, photographs, components, anything like that?'

'I've heard they've got things out of the National Security Agency at Fort Meade, so anything's possible,' Halford said. 'But it's damned unlikely. We make it pretty difficult. There's a tight system of checks and balances.'

'If something was taken — let's say some kind of secret component — how long would it be before it was missed?'

Once again he caught the wary look in Halford's eyes, masked almost as soon as it appeared. 'Unless someone was covering up, almost immediately. Are you suggesting . . . ?'

'Ronald Morris,' Garrett said flatly. 'He was being blackmailed. He handed over secret components to get off the hook. Nobody has screamed bloody murder. If what you tell me is true, that can only mean one thing. Someone covered it up. Any idea who it might be?'

Halford stared at him. His lips moved a little, but no sound emerged. It was as if he had momentarily lost the power of speech. His eyes were glazed with shock.

'You . . . you're sure of this?' he finally managed.

'Very sure,' Garrett said.

'Do you . . . know who else is involved?'

Garrett ignored the question. 'Something else has been bothering me,' he said. 'Couldn't quite put my finger on it. Then I realized, there was a common denominator to some of the deaths of

Hayling-Brittain personnel that nobody but me seems to have noticed.'

Halford had himself under control again now. He frowned. 'Really?'

'Yes,' Garrett said. 'You.'

'Me? Are you serious?'

'I'm very serious. In nearly every instance you were the only Hayling-Brittain employee to visit the scene of the crime.'

'And you find that significant?'

'It's a common denominator,' Garrett said. 'Let's discuss it.'

Halford shrugged and leaned back in his chair. 'Fire away,' he said.

'Okay,' Garrett said. 'Let's start with Ronald Morris's diary. Why did you take it?'

Halford blinked 'What?'

'You went to his house. You told his wife he had some papers that had to go back to the office.'

'She told you that?'

'Isn't it true?'

'Yes. There were some charts. Nothing important. They were needed in the planning office.'

'When I talked to Lord Bletchlock he seemed to think it unlikely anyone would go to the home of one of the dead men.'

'Lord Bletchlock doesn't run security,' Halford said. 'I do. Morris had some papers that we needed. I went and got them.'

'They weren't classified?'

Halford shook his head. 'No one's allowed to take any kind of classified material — hardware or documents — offsite.'

'Then what happened to the diary?'

'I don't know anything about it.'

'You mean, someone else must have taken it.'

'I don't mean anything other than what I said: I didn't take it.'

'What do you think might have been in it that made it worth stealing?'

'You know for a fact it's been stolen? You're sure Dorothy Morris hasn't mislaid it?'

'I'm sure.'

'Suppose you're right and someone took it,' Halford said. 'Why me? There must have been half a hundred people there after the funeral. They were all over the house. Anybody could have taken the damned thing.' He was getting angry. Good, Garrett thought. Angry men made mistakes.

'Anybody would have to know what it was.'

'There were a lot of people at that funeral from Hayling-Brittain. Maybe one of them took it.'

'What for?'

'You tell me.'

'Maybe I will,' Garrett said. 'Maybe I will. But first, I want you to tell me something. Why did you put the black on me, Halford? Why did you tell your people not to talk to me?'

'Who says I did?'

'I say you did. And I want to know why.'

Halford regarded him levelly. 'You don't learn, do you?' he said. 'Let me lay it out for you, Garrett. You can interview every member of staff from the chairman to the tea ladies, but unless I okay it, you won't even find out where the men's room is.'

'You're scared, Halford,' Garrett said. 'What are you scared of? Or should that be, Who are you scared of?'

'You won't get me mad again, Garrett,' Halford said, his voice flat and unemphatic. All the anger was gone, and he was as cold as ice. 'You're not big enough.'

'You've convinced me,' Garrett said. 'You're tough. Sharks break their teeth on you. Okay, we'll do it the hard way.'

Halford laughed harshly. 'I thought that kind of dialogue went out with George Raft,' he sneered.

' "Imagination is more important than knowledge," ' Garrett told him. 'Einstein said that.'

Halford opened a deep drawer in his desk and brought out a hard hat.

'Here, Einstein,' he said. 'Take this with you. Wear it whenever you're on one of our facilities. It can be dangerous out there.'

He put no emphasis on the last sentence. It was neither a threat nor a warning. But it wasn't a joke, either.

10

When he got to his office, Garrett picked up the phone and punched in the direct-dial number for Harry Massiter, head of F Branch at Curzon Street House, headquarters of the home security service, DI5.

'Yes?' a familiar voice said.

'Today's clearance is Xavier,' Garrett said. All security service phone lines were routed along specially laid cables which bore no commercial traffic. Anyone reaching a security office, either by accident or design, who did not begin with the appropriate codeword was instantaneously disconnected.

'It's Charles Garrett, Harry.'

'Well, well. What have I done to deserve this honour?'

'I need some help.'

'I've heard that said,' Massiter said drily. 'What have you got in mind?'

'I want someone turned over. Home

and office job. Azure phone facility, Phidias mail catch — the whole business.'

'Who's the target, Vladimir Putin?'

'A civilian.'

'Name?'

'Ian Mitchell Halford. Head of security for Hayling-Brittain at Amersham.'

Massiter gave a low whistle. 'Hayling-Brittain the defence contractors? What's he done, stolen Trident?'

'That's what I'd like you to find out.'

'Ought we to be opening an F-Branch file?'

'Don't bullshit me, Harry, I know you've got files on all of us already. Come on, what about the toss? Can you do it?'

'I'm not waltzing you about,' Massiter grumbled. 'I'm doing sums. You want us to turn this Halford over, install listeners, put a bleeper on his motor, intercept his mail. Anything else?'

'I want him on video, home and office. And footmen.'

'Round the clock, no doubt.'

'Round the clock.'

'Dammit, have you got any idea how much all this is going to cost, Garrett?

We're not made of money over here, you know.'

'Keep your hard luck stories for people who don't know any better, Harry,' Garrett replied. 'I know how much your budget really is. And it isn't what the Accountant tells the House of Commons. How soon can you get me an answer?'

'You know the drill,' Massiter said gruffly. 'Get the must-do papers over to me. As soon as I get them I'll set up an appointment with the DG.'

'I'll get right on to it,' Garrett told him. 'Oh, and Harry: no hostile ubiety. I don't want Halford to know he's under surveillance.'

'What do you think, we advertise?'

'No comment,' Garrett said. 'Listen, Harry, put a bit of speed on it and I'll buy you dinner at Gino's.'

'Gino's,' Massiter said. 'Gosh, thanks.'

★   ★   ★

When he got off the phone Garrett's message light was blinking. Since he had no use for a secretary, his messages were

178

held by Bleke's executive assistant, Liz James. He called her on the intercom and she told him that Tony Dodgson had phoned and wanted him to call back. He dialled Dodgson's direct number.

'DAC Dodgson's office.'

The dark-haired secretary with the neat figure and dimples. He'd meant to ask Tony about her.

'My name is Garrett.'

'He's been expecting your call. I'll put you straight through.'

'Pat?' Dodgson's faint Dorset accent somehow sounded stronger over the telephone line. 'Thought I'd better let you know we've got a line on the Kid. He's been spotted in old Fort Sumner.'

'What?'

'The Kid, Pat. Billy the Kid, remember?'

'Oh, for Christ's sake, Tony.' There were times when Dodgson's fixation on the American West was less than amusing. 'Aren't you ever going to grow up?'

'That's the trouble with you secret service types,' Dodgson said, and Garrett could almost see his grin. 'No sense of humour.'

'Is that what you called to tell me?'

'Getting anywhere with that Trail of Death business?'

'Banging my head against a brick wall might be nearer to it.'

'Pin your lugholes back, then,' Dodgson told him. 'I think I may have something for you.'

Garrett's eyes narrowed. Dodgson wouldn't be wasting his time with trivialities. 'I'm listening.'

'You remember when we were discussing the cases we didn't like the look of, I said something to you about it being difficult to co-ordinate the information because of all the various local forces involved?'

'I remember.'

'It occurred to me there was a lot of evidence out there that didn't get on to the R2 computer and wouldn't have shown up in their trawls,' Dodgson said.

'What kind of evidence.'

'Local police reports. Statements of relatives and neighbours. I put a Document Research team on to it up at Hendon,' Dodgson said. 'Asked them to go through all of it.'

'I'll bet they loved that.'

'I wasn't flavour of the week. You know how people love plodding through paper-work.'

'What were you looking for?'

'It was something you said about the victims. You said, What if someone was trying to subvert them, trying to get information? And I told you I'd tried the theory out on Five, and they said, Forget it, they'd checked it out and it was a non-starter.'

'But it was?'

'I thought, They've done the business,' Dodgson was saying. 'Computer trawls, cross-comparison of dossiers, A-searches. Then when I realized there was a whole body of evidence that hadn't gone into the scanner, I thought, Suppose Garrett was right, and someone really was buying information? They're not ghosts, they'd have to have names. So I told the DR team to start looking for names. And especially names that were out of context.'

'Out of context?'

'Non-family names, names the relatives were unfamiliar with, names that had cropped up but not been checked, anything. I just wanted to see if there was the remotest chance of a repeat, or a common denominator.'

Garrett realized he was holding his breath. He let it out softly, slowly. 'And was there?'

'Ajai Mehta's family remembered him talking about meeting someone called George. Nobody in the family by that name, and as far as they ever knew, Mehta had no friends called George. Then, bingo! Malik's family remembered him talking about a George nobody knew.'

'George first name, or surname?'

'Don't know. I'd say first name. Pat, that's not the end of it. We found four occurrences of the name George in the twenty-two statements. You know what that is, Pat? Eighteen point one eight per cent.'

'Too high to be coincidence.'

'That's right. So I fed it into the computer against the AK search files.'

There were a number of ways of conducting A-searches: AKF would yield all known facts on the subject, APD, all personal details. Dodgson would have used AKA to obtain all known associates; this subdivided into AKC, all known colleagues; AKF, all known friends: AKR, all known relatives, and so on.

'And?'

'Negative. Nobody anywhere named George.'

'Then we've got something,' Garrett said, fiercely. 'By God, Tony, I think you may have cracked it.'

'Wait. There's more.'

'Let me guess,' Garrett said. 'You found another name.'

'How the hell did you know that?'

'Was it Andrew? Or André?'

'What are you, Garrett, psychic?'

'We got a break from Morris's wife,' Garrett told the policeman. 'She told us he was being blackmailed. One night she heard her husband talking to someone. He was very distressed afterwards. He wouldn't tell her who it was. It was so unlike him that she remembered it.'

I heard him on the telephone one evening. He was very tense, very angry. I heard him say, 'No, André, I categorically refuse.' Then I saw his face: it had gone the colour of wood ash. I had never seen him so . . . distressed. The man on the phone said something else. Ronald said, 'I can't, André, I can't.' His voice was just a whisper. I asked him what was wrong, but he just shook his head. 'I can't talk about it, Dorothy,' he told me. 'Just stay out of it.' I asked him who André was, but he just shook his head.

You're sure he said 'André'? Garrett asked her.

It might have been Andrew. But I think it was André. It's such an unusual name.

'Interesting,' Dodgson said. 'None of that was in her statement.'

'Quite a few things weren't,' Garrett told him. 'I'll fill you in on them later. How many times did the name André appear in the trawl?'

'Twice. In the case of Wakenshaw, the fellow who drove off Beachy Head, the name was given as Andrew. Lawrence Peterson also appears to have known someone called Andrew or André. In view of the way he's supposed to have killed himself, I thought it was significant, and even more so when his wife said she was quite certain he knew no one of that name.'

'I think you're right.' Sometimes it was a brilliant flash of intuition. Sometimes it was luck. And sometimes you just had to thank whatever God you believed in that there were steady, unspectacular, methodical coppers who weren't afraid or ashamed to use methods that the Curzon Street high-flyers sneered at. 'You want me to ask our computer geniuses to see what they can do with this?'

'Bet your ass I do,' Dodgson told him, inelegantly. 'Let me know what you come up with.'

'You'll be the second to know,' Garrett promised. 'I'll call you later, Tony.'

He put down the phone and went straight to the office of Tom Ashley, the computer expert whose secondment to PACT from the Royal Armaments Research and Development Establishment at Chertsey had been one of the first appointments Nicholas Bleke arranged after he took control of the organization. Ashley was a tall, gangling man who always reminded Garrett of one of those long-legged waders you saw in wildlife movies.

'Hello, Charles,' he said. 'What brings you into the air-conditioned nightmare?'

'We all come for the same reason, Tom,' Garrett grinned. 'On the offchance one of those Princess Diana clones you have working in there will smile at us.'

'Show me where it says computer operators have to be short, fat and hairy.'

'Some people might call you sexist,' Garrett said, 'but I like you.'

'Trying to get on my good side, huh?' Ashley said. 'You must want something pretty badly.'

'And pretty fast, too,' Garrett told him. 'How busy are they?'

He nodded towards the time-coordinated sliding doors that led into the Lonsdale House computer facility. It was a window-less, atmosphere-controlled enclave whose staff of forty-four included some of the best programmers and analysts in Britain.

'We only work at one speed,' Ashley said. 'Flat out.'

'I need a TREVI trawl, Tom,' Garrett said.

'I'll get you a Cryptag and you can do it yourself.'

A Cryptag was the interactive device which unscrambled the information on the protected computer disks and simultaneously logged the material accessed and the operative using it.

Garrett shook his head. 'I haven't got time.'

'Who has?' Ashley said. 'Okay, sit down and tell me what's so urgent.'

Garrett told him what he knew. Ashley was a highly intelligent man; the fuller the picture he had of the object of his search, the likelier he was to identify the right option for finding it in the vast maw of the TREVI computers.

'It's connected with the death of a man named Ronald Morris. Former ministry mandarin turned marketing executive of Hayling-Brittain. A series of deaths, actually.'

'I read about all that in the papers,' Ashley said. 'What do they call it? 'The Trail of Death'. They were suggesting a ministry cover-up.'

'There's no cover-up, but there is a security aspect to it, something that the papers don't know about. We've learned Morris had been manoeuvred into a honey trap involving a boy prostitute. Someone took photographs and used them to coerce him into stealing secrets.'

In pre-*glasnost* espionage parlance, a honey trap was a carefully staged sexual entrapment operation, using either female or male bait, depending on the sexual proclivities of the target.

'A honey trap,' Ashley said, shaking his head. 'Why do you suppose they keep on falling for it?' he asked. 'You'd think they'd know, for God's sake.'

'I sometimes think deep down they do,' Garrett said. 'They know it can't be for real. But they want it to be, so they make themselves believe it is.'

'Okay,' Ashley said. 'I'll see what TREVI's got. What can you give me to work with?'

'Two names,' Garrett said. 'George. And Andrew. Or André.'

'George and Andrew what?'

'That's all I know.'

'George and Andrew-or-André,' Ashley said, tapping his lower lip thoughtfully with a pencil. 'It's not much, Charles.'

'You think I don't know?' Garrett said. 'I'm clutching at straws, Tom.'

'George isn't a popular name any more,' Ashley mused. 'It's because there haven't been any kings called George since the Fifties, you see. You're sure it's George, the English version, not Georges, the way the French spell it?'

'I'm not sure of anything,' Garrett said. 'Why do you ask?'

'Because of the other name. Nobody in England calls their kid André. Andrew is much likelier here. It's Andreas everywhere else. But if it's André, maybe it's Swiss, or French. And maybe the George is a French Georges.'

'Try it both ways,' Garrett told him. 'Try it any way you like. Just see if there's a firm out there, a team with two men on it named George and Andrew or Georges and André, or Georgi and Andreas, or any combination of them all. If there is, there's just a chance DGSE, DST or

TREVI may have something on them. I know it's a long shot, but give it a try.'

Ashley shrugged. 'You know what the frog said to the princess.'

Garrett looked at him.

'Kiss me,' Ashley grinned, 'but don't expect miracles.'

11

Birdcage Walk, which once housed Charles the Second's aviary, is a wide avenue that runs east-west from Buckingham Palace toward Parliament Square. Flanked on one side by St James's Park, and on the other by Wellington Barracks, headquarters of the Grenadier, Coldstream, Scots, Irish and Welsh Guards, its eastern end is Storey's Gate. To the south, paralleling Birdcage Walk, is Tothill Street, dominated by the bunker-like Home Office with its concrete ramparts. Sheltered in this small and relatively unknown quarter of London are the discreet Georgian premises which house the offices of some of the country's most senior civil servants.

Garrett walked across the suspension bridge in the park, drinking in one of the most exquisite views in London. Kids in T-shirts and cut-off jeans queued by the ice-cream vans. As he walked by, Garrett wondered idly how many of them knew that the park they were sunning themselves in was called after St James the Less, in whose name a hospital for lepers had once been built nearby.

Queen Anne's Gate was like a quiet garden into which the madding crowd had not penetrated. He walked past the Queen's statue, and the mansion block named after her. Turning into Old Queen Street — subject of many a ribald joke among the guardsmen barracked nearby — Garrett rang the bell of an elegant old house whose door bore a brass plaque with the less than informative legend: PS 2/ ARMY: MINISTRY OF DEFENCE. When the buzzer sounded he entered a cool, marble-floored hallway with striped satin wallpaper and discreet watercolours. A security guard checked his ID and took the statutory thumbprint on the desktop scanner before allowing Garrett to go through an elegant Adam doorway into the office of his friend, Brigadier Derek Warren.

'Charles, m'dear chap!' Warren said, jumping to his feet, hand outstretched.

'Good to see you, good to see you!'

He was a small, neat, precise man, dressed in a faultlessly tailored uniform that could only have come from Gieves. Salt and pepper hair, moustache to match, rimless glasses and shrewd pale blue eyes gave him an air of alert watchfulness that was an accurate representation of his true personality. Derek Warren was coming up to his thirtieth year as a senior military intelligence officer; there was very little he didn't know about how the machinery of defence procurement worked.

Garrett sat down in the George II-style leather wing chair to which Warren directed him and watched as his host took two heavy crystal tumblers from a glass-fronted cupboard and set them on the table.

'Still a Glenfarclas man, Charles?'

Garrett smiled assent; Warren unstoppered a beautiful Waterford decanter and poured them both a healthy dram. He handed one glass to Garrett and took the other himself.

'Cheers!' he said, going back to his

chair behind the lovely old Louis XVI mahogany bureau that served as his desk. The whole place was more like the drawing-room of a country house than an office, Garrett thought, with its tall Georgian windows looking out on to a neat walled garden, the low occasional tables and built-in bookcases, the deep, soft sofa with its cream linen cover, the Hepplewhite design shield-back chairs with their striped silk seats. The difference, of course, was that the magazines piled on the table were specialist publications from all over the world, and that most of the books in the late Regency break-front bookcases were equally esoteric. On one wall hung a Frank Wootton painting of three Spitfires flying across a bright summer sky. By comparison with most of the other furnishings, it seemed almost indecently modern.

'How've you been, Derek?' Garrett asked.

'Busy as hell,' Warren said. 'Just got back from Malaysia. We've been 'battling for Britain' again.'

'What are we selling them this time?'

'Ground attack fighters, air defence missile systems, ground-to-air missiles, 105mm light guns — a thousand million pounds' worth. Shall I go on?'

'Quite a deal,' Garrett observed.

'Big. But not the biggest,' Warren said. 'We've got one shaping up fifteen times the size.'

Garrett let out a low whistle. 'Fifteen thousand million pounds?' he said. 'Pity you don't get commission.'

'Danger money, you mean,' Warren said. 'Nothing but a bloody jungle out there. Kickback payments, Third World barter deals, uncontrolled subsidies — a bloody jungle. Well, enough of that. Tell me what you're here for.

I want to pick your brains a bit.'

'Fire away.'

'Tell me about the Hayling-Brittain organization,' Garrett said.

Warren frowned. 'Take a while, that. They're the biggest thing in defence.'

'That's why I'm interested.'

'Won't bore you with their history,' Warren said. 'Imagine you've got all that from Companies House anyway.'

195

'I'm more interested in their relationship with the ministry,' Garrett said.

'Chairman's Lord Bletchlock,' Warren told him. 'Formerly Lieutenant-Colonel Arnold Bletchlock, and before that, plain old Walter Horn from Königsberg, Ost-Preussen.'

'Do you know him?'

Warren looked up sharply, as if suspecting a trick question. 'We used to be great pals,' he said. 'Till he turned into another Aristotle Onassis. Haven't seen him for ages. Why d'you ask?'

'I gather he does a lot of head-hunting in this part of the world.'

'Don't you start,' Warren said. 'Bad enough the Sundays are at it again.'

An all-party Treasury and Civil Service Select Committee had urged the Ministry of Defence to tighten up the rules on civil servants taking up jobs with defence contractors and big City firms. The system by which the big companies contacted officials before they retired from their ministry jobs, with a view to recruiting them, was known as the 'revolving door'. Civil servants and

196

military officers went in one side, emerging on the other as businessmen soliciting the very ministries they had so lately quit. Several leading newspapers had published articles indicting the system in the wake of revelations that several senior executives of the Hayling-Brittain corporation had been accused by Scotland Yard's Serious Fraud Squad of defrauding the government.

'Have Hayling-Brittain offered you a job yet?' Garrett asked, with a grin.

'No, and they won't,' Warren said vehemently. 'Wouldn't work in the private sector for a gold clock. Wearin' a bowler, commutin' every day, that's not my cup of tea at all. When I pack it in, the most strenuous exercise I'm going to take will be dead-heading my roses.'

'Just as a matter of interest, what does the ministry spend with Hayling-Brittain per annum?'

'Defence budget stands at about thirty billion,' Warren said. 'Something like forty-five per cent of that goes on weapons and equipment. The ministry is Great Britain's largest single consumer.

We buy nearly half of all this country's aerospace production, twenty per cent of all shipbuilding, a fifth of all electronics. I'd say about ten percent of that goes to Hayling-Brittain.'

Garrett gave another low whistle. 'That's serious money.'

'They provide serious products,' Warren replied. 'Not to mention the ongoing research and development work funded by the ministry.'

'How big are they in the scheme of things, Derek?'

'Giant,' Warren said. 'You see, Hayling-Brittain is really a sort of octopus, a conglomerate of linked industries that range from car radios and tractor parts to the most sophisticated guidance systems and satellite communication equipment. Space and defence systems, avionics, weaponry, there are plants all over the country — Bristol, Manchester, Leeds, Birmingham, Portsmouth, the West Country, you name it. Their annual turnover is in multibillions. They're linked with firms in America, France, Germany, Sweden and God alone knows where else.'

'Are you allowed to tell me anything about what they're up to on behalf of the ministry at the moment?'

Warren looked defensive. 'Difficult one, that,' he pointed out. 'My masters don't care to have too much light cast on their little secrets.'

'What I'm thinking of,' Garrett said, 'is a state-of-the-art guidance system originally designed for the Stingray torpedo, but since massively enhanced and probably miniaturized. How am I doing?'

'Admirably,' Warren said, and there was respect in his voice. 'Where did you get your information?'

'I don't care to have too much light cast on my little secrets, either,' Garrett told him.

'Touché,' Warren said, with a rueful smile. 'What's your security clearance now?'

'You want to see my card?'

'I'll trust you,' Warren said. 'Let's go for a walk.'

They walked out of his office and into Old Queen Street, turning left into Storey's Gate and across Birdcage Walk to

199

the park. Wildfowl chattered on the calm surface of the water.

'Saw a wryneck here the other day,' Warren said as they strolled along the lakeside. '*Rara avis.*'

They reached the little bridge spanning the ornamental water where Garrett had stopped earlier, and Warren leaned against the metal railing. Garrett concealed a smile; how many espionage movies had he seen where spymaster and joe met to talk at exactly this spot?

'What I'm going to say now is for your ears only, Charles. You understand?'

'Absolutely.'

Warren nodded. 'The weapon you're talking about is called Cosmos. I needn't tell you that it's ultra-classified. If you were to ask them about it, Hayling-Brittain would deny its existence. So would the ministry.'

'It must be something extra special.'

'It would appear so,' Warren said drily. 'Let me ask you a question. What's our biggest defence budget expenditure?'

'Nuclear subs?'

'Right first time. Why?'

'Because of all defence installations, they are the most difficult to find and destroy.'

'Right again. So if someone came up with a foolproof weapon that could do just that . . . ?'

'Cosmos?'

'An electronic anti-submarine missile that acts independently as a hunter-killer.'

'They've got such a weapon?'

Warren nodded.

'And it works?'

Warren nodded again.

'How?'

'You don't need to know,' Warren said. 'Just take my word for it, the success rate is amazingly high. It's compact, simple, deadly. It can be launched from the surface or below, from a remote-controlled aircraft, a robot submarine, a radio-controlled boat, a drogue or a balloon. It doesn't seem to make any difference how it gets into the water. Once it's activated, it will find anything moving underwater up to a range of three miles.'

'How is it armed? Conventional or nuclear?'

Warren shrugged. 'I'd guess a limited nuclear warhead. Conventional explosives might not damage an enemy sub enough to sink it or prevent it firing its missiles.'

'Is it in production?'

'Final proving runs.' Warren's sentences were getting shorter, an unmistakable sign which told Garrett he was reluctant to reveal any more. Even though they were old friends, Derek was uneasy talking secrets.

'Just tell me one more thing,' Garrett pleaded. 'Who knows about it at Hayling-Brittain?'

'Officially, Cosmos does not exist,' Warren told him. 'The manufacture of its components has been rationalized in such a way that no unauthorized person can know enough even to visualize the finished weapon, let alone familiarize himself with its configurations, its purpose or its effect. Once assembly has begun, no construction worker is allowed to work on the weapon or any of its components for longer than one hour at a time, or allowed to see it after final assembly.'

'What about the big picture? Someone at Hayling-Brittain has to know.'

'Only five people. Bletchlock, of course. Eric Mackenzie, head of product development. Desmond Elliott, head of testing. Ian Halford, head of security. Timothy Manderson, senior ministry liaison officer. That's it.'

Garrett felt a surge of elation. At last, the pieces of the puzzle were beginning to fall into place. 'Thank you, Derek,' he said. 'No more questions.'

Warren nodded abruptly. Garrett knew the gesture well. It indicated that Warren considered the interview terminated; they would now revert to conversational mode.

'One more thing, Charles,' Warren said, staring down at the brackish water. 'I want you to forget everything you've just heard — and especially who told you.'

'What did you say your name was?' Garrett said.

12

Just opposite the staff entrance to Curzon Street House, on the corner of Half Moon Street, is an old building. It houses an unassuming Italian restaurant with two small dining-rooms on the ground floor and a couple more upstairs. The restaurant, Gino's, is known at DI5 as the Safe House, and is used a lot by middle-echelon personnel who need a place to talk away from the ever-open ears of colleagues. The food at Gino's was simple but good, the waiters were noisily friendly, the wine list unspectacular but adequate. Garrett had reserved a table in a corner of the upstairs dining room. He arrived before Massiter, ordered a bottle of Orvieto and settled down to wait for his friend to arrive.

Massiter came hurrying in about ten minutes later, a tall, dapper man in a well-cut blue double-breasted suit. Dark wavy hair, brown eyes, small features, neat ears; the kind of face women instinctively trust. He sat down, laid a thin document case on the table to his left, poured himself some wine, then looked at Garrett, shaking his head.

'I wish I had half the clout you people over at Lonsdale seem to have,' he said grudgingly.

'You got clearance?'

'The DG rubber-stamped it,' Massiter said. 'Black bag job, anything we like. Muttered something about it being no use arguing if it was one of Bleke's operations, anyway.'

'When can you get started?'

'We're already rolling. A4 is putting watchers on your man instanter. Interchangeable tail. Strollers, taxi drivers, the works: round the clock surveillance for ten days. After that we'll review the situation.'

'Fair enough,' Garrett said. 'What about turning over his drum?'

'I had a word with Paul Maskell. Seems he's an admirer of yours.'

Garrett smiled. 'He owes me a favour or two,' he said.

A long time ago, Maskell had worked with Garrett in Berlin. He was now the head of DI5's Section A-1, euphemistically known as 'Property'. One division within his section was called the Latchlifters. It was staffed by breaking-and-entering specialists who could make a cat burglar sound like *Tyrannosaurus rex*.

'A-1A has the take,' Massiter said. 'They'll process Halford's office tonight. They've got to wait till he's at work tomorrow before they turn over the apartment.'

'Fine,' Garrett said. 'Give me a rundown.'

'Fibre optic auto-iris pinhole lenses and VCRs in the apartment and at his office. Data communications surveillance: computer, fax, telex, etcetera. High-frequency RDF on his car. The equipment is being couriered in from Sandridge now.'

All DI5 — DI6 — Special Branch bugging and electronic surveillance teams worked out of an anonymous-looking building in Grove Park, a side-street in the South London suburb of Camberwell; the surveillance and technical equipment they used came from the Home Office 'police research centre' at Sandridge, near St Albans in Hertfordshire.

'When will they be ready to roll?'

'A Tinkerbell crew will go in at the same time as A-1A tonight,' Massiter said. 'They'll rig the apartment tomorrow. I've already authorized a postal trawl. All mail will be rerouted. From about ten o'clock tomorrow morning, your friend Halford won't be able to scratch his bum without us knowing.'

The nickname 'Tinkerbell' had belonged originally to the telephone-tapping facility at Ebury Bridge Road in London; these days most of the System X technical staff were headquartered in an anonymous building in Oswestry from which practically any telephone in Britain could be tapped. The Tinkerbell equipment would transmit every word spoken in Halford's office or apartment to voice-activated tape recorders. Data surveillance equipment would monitor every letter, every fax, every e-mail that was sent or received. All letters addressed to him would first pass through the Post Office letter opening department, Room

202 in Union House, near St Paul's Cathedral, where they would be opened, copied and resealed before delivery.

'What about R2?'

'I've passed the word to Mac McCaskill. A hard copy of Halford's dossier will be on your desk by the time you get back to the office. If you need anything extra, Mac will dig it out for you.'

'Mac' McCaskill was the unflappable Scot who headed the DI5 Research and Analysis computer facility at Euston Tower. It was an ideal location. The Department of Social Security occupied most of the first twenty floors of the building, and the Post Office had the rest. Sandwiched in between, on the mirror-windowed twelfth and sixteenth floors, were McCaskill and his staff. It was a useful environment; there was very little information about most UK citizens that could not be located on that interfaced network of high-powered computers.

'Good. Listen, Harry, when the Latchlifters go in, there's something I want them to look for.'

'Go ahead.'

'A diary. It belonged to a man named Ronald Morris. It's gone missing, and I think our hero may have it.'

'What kind of diary?'

'De luxe business diary. Blue leatherette cover.'

'That all?'

'It's got his initials on it, bottom right-hand corner of the front cover. His wife said it was just a business diary, but I think there may be more to it than that.'

'What do you mean? Secret writing, coded entries?'

'Find the diary and then we'll know,' Garrett replied brusquely. He gestured at Massiter's document case. 'What's in that?'

'Paperwork, of course. You have to sign the authorization. The DG says if this one blows up in anybody's face, it isn't going to be his.'

'Dear old Patrick,' Garrett said. 'He'll never get into *Who's Who* if he goes on like this.'

'You going to talk all night?' Massiter said. 'Or order another bottle of wine?'

A little after nine-thirty, Harry Massiter

jumped into a cab in Curzon Street that would get him to Marylebone in time to catch the ten ten to Great Missenden. It was a balmy evening, with just a growl of thunder lurking on the far side of the clouds piling up to the south, and Garrett decided to walk back to Whitehall Court. One of the things he liked most about living in London was being able to walk anywhere. There weren't too many places left in the world where you could do that any more. He turned up Half Moon Street to Piccadilly, and crossed over into Green Park. It was fully dark now, and there was nobody about. The lights of the Royal OverSeas League spilled brightly out over its back garden. He was halfway down Queen's Walk, fitfully lit by a single street-lamp, when the two men ran out to kill him.

Both men were short and dressed in dark clothing. Woollen ski-masks concealed all but their eyes and mouths. He saw the wicked gleam of a knife, and moved without conscious thought, every sense alert. The man behind was always the most dangerous. He pivoted on his left foot and lashed out with his right. His foot connected with the arch of the man's groin with a sound like an axe being buried in a tree stump. A dark, hurt, glottal grunt burst from the man's mouth. He doubled over and fell to his knees, retching. The looped garrotte he had been lifting to drop over Garrett's head fell to the ground with a small clatter.

Garrett whirled around. The second man hesitated, the saw-edged commando knife in his right hand weaving uncertainly. The knife made a soft *whuck* as he struck out in a killing arc at Garrett's body.

Garrett swayed aside, letting the deadly blade pass, making no attempt to intercept it or the man's arm. One error of judgement there, and he'd end up with no fingers. Instead, he lashed out with his foot, kicking the man behind his left knee, spilling him to the ground. In a continuation of the movement, Garrett grabbed the top of the ski-mask in his right hand and brought up his knee, yanking the man's head forward to meet it. He felt bone crunch as the man's face smashed against his kneecap. Fingers intertwined, he raised his fisted hands high and brought them down on the point where the man's neck and right shoulder joined. His assailant screamed in agony as the impact shattered his clavicle.

As the man fell forward, hands outspread to break his fall, Garrett stamped on his right hand. A second howl of pure pain split the darkness, and the big knife clattered to the ground. Garrett kicked it aside as he spun round on the balls of his feet, ready for any counterattack by the first man he had downed. He was just in time to see the man lurching across the open ground toward Constitution Hill about a hundred and fifty yards away. Garrett started after him, then stopped as the figure weaving between the trees disappeared into darkness.

Sliding the ASP combat version of the Smith & Wesson M39 out of his shoulder holster, he ran back to the path to see the man he had felled running back into the dark alleyway, feet whispering on the old paving stones. Garrett leapt after him, ready to lay down a killing arc of lead, but even as he came automatically into the firing position he heard voices and knew he dared not shoot: the narrow passageway opened out near the entrance to the Stafford Hotel. He could not take the chance of wounding innocent bystanders.

'Bang, bang,' he said softly, as the silhouette of the running man disappeared. He went back to the path in the park. There was no sign of the garrotte. A dull metallic gleam caught his eye: he bent down and picked up the knife they had been going to kill him with. It was a solid, heavy weapon, about fifteen inches long overall. The haft incorporated a spiked steel knuckleduster; the grip was covered with insulating tape. There were ugly sawteeth on the upper leading edge of the wickedly curved ten-inch Bowie-style blade. It would have ripped him open like a plastic bag.

He hunched his shoulders; all at once the balmy evening felt cold and inimical.

He headed purposefully down to the Mall and picked up a taxi, resolutely not thinking about anything as it threaded its way to Whitehall Court. He got out, paid the cabbie and hurried upstairs to his apartment. Only then did he let the reaction bite. Death had flown over, looking for company, then decided: *not you, not this time*.

At least I hurt the bastards, he thought. That's something. Now forget what happened, concentrate on why. Could it have been, as he had first thought, an ordinary mugging? Not a chance. Which meant someone had put out a contract on him, and the two assassins were trying to fulfil it. Since they could not have known for sure that there would not be someone else around, the attempt on his life had been pure opportunism. So whoever was paying them had told them kill him wherever and whenever the chance presented itself. Which led to an even more interesting question. No one had known he would be walking through Green Park. He hadn't decided himself until he left Harry Massiter. Which in turn meant . . .

Damn.

Someone had him under surveillance. Someone who wanted him dead. And next time he might not be so lucky.

13

The house — one of those large, beautifully proportioned country mansions the French call a *manoir*, dated from the early seventeenth century. It lay on a winding road about six kilometres outside the little town of Ribérac in the Dordogne, south of Angoulême. Set in about fifty acres of well kept woodland and meadows, the estate had been the home of the Duhamel family for five generations; when the last surviving member of the family had died an old maid six months ago, André Dur had bought the place without hesitation. It was worth every penny it cost him to have so discreet, so isolated a base from which to operate.

It was approached by an arched entrance flanked by a *pigeonnier*, restored and converted to a guest suite with its own sitting-room, kitchen and bathroom. Beside the manor were a guest-house and a small barn used to garage the new owner's silver-grey Peugeot. At the rear, beyond the terrace and the rose garden, was a walled enclave housing a large swimming-pool.

A tiled hallway, dominated by a double turned wooden staircase with a wrought-iron rose balustrade, lay behind the imposing oak double doors. To the left was the beamed dining-room.

To the right of the hallway lay the drawing-room with its superb original walnut floor, and the library with its corner fireplace beyond. It was here that André Dur sat now. Dressed in a light tan jacket with leather elbows and shoulder patch, and tan slacks tucked into laced leather boots, he looked every inch the *haut bourgeois* that everyone in Ribérac thought him to be.

'I told you not to use this number except in an emergency!' he snapped into the telephone. The tense drumming of his fingers on the arm of the chair as he spoke emphasized his anger.

'It is an emergency,' the caller said.

'It had better be,' André said, his tone

still biting. 'You are calling on a landline, I trust?'

'I'm at London Heathrow.'

André nodded. No one would ever deem Georges Barbier brilliant, but he was far from stupid. 'What is the emergency?'

'It's about the Englishman. Halford.'

'What about him?'

'Listen, I'll explain. They have opened a new inquiry.'

'Another? Why?'

'I don't know, André. Halford couldn't find out.'

'Couldn't find out?' André drew the words out, stressing his disbelief.

'He tried every contact he's got. Scotland Yard, the ministry, DI5, everybody. Nobody knows.'

'Somebody knows. He hasn't asked the right people, that's all. Who is making this inquiry?'

'A man named Garrett. Charles Garrett.'

'Who does he work for?'

'He carries Ministry of Defence identification. With very high security clearances.'

André's mind was busy. Ministry of

Defence. Did that mean the security service? But they had already conducted an inquiry. As had the ministry itself. There was something strange about this.

'Go on,' he told Barbier, not failing to notice the slight hesitation that followed.

'There are . . . we have a problem.'

'What sort of a problem?'

Once again, André noticed his caller's hesitation.

'Halford. He took unilateral action.'

'For God's sake, man,' André spat. 'Get to the point.'

'He hired two men to kill Garrett.'

'He killed a ministry official? In the name of God, is he mad?'

'They didn't kill him. The men he used were amateurs. One of them is in hospital.'

'*Merde!*' André breathed. 'Did . . . is there any chance they were identified?'

'They say no, André. It was dark. They wore ski-masks. The whole thing didn't take more than a minute.'

'All right,' André said, forcing himself to hold his temper in check, to think slowly, rationally: an angry outburst would solve nothing. The top priority now was to limit the damage.

'All right,' he said, as calmly as he could. 'Start again. At the beginning. Tell me exactly what happened.'

'Garrett told Halford that he knew Ronald Morris was being blackmailed and that he took components out of the facility at Amersham.'

'Morris? Which one was that?'

'The one who liked street boys. He brought us the depth-setting gauge and the self-actuated gyroscope.'

'How did Garrett find this out?'

'It appears Morris told his wife he was being blackmailed. And why. Halford didn't know how much else she'd told Garrett. So he — '

André frowned. Damn the man! There were some things you just could not plan for. He thought for a long moment. He could hear Georges feeding more money into the telephone, and the *bing-bong* of the airport PA in the background.

'What do you want me to do, André?' Barbier asked into the lengthening silence.

'Listen carefully.' André's voice was

decisive. 'I'll come to London right away. Call everyone together, but do nothing until I get there, do you understand? Take no action.'

'*D'accord*,' Georges said. 'When will you arrive?'

'There's an Air France Airbus, Flight eight-twenty, that gets into Heathrow at half past eight, Terminal Two. Meet me there.'

He put the telephone down.

Why were they launching a new investigation this late in the day? What had happened to prompt it? Who was this Garrett? No ordinary civil servant, clearly. André shook his head. There was a factor missing, an element he could not identify. It perturbed him.

Until now, everything had gone perfectly. André had come up with the plan, a foolproof way to stitch his own indistinguishable pattern into the fabric of the series of fatalities the newspapers dubbed The Trail of Death. For one million francs paid into a numbered account in Switzerland, Halford had identified the appropriate personnel, provided the information they needed to compromise them, and removed any evidence that might have assisted those investigating the deaths. Each carefully constructed link of the chain had been joined to the others on schedule, each door carefully closed behind them.

Halford's stupidity must not be allowed to jeopardize the mission. Nothing must stop it. No one. It had taken too long to put it together. He looked around. He hated leaving: he had never really had a home before, and he loved it here, making occasional trips into town, taking the Peugeot in for service at the garage on the rue Larobertie.

He looked at his watch. He had about an hour. He went into the kitchen and told his housekeeper that he had to leave. Her narrow face set like a trap; she was in the middle of preparing supper. All that food, *monsieur*! Those lovely plump wood pigeons she had been going to cook in red wine!

'Please take them home, *chère Madame*,' André told her. 'Give them to your husband with my compliments. And take a couple of bottles of the red to go with them.'

He went up to his bedroom, and put a disc into the CD player. As the dancing strains of the Vivaldi filled the room, he changed from his country clothes into a blue denim shirt and a light windbreaker jacket, lightweight cotton slacks and black leather loafers — they were having a heatwave in England, a country where apparently no one had ever heard of air-conditioning — and threw a few things into an overnight case. As he worked, his mind was busy turning over propositions, reviewing options, assessing risks.

The operation would move to its penultimate phase as soon as he got to England. But first, in order to motivate Halford, it was necessary to remove the threat posed by this man Garrett. What was the best way to bring the fly into the spider's web? Simple: offer him proof that there was indeed a link between the mysterious deaths of the Hayling-Brittain scientists. But it would have to be convincingly packaged.

André smiled. A plan that would

simultaneously solve the problems posed by Garrett and Halford was already beginning to take shape in his agile brain. He snapped shut the locks on the briefcase, carried the bags downstairs and put them on the back seat of the Peugeot.

An hour and a half later, he crossed the Garonne by the Pont d'Aquitaine. The lake of the Parc des Expositions with its cluster of luxury hotels slid past. Skirting Bordeaux, the motorway looped south towards Mérignac airport, eleven kilometres from the centre of the city. When he had parked the car and checked in, he went across to the bank of pay phones by the news-stand and made a long-distance call to an unlisted number in a building on the boulevard Mortier in Paris. He told the man who answered what he wanted.

'It'll take at least an hour, maybe two,' the man replied.

'I'll call you again when I get to Charles de Gaulle,' André said, and hung up. The man he had spoken to worked for the Direction Générale de Sécurité Extérieure. He also worked for Action

Directe. As an *analyste*, responsible for dossier maintenance, he had access not only to all DGSE files but also to those of the domestic equivalent of England's Special Branch, the Direction de la Surveillance du Territoire, and those of the Europolice databank, TREVI. If Garrett was a security service specialist, the odds were that there would be some information about him on file in one of them.

André smiled as he passed through the airport security check, enjoying a moment of superior scorn for the earnest guards burrowing in hand baggage. Taking *plastique* or guns on planes was for amateurs, the thick-ear bombers of the IRA or the mindless assassins of the mullahs. The most dangerous weapon, he thought, is the one inside my head.

He went into the departure lounge. He had already decided that Halford's blunders and Garrett's investigation were nothing more than minor distractions. He would proceed, boldly. The bloodhounds blundering behind you always had first to locate your scent, follow your spoor. By the time they found his, he would have struck a blow for freedom from which the imperialist Americans and their lackeys, the Pentagon-led sheep of the British government, might never recover. That he might die bringing it about was part of the excitement. He could do it. He would do it. All he had to do was believe in himself. He smiled again, and silently repeated the words of his boyhood hero, Georges-Jacques Danton. 'the Mirabeau of the mob'.

De l'audace, et encore de l'audace, et toujours de l'audace!

14

The worst part of Garrett's job was waiting. Waiting for the phone to ring, waiting for an agent's report, waiting for a computer trawl to rake up a piece of information that would provide the vital lead, waiting for an enemy to make an ill-considered move, waiting for a break. They were still waiting.

Massiter's blitz had so far yielded mixed results. Although the A-1A lifters had gone through Halford's office and flat, they found no trace of Ronald Morris's diary, nor — as Garrett had hoped they might — any indication that it was Halford who had hired the two thugs who tried to kill him in Green Park. Halford was clearly too streetwise to leave incriminating material lying around.

The round-the-clock surveillance paid off with a big surprise: Halford's mistress was none other than the mascot of the first team, Lord Bletchlock's sexy secretary Elaine Harding. The two of them had begun their liaison in the summer of '86. By all indications, Elaine the lily maid was a lady with very expensive tastes. A flat in Chesterfield Gardens, Mayfair. Charge accounts at all the most exclusive stores. Regular vacations in faraway places: Mauritius, the Barrier Reef, the Gulf Coast of Florida. And first class, of course, all the way.

Well, there was no law against having a mistress, nor against her having expensive gewgaws, providing you could afford it. But Elaine Harding earned less than thirty five thousand a year. And as for Angela Cummings-designed bracelets and timeshare apartments on Sanibel Island on Halford's salary of sixty five thousand, no way. Which led inevitably to the question: where was the money coming from? Halford's bank records showed that he had been considerably overdrawn between September 1984 and March 1985; since then, his account had been a model of equilibrium, with no sign of the scale of expenditures that would have been necessary to furnish Elaine Harding with her glittering toys. Conclusion: he was paying for them out of a slush fund, serious money stashed away somewhere else — America, or possibly Switzerland. The security chief had visited both countries more than once in the last six months.

Garrett now knew pretty much everything there was to know about Ian Mitchell Halford. The dossier sent over by Neal McCaskill at R2 had given him all the salient facts of the man's background. Garrett pushed the bulky R2 dossier aside with an impatient sound of anger. He needed something more three-dimensional than career statistics. He called Tony Dodgson.

'Tony, did you know a DCI called Ian Halford in your Sweeney days?' Dodgson had once been a Flying Squad detective, based at West End Central.

'I knew him, all right,' Tony said. 'The Snout, they called him.'

'Not what you'd call a compliment,' Garrett said. In police parlance, a snout was an informer. 'How did he get the nickname?'

'He blew the whistle on every officer on the take in London West End Central. Names, dates, amounts: the business. Needless to say, all hell broke loose. Then one of the serious newspapers got wind of what was going on — maybe from Halford, I wouldn't put even that past the bastard — and mounted an investigation of its own.'

In the storm which followed, two commanders resigned in disgrace — the most senior officers ever to do so — together with some twenty detectives involved in accusations of bribery and corruption connected with vice in Soho and Mayfair.

'As a direct result of all this, the Home Secretary appointed a new Commissioner of Police, a new broom to sweep out the filth.'

'I remember that,' Garrett said. 'Robert Mark, wasn't it?'

' "The Lone Ranger from Leicester",' Dodgson said. 'He wasn't a popular fellow.'

It wasn't difficult to understand why: the new Commissioner had announced without ceremony that his three main objectives were to stop the corruption, to break the power of the Criminal Investigation Department, and to establish the supremacy of the uniformed branch. He set about the task with commendable zeal.

'One of the first things Mark did was to set up a new department to take over the investigation of all complaints against police officers,' Tony went on. 'That was *all* police officers, in division or at the Yard.'

'A-Ten,' Garrett said. 'Right?'

'Right,' Tony replied. 'He put a uniformed commander in charge. And Guess Who as his executive officer.'

'Giving the good doggie a bone.'

'And a lot of power,' Dodgson said. 'Which Halford grabbed with both hands. He made life hell for a lot of people over the next five years. Everybody in the force breathed a sigh of relief when he resigned.'

Halford had himself reached the rank

of commander by then; his appointment as head of operations for a private security company named Gardright was a doddle compared to what he had been doing. Five years later, when Gardright was taken over by the larger company, he became head of security at Hayling-Brittain.

'Does he still have friends in the force, Tony?'

'Friends, no. Connections, certainly. He'll have a big funeral.'

'What do you mean?'

'Everybody will go, just to make sure the bastard is dead. Listen, while I've got you on the phone: any news on Andrew and George yet?'

'We're still waiting. Can I ask you a personal question?'

'Sure.'

'That new secretary of yours.'

'Joanna? What about her?'

'How long has she been working for you?'

'About six months. Why?'

'She thinks you're wonderful.'

'Everybody does.'

'Be serious,' Garrett told him. 'She's an attractive woman. Or didn't you notice?'

'Who the hell am I talking to, Claire Rayner?'

'Take her to dinner. Buy her some flowers. Watch what happens.'

'She'd laugh.'

'Try it.'

'Maybe I will,' Dodgson said, his tone thoughtful. 'Maybe I will at that. And listen . . . thanks, Pat.'

'Hell,' Garrett grinned. 'Just call me Yentel.'

Garrett returned to the R2 dossier with a sharper picture in his mind now of the man whose life it detailed. From what Dodgson had said, and from reading between the lines of the dossier, it was clear Halford had been almost universally detested during his time with the police. Nor had he done much to win friends and influence people at Hayling-Brittain, either. He was apparently one of those odd men who do not seek or appear to need the approbation and support of friends. His marriage to a Tottenham girl he had known all his life had broken up

233

and she had since remarried. There were no children.

He lived in a comfortable apartment in a mansion block near Chelsea Bridge. He drove a company-owned Jaguar. He appeared to be a creature of habit, driving out to Amersham each day, arriving at eight-thirty, and was invariably there until seven or eight at night. Apart from playing squash three times a week at Dolphin Square with a young publishing executive, he had no hobbies. Unless, of course, you counted Elaine Harding. Maybe she left Halford no time for hobbies.

Garrett frowned: the involvement of the woman bothered him. It was easy enough to see why Halford would be attracted to Harding, but — apart from the money — what did she see in him? Beautiful, intelligent, available — she could have her pick. Yet she chose someone who, on the face of it, had all the charm of a used toothbrush. Was it only money? Or was she part of the larger thing?

Move on.

Only five people at Hayling-Brittain

knew the full story on Cosmos. It could be fairly safely assumed that Bletchlock was above suspicion. Checking on the others had been a matter of simple routine; their dossiers and lifestyles gave every indication of being entirely normal. Acting upon the assumption that Halford was the leak, it was possible to construct a hypothetical scenario. Up to his neck in debt from trying to keep up with the demands Elaine Harding is making on him, Halford is approached by someone: call him André. André offers Halford a financial lifebelt if he will identify Hayling-Brittain personnel who have personal problems which might make them suggestible to a similar approach, or who might be blackmailed into providing him with telemetry, guidance systems, computer software, or other components of the Cosmos system.

What the watchers had to hope now was that Halford would give them a lead to the real target. So far the surveillance teams keeping a watch on him had come up with nothing, nothing, and more nothing. It was frustrating, but frustration was at the heart of surveillance work. Four days, Garrett thought. Massiter would have to review the operation in another six: the drain on DI5 resources was considerable. He looked up as the door opened and Tom Ashley stuck his head round it, eyebrows raised.

'Got a minute?'

'Any number of them,' Garrett said grouchily, shoving the surveillance report into a folder. 'Come in, Tom. What have you got?'

'Good news and bad news,' Ashley said. He dropped a wad of listing paper covered in computer printout on the desk and collapsed into one of Garrett's armchairs like a shot stork. 'Which do you want first?'

'I'm having a trying day,' Garrett said. 'Give me the good news first.'

'The good news is that TREVI has come up with an operation with an André and a Georges. It was the French spelling in both cases, by the way.'

Garrett nodded. 'And the bad news?'

'Have you ever heard of the Partisan Combat Cell?'

'I've heard of them,' Garrett said harshly. 'They're bombers, and very nasty ones.'

'In that case, I suppose you also know they were part of Action Directe?'

'That, too,' Garrett said. 'So who is André?'

'It's all in the printout,' Ashley replied. 'TREVI says his name — a *nom de guerre*, really — is André Dur. He was a member of Action Directe.'

'So Dur quit Action Directe in eighty-four,' Garrett mused. 'Was that before or after Lisbon?'

'At,' Ashley said. 'Or in, as the case may be.'

In August 1999, a new terrorist alliance calling itself the West European Anti-Imperialist Front had been created in Lisbon. The new organization's avowed principal purpose was to oust NATO from Europe. André Dur's PCC unit was nominated its independent executive arm.

'More work for the undertaker,' Garrett said. 'Thanks, Tom. And thank your princesses, too.'

When Ashley was gone, he scanned through the computer printout. He skipped the introductory paragraphs and concentrated on what the report had to say about André Dur's splinter organization, the Partisan Combat Cell.

Dur had gone into action almost immediately after the Lisbon conference with an attack on the offices of Interfax, a data systems company in Luxembourg. Over the ensuing six years, PCC had carried out more than forty bombings and assassinations, all of them aimed at US Army-associated targets — companies supplying materials to, or dealing with, US Army installations or personnel. The group was thought to have about ten members, at least one of them a woman.

Garrett looked down the list of PCC attacks — the assassination of a member of the European Parliament known to be a pro-American hawk, the sabotage of a Lille factory manufacturing secret US Army anti-tank defence systems, the private jet of a German industrialist blown out of the sky. Whatever else it might be, André Dur's terrorist cell was no jargon-happy gang of ultra-left loonies looking for something to blow up with C4 plastic explosive. This was a sophisticated and dangerous organization which did extensive fieldwork, carefully researching every target and opportunity before making its strike. Its members were professionals; its leader clearly an intelligent and resourceful man.

'André Dur,' Garrett murmured. There was a photograph paperclipped to the top of the first page of the TREVI dossier on the terrorist. It was a blurred surveillance picture, and even with ME — maximum entropy, the photographic enhancement process invented by two Cambridge scientists, widely used now in security services throughout the world — revealed little other than the man was quite young, good-looking in an early Marcello Mastroianni sort of way, with dark blond hair and — although it was impossible to appreciate them in the photograph — brilliant blue eyes. He turned to the dossier.

DUR ANDRÉ JOHN:

Born 27 August, 1976 at 23 rue de la
Croix de Fer, Brussels.

1. Father John Durham, born 7 September, 1949 at The Old Vicarage,
   Alton, Hampshire, nationality British. (Parents British: see supplement
   for DURHAM, John, TREVI-dossier
   888325z49/B.)
2. Mother Amy Tan Jackson, born
   2 January 1959 at Vibhavadi
   Rangsit Road, Bangkok, Thailand,
   nationality Thai. (Parents [F]
   English [M] Thai: see supplement
   for JACKSON. Amy Tan, T-dossier
   888326x23/0.)

Education:

1. Lyceé Robert, avenue Montaigne,
   Brussels.
2. American College, Vevey, Switzerland.
3. Sorbonne, Paris.

Attainment:
1. *Licence ès lettres* (equivalent Bachelor of Arts).
2. *Maîtrise* (equivalent Master of Arts).
3. Languages spoken fluently: English, French, German, Italian.

Known qualifications and skills:
1. Private pilot's licences: CAA-UK/ AAE-Europe/FAA-US.
2. Firearms and explosives: proficient but degree of expertise unknown.

Physical:
    Height 178 cms (5′ 11″).
    Weight 82 kilos (180 lbs).
    Hair dark blond, turning prematurely grey.
    Eyes: violet.
    Identifying marks: none.

Background:
He is thought to have been trained in the techniques of terrorism in the Contremaestra mountains of Cuba by Colonel José Montaño, head of covert operations and second in command to

Ramiro Valdez, head of Dirección General de Inteligencia, the Cuban secret service. Subsequently he spent six months at Patrice Lumumba University in Moscow perfecting his skills.

He is reputed to be a considerable womanizer, but has never made any permanent attachment.
(T-dossier AKA 4447623/D)

Associates:
Known or former members of PCC include:

Georges Barbier (T-dossier 392175y68/F).
Adam Marais (T-dossier 398123x45/F.)
Charles Trennet (T-dossier 597234c32/F).
Madeleine Bonnard (T-dossier 387241v45/F).
Marc Certaine (T-dossier 375641b28/F).
(See appropriate supplementary AKA dossiers.)

There was more, but it didn't look as if it would be much help. Computers were like accountants: they could only tell you what you told them in the first place. The dossier contained the bare bones of the man, but nothing to indicate his present whereabouts, his base of operations, his current associates or the strength of his so-called 'combat cell'. Obviously not. If TREVI knew any or all of that, André Dur would be doing hard time in a top-security prison.

Garrett put the printout to one side and walked across to the window, brows knitted in thought. Below in Berkeley Square, the traffic moved in its incessant circle. No nightingales singing, although pigeons waddled on the paths where office workers were eating their sandwiches.

The parameters of André's scenario were beginning to take shape in Garrett's mind, the exact intent buried somewhere in the series of bizarre suicides and accidents the tabloids called the Trail of Death. What exactly the connection was between it and André, between André and

Halford — if there was one — Garrett could still only guess. Fact: André was a terrorist. The scenario suggested he wanted components from Cosmos, perhaps that he wanted a complete weapon, or even that he already had one. What did he want it for? To sell to the highest bidder? It wasn't likely. Then what? Cosmos was a highly sophisticated submarine hunter-killer, useless without a target at which to point it. An unexpected thought chilled his blood. *Did he have a target?*

He picked up the telephone and called Jessica.

'Help me if you can, I'm feelin' down,' he said.

'Just my luck,' she said, recognizing his voice immediately. 'Ringo Starr. And you're supposed to use the codeword.'

'Avatar,' he said. 'You ever wonder who thinks them up?'

'Yes, I've seen some of his work on the side of Tube trains.'

'Listen, Jess, I'm serious about needing help.'

'Are you private or National Health?'

'National Health, but wait till you hear what I'm cooking for supper.'

'Don't tell me, let it be a surprise,' Jessica said. 'I wanted to talk to you anyway. I've just had a call from Dorothy Morris.'

'And?'

'She said someone called her. Claimed to have information about the death of her husband.'

'Man or woman?'

'A man.'

'No name?'

'No name. He said he has Ronald Morris's diary, and that it proves he was murdered. He offered to sell it to her.'

'How much?'

'A thousand pounds in cash, old notes. He told her he will contact her again and give her further instructions.'

'That's all?'

'She asked me what she should do. I told her I'd talk to you.'

Only Halford knew about the diary, he thought. 'Did the caller say anything else?'

'He said no police. She agreed.

Anyway, she doesn't trust them.'

'She doesn't trust the police, but if a complete stranger telephones her, she'll go straight to the bank and draw out a thousand pounds.'

'Don't expect her to make sense, Charles. She's going through a bad time. Grief is a strange emotion. You start off numb. Then you get angry. After that you fall apart: that's when it really gets to you. And much later, you adjust. She's in the angry stage at the moment. She's hating her husband for dying and leaving her to cope all alone, hating everything about her life. She needs to blame someone, and it looks as if the police have been elected.'

'I'll talk to her,' Garrett said. 'Now, about tonight. You want me to pick you up?'

'Six-thirty,' she said. 'Outside Kelvin?'

'How will I recognize you?'

'I'll be the one standing on the corner with the come-and-get-it look in my eyes,' she said, and he could almost see the hoyden grin. 'Breathing heavily.'

'I'll try to get there before the riot

starts,' he said, and rang off. Next he dialled Dorothy Morris's number. She answered on the third ring.

'I've just talked to Dr Goldman, Dorothy,' he said. 'She told me about your telephone call.'

'I haven't stopped thinking about it since it happened,' she said, and he could hear the tension in her voice. 'Do you think it's possible, Mr Garrett? Could this man know something about Ronald's death?'

Garrett kept his voice neutral. 'I don't honestly know,' he told her. 'When did he call?'

'It was about three o'clock.'

'Tell me exactly what he said. Word for word, as nearly as you can remember.'

'He asked if I was Dorothy Morris. I said Yes. He said I wouldn't know him and he preferred not to give a name.'

'What kind of voice?'

'Soft. Educated.'

'English?'

'I think so.'

'Go on, please, Dorothy.'

'I asked him what he wanted. He said Ronald had been murdered. He said, I know who did it, Mrs Morris, and I have his diary to prove it.'

'And then?'

'I said, Tell me who did it. He laughed at that. He said, I want money. I told him I didn't have a lot. He said, You have enough. I only want a thousand. Go to the Midland tomorrow and draw out one thousand pounds in used notes. He repeated that: Be sure you get used notes. As soon as you have the money, I will call again. I said I'd do it. He said, There's one more thing: don't tell the police. If you tell the police I will know.'

'He used those words: 'I will know'?'

'That's right.'

'Tell me something, Dorothy, do you bank with Midland?'

'Yes, I — ah, you mean, how did he know?'

'Good question,' Garrett said. 'Did you ask him for any sort of bonafides?'

'What do you mean?'

'Something to prove he actually has the diary.'

'No. I was too excited. Should I have done?'

'It doesn't matter. You handled it perfectly well.'

'What shall I do now?'

'Follow instructions. Go to the bank, get the money, wait for the call. We'll be watching. In the meantime — with your permission — I'm going to send a technician to your house. He'll put a recording device on your telephone.'

'When will he come?'

'Later today. There'll be another man with him. He'll stay with you. I don't want you to be alone when that telephone rings.'

I also want to try to get a trace on it while he's talking, he thought, but he did not tell her that.

'I — very well.'

'Don't worry, Dorothy.'

'I wish it was that easy, Mr Garrett.'

'My first name is Charles,' he told her. 'Call me on this number if there is anything you need.'

He hung up and leaned back in his chair, staring at the ceiling. He was smiling, although there was not the slightest trace of amusement in the smile. The waiting was over. The enemy had made a move, and the action had begun.

15

All his decisions made long before he arrived, André Dur wasted no time when he got to London.

After making some telephone calls, he went down to the hotel entrance and waited until Barbier drew up in an inconspicuous Vauxhall Cavalier 1.6GL he had rented from Hertz in Russell Square.

'You've arranged the meeting?' André asked, as he got into the car. Barbier nodded. He was a big, muscular man who looked like exactly what he was, an ex-boxer. He had been with André from the beginning; the ideal lieutenant who always obeyed orders implicitly, reported faithfully, served uncomplainingly. You could not buy that kind of loyalty.

'Four o'clock,' Barbier said. 'As you said.'

'Good,' André said. 'And Catherine?'

'She arrives at two. I'll pick her up at the airport.'

'What about the house?'

'All in order. We can move in this evening.'

'Okay. You have the briefcase?'

'Here. Everything you asked for is in it.'

'*Bon.*' André said. 'Drop me off at Leicester Square.'

He found what he was looking for without difficulty in the Central Reference Library. In the Business Directory, three organizations were listed as the tenants of Lonsdale House, Berkeley Square. One was a service company, Business Data Computing Information Systems Ltd, which occupied the lower two floors. Above them was Diversified Corporate Facilities Ltd, import-export factors. The remaining floors were occupied by a property leasing and rental agency: Millbank Investments Ltd. So far, so good.

Next, he checked the street-by-street directory. Here, however, Lonsdale House was listed as 'central government offices'.

To make absolutely certain he turned next to the appropriate Civil Service directories, checking carefully for any

251

reference to Lonsdale House. There was none. Now he knew for a fact that Diversified Corporate Facilities was a front. Something secret: some unlisted extension of the labyrinth which the security services did not wish the world to know about. And Charles Garrett was a part of it.

Before he left Charles de Gaulle airport for London, André had again telephoned his informer at the building known as La Piscine, the swimming pool, headquarters of the French security service. Jules — an Action Directe sympathizer who had been placed 'on the inside' years ago — confirmed that a Charles Garrett was 'known'. He had been involved a couple of years earlier in a DGSE counter-terrorist operation that went wrong at a little seaside town called St Valery-sur-Somme.

'Can you get me a copy of his dossier?' André asked.

'Not possible,' Jules told him flatly. 'My classification isn't high enough to access his file, and even if it was, the dossier is interactive.'

In other words, if Jules accessed the file, his having done so would be automatically logged and referred to the subject. Interesting, André thought.

'You can't even find out who he works for?'

'The British, obviously. But nothing more. You know how they classify?'

'Yes.' Security clearances were rated upward from C to A, in six-numbered codings: C-1 was the lowest grade, permitting its holder access only to 'soft' intelligence. The really highly classified material was rarely made available to anyone below A-3 classification.

'Garrett is A-6,' Jules said. '*Un vrai gros bonnet.*'

So: Garrett worked for a large security service establishment which officially did not exist, protected by an elaborate cover and an interactive dossier, and operating with the highest security clearances. *Un vrai gros bonnet*, indeed. Once again, André blessed his own foresight for having always communicated through drops and telephone cutouts.

He walked down to Piccadilly, where

he hailed a cab that took him along Knightsbridge to the Victoria and Albert Museum.

'*Chef*,' Barbier said, as he walked in.

André turned and there she was: Catherine. Her full lips were cool as she kissed him and he felt arousal as he touched her body.

'The others are upstairs,' Barbier said.

André nodded and preceded them up the staircase immediately to the left of the entrance. This led to the upper ground floor area, and in turn to a gallery on the floor above. It was empty except for four men.

'Gentlemen,' he said. 'Welcome to London.'

He had asked the *Conseil Exécutif* for unusual men with unusual skills. The Council promised him the best men they could find: no musclemen, no *plastiqueurs*. If there was any 'wet' work to do, Barbier would take care of it.

'Jacques Delormes,' Barbier said, introducing the first man. Delormes was a tall, dark-haired fellow in his mid-forties, an expert in underwater electronics. One by one, Barbier introduced the others: Henri Delaguerre, shorter, grey-haired, with slightly bowed legs and deep squint creases around washed-out blue eyes, a former charter skipper who these days hired out to the highest bidder.

Standing next to the stocky Delaguerre, Paul Gérard looked positively wasted; in fact, he was a brilliant electronic engineer, one of the designers of the original Ariane rocket that had taken French technology into space.

The last of the quartet was a man André had worked with before, one of the best all-round weapons experts he had ever met. His name was Laurent Schaimes, but he was known by the nickname 'Lucky Luke' after the cartoon character of the same name.

'Lucky,' André said, embracing him. 'How are you?'

'Shot to hell,' Schaimes grinned. He was a big man, wide shouldered, tough looking. 'Just an old crock.'

'Barbier has explained what is to be done?' André said. There was a chorus of assent.

'When do we start?' Delormes asked.

'I'm moving the operation forward,' André told him. 'Assembly of the weapon will commence immediately. Gérard, I want you and Lucky to go at once to the safe house. Everything you need is waiting for you there. Delaguerre, you and Georges will go with them. Your task is to pick out the boat. Delormes will go with you. I want the best of everything — whatever Gérard says we need — on the boat. Aim to be ready to sail four days from now.'

'Four days,' Gérard said. 'It's really not enough time.' His thin voice was set to become a whine, given the slightest opportunity.

'Are you telling me you can't do it?' André snapped. 'If you are, say so now and I'll have you replaced immediately.'

'No, no,' Gérard said, his narrow face twisting into a placating grimace. 'I can do it.'

'Get on with it, then,' André said curtly, turning away. 'Today is Monday. We move on Friday. *D'accord?*'

'Okay, *chef*,' Barbier said. 'And you?'

'There are one or two loose ends to tie up here in London,' André told him, with a small smile. 'Catherine and I will take care of those.'

'Halford?'

'We'll join you on Thursday,' André said, deflecting the query. 'Are there any other questions?'

'One big one,' Lucky Luke said. 'Money.'

André opened his briefcase, and from it took out four bulky manila envelopes. He gave one to each of the four men.

'One thousand sterling each,' he said. 'That ought to cover your expenses. Georges will be the bagman. Ask him for whatever you want.'

He stood and watched as they trooped out of the gallery and disappeared down the staircase. Catherine moved closer to him. He could smell her perfume. She always wore Chanel.

'And us?' she murmured, taking his hand. He lifted her hand to his lips and kissed her fingers.

'Everything is ready. We have tonight to ourselves.'

'And tomorrow?'

His expression hardened, and the violet-blue eyes turned as cold and empty as a winter sea.

'Tomorrow,' he told her, 'we have work to do.'

16

A little after 6 a.m., André Dur checked out of the apartment in Down Street, his bills paid the preceding evening with the credit card he had taken off the body of Charlie Ballard. The receptionist who had handled the transaction then would have had trouble recognizing him as the same man now, for André's dark blond hair was now dyed brown, Ray-Ban mirror sunglasses concealed the bright violet eyes, and instead of the impeccable lightweight suit of the night before, he was now wearing a loose-fitting cotton T-shirt, Levi 501s and white Adidas Oregon running shoes.

He opened the car, a Volvo 760 brake, and threw their cases into the trunk as Catherine got in. Like André, she was casually dressed in T-shirt, shorts and sandals. Half an hour later they were bypassing East Grinstead and spearing south through Ashdown Forest. Near

Ringles Cross, André swung east on to the A272, and about ten minutes later they were coasting along Heathfield High Street. He checked his watch: eight twenty. So far, so good.

* * *

As André Dur checked his watch in Heathfield, Ian Halford pulled his Jaguar XJS to a stop outside the Rickmansworth newsagents' shop where he stopped every morning and went inside. The DI5 watchers who had followed him from London slid to a stop outside a cut-price wine store half a block away and waited. The newsagent was a smiling Muslim named Mullik, whose wife and daughter also worked in the shop.

'Beautiful day, sir,' he said, as Halford came to the counter. 'Going to be hot again.'

'Looks like it,' Halford said. 'Anything in the paper today?'

'I believe so,' Mullik said, handing him a copy of the *Daily Telegraph*. Halford paid and went out. He laid the newspaper on the passenger seat, and sat for a moment reading the front page. Then he checked his mirror and moved off into the traffic. After a moment the DI5 surveillance car, a silver-grey MG Maestro, slid into line and followed him through the one-way system back to the main Amersham road.

At the top of the hill was a bus station; beyond it there was a roundabout, but instead of taking the Amersham road as he normally did, Halford floored the accelerator and the big car took off down the hill, weaving like a shark between slower-moving vehicles, and by the time he hit the bypass he was already doing well over seventy miles an hour. Hemmed in by the early morning rush-hour traffic, the two men in the Maestro behind him were left stranded, helpless. By the time they had negotiated the traffic island, the big Jaguar was gone.

★ ★ ★

The entire half-mile length of Heathfield High Street was bordered by double yellow lines which permitted no parking;

André drove to the traffic roundabout at the east end of the street, swung right at the roundabout and turned into a narrow road alongside a Safeway supermarket which led into a pay-and-display parking area. He checked his watch again: eight-thirty. Right on schedule.

*   *   *

At eight thirty-four precisely, the news that Ian Halford had ditched his tail was patched through to Charles Garrett, who was working alongside Chief Superintendent Peter Thorne, the SO.13 co-ordinator who had been given command of this operation. Thorne had commandeered the upstairs floor of the Heathfield post office on Cranbrook Road, about fifty yards north of the Midland Bank building, as his headquarters, and it was on the police radio installed here that the news came in about Halford.

The newsagent, Garrett thought. A picture of the surveillance reports flashed through his mind, the regular calls each day at the little shop in Rickmansworth. It should have touched a nerve, of course. The damned place was a drop.

'Pick the newsagent up,' he told the DI5 liaison officer. 'Give him the treatment. Then show him the photograph of André Dur. And let me know what he says.'

'We'll get right on to it,' the officer told him. 'What about Halford?'

'What steps have you taken?'

'Full alert. All forces, all units. We'll advise you immediately the car's sighted.'

Garrett shook his head. Halford wasn't that stupid. The security man probably had a switch car ready.

'Get on to Hayling-Brittain,' he said urgently. 'Halford didn't leave empty-handed. He's got something: a component, something Dur needs badly. And one more thing: round-the-clock surveillance on Elaine Harding. If she so much as looks like making a move to leave London, I want to know about it, and I mean ten seconds after she decides it herself.'

'We've got it,' the man at Curzon Street House told him.

Garrett looked up. The two female and six male SO.13 officers who had been placed at Thorne's disposal were watching him expectantly.

'All right, Peter,' he said, his voice harsher than he intended. 'Let's get this show on the road.'

★   ★   ★

André got out of the car and locked it. With Catherine beside him, he used the walkway alongside the supermarket to return to the main street. At the western end of the shopping parade, across the street, was the Waggoner's Arms. They crossed over and walked round the back to the pub's car park. A battered-looking Land-Rover was parked to one side near the exit. The lights flashed, on-off. Barbier was in place. André raised a hand and turned back to the main street.

They walked back on the north side of the street all the way to the post office, a redbrick building which was the last commercial property on this side of Cranbrook Road. In front of it was

264

another zebra crossing; using this put them within a few yards of the entrance to the car park at the rear of the Midland Bank. This was where Dorothy Morris would park when she arrived to collect the money.

'You still think there will be surveillance?' Catherine asked.

'I'm sure of it,' he replied. 'But we have two things in our favour. They'll be looking for me, not you, and they won't be expecting trouble here.'

'Where do you think the watchers will be?' Catherine said, as they strolled toward the junction.

'They're probably already in place. One man or more with the woman. One or more upstairs in the post office, another up there,' André said, pointing with his chin at the upstairs rear windows of the Midland Bank which overlooked the car park. 'They may have others posing as pedestrians.'

'And where will we be?'

'Shopping,' he grinned.

★   ★   ★

Peter Thorne looked at the big electric clock on the wall of the post office. Eight forty-five.

'All right, people,' he said. 'You know what to do.'

The plain-clothes counter-terrorist squad officers nodded their understanding and filed out in ones and twos. All of them were armed. Three would take up positions on the street watching keenly for anything at all out of place on an ordinary weekday morning in a small Sussex country town. Two officers took position in an unmarked car in a corner of the Midland Bank car park. When she left, they would escort Dorothy Morris's car, ready for instant action should there be any attempt to hijack it.

Of the remaining three officers, two men and a woman, one was stationed with high-powered binoculars at the window of the post office, another in an upstairs room at the rear of the bank, and the woman officer inside, posing as a member of staff. In addition to the street surveillance, Peter Thorne had posted unmarked radio cars about half a mile out, beside every one of the seven roads leading out of town.

At eight fifty-eight, the SO.13 co-ordinator confirmed that all the operatives were in place. At a minute past nine, Jim Brough, assistant manager of the Safeway super-market, looked over his shoulder to make sure all the girls were at their places by the cash registers, rang the opening-time bell, then unlocked the plate-glass front doors and switched on the automatic beam. Within a few minutes, customers were trickling in. André and Catherine moved through to the main body of the store. Through the big plate-glass win-dows of the wine department they had a clear view of the Midland Bank building opposite. Nine eighteen.

★　★　★

'Are you ready, Mrs Morris?'

Dorothy Morris nodded. How quickly nine twenty had come round, she thought. She felt a little tense, but otherwise fine. Stephen Barlow, the tall, dark-haired young Special Branch officer who had been sent down to stay with her, opened the hall closet and switched on the burglar alarm; the insistent warning beep filled the hallway. Dorothy went out to the car and watched as the detective locked the front door.

'I'll drive, shall I?' she said.

'Fine,' he replied, handing her the house keys. He got into the Mercedes and belted up. As Dorothy got into the car, he spoke into his walkie-talkie. Leaving now, on schedule, over and out, she heard him say. When she turned left on to the Battle road, Detective Barlow spoke into his walkie-talkie once again.

'Leader this is Butterfly. Just turned on to B-two oh nine six. We should be arriving at destination in about ten minutes.'

'Understood, Butterfly,' someone replied, the voice harsh and tinny. 'Come on in.'

* * *

At nine thirty-six, Dorothy Morris's dark blue Mercedes 200 turned into Cranbrook Road, then right again into the car park behind the Midland Bank building.

There was no rear entrance to the bank. Accompanied by the young detective, Dorothy walked round to the front entrance and went in. It was nine forty-three.

★   ★   ★

As Dorothy Morris went into the bank, André Dur touched Catherine on the shoulder. She nodded and went out of the front door of the supermarket, turning right. She crossed Cade Street on the zebra crossing about fifty yards east and went to the cash dispenser set in the south wall of the Midland Bank. She stood before it, staring down like someone trying to work out how to operate it.

★   ★   ★

Inside the bank, Dorothy Morris went to the Enquiries window and pushed the bell. The female DI5 officer posted behind the counter saw her, nodded, and brought across a bulky No. 3 Jiffy bag which she slid through the slot beneath the glass panel.

'Don't touch the money, Mrs Morris,' she said, quietly.

Dorothy Morris nodded; they'd told her the money would be treated with some kind of chemicals. Detective Barlow smiled and held the swing door open for her. She went out into the bright sunlight and he fell into step beside her as they walked back toward the car park. As they did, Catherine Devieux fell into step behind them. Nine fifty-one.

★ ★ ★

Georges Barbier started the engine of the mud-spattered Land-Rover, eased out of the narrow entrance and turned left into the High Street, moving slowly.

★ ★ ★

Abandoning the trolley full of shopping, André Dur went out of the rear entrance of the supermarket to his car, drove round the feeder road and turned right on to Cranbrook Road opposite the bank. He saw Dorothy Morris and the detective walking together about halfway along the north side of the long bank building, with Catherine perhaps two yards behind them. He checked carefully to make sure there was no backup tailing Catherine, then tooted the horn, once.

On his signal, Catherine took a 9mm Walther P5 pistol from her shoulder bag and shot Barlow in the back of the head. Blood sprayed outward as he fell on to his knees, and then rolled on his back, groaning. In the same moment, Catherine grabbed Dorothy Morris, slamming her against the side of the Volvo and driving the breath out of her body as André stopped with a sudden squeal of brakes. Catherine jerked the rear door open and thrust the half-stunned woman forward on her face across the rear seat, jumping in on top of her.

'Go!' she screamed to André, 'go, go, *go!*'

André floored the accelerator and the big Volvo leaped forward with a huge roar, tyres biting into the soft tarmac. The

271

whole thing had taken no more than ten seconds.

As though Catherine Devieux's shot had been a starting pistol, Garrett sprinted out of the upstairs room in the post office building, bounding three at a time down the concrete steps to the street. Behind him he heard Thorne barking orders to the officers in the unmarked police car in the bank car park. The officer driving it was Sweeney-trained, and he was on the move within seconds. Lights blazing, siren baying, he roared to the exit. As he came out, wheels locked right, everything perfect, the battered old Land-Rover driven by Barbier roared up from the roundabout, doing about seventy miles an hour. Reinforced 'roo bars protecting its front end, it smashed the Escort aside as if it were a child's toy. The Land-Rover bounced up on to the sidewalk and off again, then sped off up Cranbrook Road in the wake of the Volvo.

One of the two officers half fell out of the car, trying to lift his pistol to take a shot at the disappearing vehicle. He collapsed alongside the wrecked Ford as Charles Garrett sprinted across the car park behind the post office to his own car. He threw it into gear and swung out on to Cranbrook Road, horn blaring; astonished morning shoppers jammed on their brakes and shouted imprecations as he powered past them. He snapped on the radio in time to hear Peter Thorne alerting the SO.13 stakeout car, a mile or so up the Cranbrook road at the village of Broadoak.

'Victor Bravo, watch for a silver-grey Volvo 760 brake, registration G-George oh-one-oh-five-seven, B-Beta, T-Tango, K-King, repeat — '

'Victor Bravo, we have the Volvo in sight, Central,' Garrett heard the stakeout car reply. 'Approaching at high speed. Moving to pursue . . . now!'

'Victor-Bravo, Victor-Bravo, exercise caution, suspects armed and dangerous.'

'In pursuit now, Central!' Garrett could hear the tension in the officer's voice.

'Victor Bravo, do you have a grey Land-Rover, old model, anywhere in sight?'

'Affirmative, Central. Grey Land-Rover behind us. He's — Central, Land-Rover approaching us at speed, overtaking — ' The voice rose in alarm. 'Watch out! *Christ, he's going to ram — !*'

Silence, nothing. The radio hissed emptily.

'Victor Bravo, respond!' the controller shouted. 'Victor Bravo, respond!'

There was no reply. Garrett's lips clamped into a thin line and he pushed the speedo needle up past the ninety mark. About half a mile ahead a pillar of black, coiling smoke climbed straight up into the bright blue morning sky. He stopped the car, put on his hazard warning lights, and ran toward the police Escort, which was upside-down and burning furiously on the central reservation. Off to his left, the Land-Rover lay on its side in the ditch beside the road.

Shielding his face with his jacket, Garrett got as near to the burning police car as he could; the soft *sisss* as the intense heat singed his hair and eyebrows driving him back. The doors of the vehicle were still shut, and the flames and smoke that filled the interior made it impossible to see anything inside. They must still be in there, he thought, and if they were, they had never had a chance. He ran across the road toward the Land-Rover, gun in hand, hearing sirens coming toward him from the direction of Heathfield. He yanked open the door, his face locked in a grimace of anger. There was no one there.

As he turned away, a sleek black police Jaguar slid to a stop, followed by a turbo-powered Transit van with an orange stripe down its side. Its rear doors were thrown open with a bang and uniformed officers erupted out of it, yelling to each other as they ran towards the burning Escort with fire extinguishers and first-aid kits while others coned off the road and positioned the van to control oncoming traffic.

Peter Thorne came across from the Jaguar to where Garrett was standing by the wrecked Land-Rover.

'Nothing?' he said, his voice disbelieving. 'Three good men dead, and we come out with nothing?'

Garrett shook his head, concealing his own anger. Peter Thorne banged an impotent fist against the side of the Land-Rover, then stalked away. Garrett watched him go, then went back to his car. He leaned his head back against the headrest and closed his eyes, trying to concentrate. There was still a series of unknowns here that he couldn't make sense of. Why had the terrorist kidnapped Dorothy Morris? Hostage? Decoy? Red herring?

A few minutes later, a local police officer came over to tell him that an East Sussex police patrol had found the Volvo abandoned by the roadside a few miles south of Cranbrook. The envelope containing the money was still in its envelope on the rear seat. A police tow truck was bringing it back to Heathfield. As the policeman left, Garrett noticed that the dashboard transceiver light was flashing. He switched on and was immediately patched through to Lonsdale House.

'Garrett?' It was the unmistakable voice of Nicholas Bleke. 'Where are you?'

'Heathfield, East Sussex,' Garrett reported.

'Is this urgent, sir?'

'Wouldn't bother you otherwise,' Bleke said curtly. 'I've just heard from Massiter at Curzon Street. It's about the newsagent, Mullik. He spilled. The shop was a drop. He was being paid to pass messages to Halford. He identified the man who paid him from a photograph.'

'André Dur,' Garrett said.

'You knew?'

'It had to be him,' Garrett said.

'Something wrong?'

'I got SO.13 to set up a stakeout,' Garrett told him. 'It just blew up in my face. I've got three dead policemen to explain, and it looks as if Dur has Dorothy Morris, too.'

'You had a chance to take him?'

'A half chance,' Garrett said. 'I blew it.'

'You may get the other half,' Bleke said. 'We've had a break at this end. It's Halford.'

Garrett felt adrenaline pump through him. 'What about Halford?'

'You were right. He took a copy of the assembly procedure manual for the Cosmos missile with him when he went missing.'

'Then we're in real trouble,' Garrett said. 'Dur now knows how to operate Cosmos.'

'Maybe not. It would appear Halford has had second thoughts. He called Massiter. He's afraid Dur will kill him as soon as he hands over the manual. He says if we give him immunity, he'll help us to nail Dur.'

Garrett frowned. 'Massiter's sure it was Halford?'

'That's what he said. Halford wants a meet. You, solo. No surveillance, no backup.'

'When, where?'

'You're to be at a public telephone box outside East Grinstead station, up side, at exactly noon. You'll get further instructions then.'

Garrett looked at his watch. Eleven oh-eight. 'I'm on my way,' he said.

'What do you want me to tell Massiter?' Bleke said.

'Nothing,' Garrett said flatly. 'We've tried it their way, and all we've got to show for it is dead men. It's time to cut a few Gordian knots.'

'All right,' Bleke said decisively. 'Go ahead. But I hope you realize I'll have a hell of a lot of explaining to do to the Minister if you don't deliver.'

'I'll deliver,' Garrett said.

17

Garrett knew East Grinstead reasonably well: at one time the Old Felbridge Hotel there had been used as a debriefing centre for defectors.

He found his way easily through the town's otherwise bewildering one-way system, and slid into a parking space outside the British Rail station at eleven fifty-two. There were two phone boxes outside the booking hall. At noon exactly, the phone on the right rang. Garrett snatched it off its hook.

'Garrett?'

'Halford?' It didn't sound like him. 'Where are you?'

'Not so fast. I want to be sure you're alone.'

'I'm alone.'

'We'll see. There's a phone box outside Gipsy Hill station, West Norwood. Be there at twelve-forty.'

The connection was broken. With a

curse, Garrett slammed the phone back on its hook and ran for the Audi. He put on his headlights, clamped a portable strobe flasher on the roof above the driver's door, and roared out of the station, forcing his way through the traffic, horn blaring when slow-moving buses or trucks barred his way. He looked at the dashboard clock: he had three minutes in hand as he turned on screaming tyres into Gipsy Hill, slammed to a halt in Sainsbury Road, and ran for the station. He heard the telephone ringing as he skidded into the booking hall, saw a crewcut young man dressed in jeans and a grubby athletic singlet going across to answer it.

'Leave it!' he yelled. The man froze in his tracks, then turned, a frown putting a crease between his piggy eyes.

'Oodafuckyafink — ?'

Garrett shortarmed him aside and snatched up the phone.

'Halford!' he panted. 'Where the hell are you?'

'Very good, Garrett,' the voice replied. 'Very good indeed. Next stop, Acton

Town tube. One-thirty. We're watching you, Garrett. Don't use your carphone.'

'Where's Dorothy — ?'

It was no use: the connection was broken again.

The traffic was heavy and moving slowly in Camberwell. By the time he reached Vauxhall Bridge, half of the time Garrett had available to reach west London was already gone; although he drove like a maniac, it was one thirty-four when he skidded to a stop in Gunnersbury Lane and ran back across the pedestrian crossing into the station booking hall. There were several phones on the wall to his right. None of them was ringing.

'Damn, damn, damn!' he ground out. The ticket collector looked at him uncertainly, then smiled.

'Hey man, yo name Garrett?'

'Yes, it is,' Garrett said.

'Dis feller phoned you,' the West Indian said. 'You got to go to . . . wait now, I wrote it down yere someplace.' He rummaged in his uniform pocket, then brought out a creased yellow Travelcard.

'Dassit, man,' he grinned. 'Phone outside em post office in airfield. Okay?'

'Harefield?'

'Dassit.'

'He say when?'

'Oh, yeah,' the man said. 'He say two o'clock, don' be late, right?'

Garrett nodded. 'Thanks,' he said, and ran. Harefield was about ten miles west of him as the crow flew, maybe twelve by road. It was a route he knew well; he kept a light plane at Denham airfield, just a few miles from Harefield.

This time he was early. The phone rang right on time.

'Where are you, Halford?'

'Quite near. The Fisheries Inn, fifteen minutes.'

'Wait, I — '

The phone had been hung up again. Garrett cradled the receiver, stared at it for a moment. It would be but a matter of moments to contact Lonsdale House, let Bleke know where he was, get some backup organized, but he couldn't bet Dorothy Morris's life on it. He went into a newsagent next door to the post office and asked if they knew where the pub was.

'Turn left at the crossroads, down Mount Pleasant, you'll come to a bridge,' the shopkeeper told him. 'The Fisheries is on the other side of the canal. Just follow your nose.'

He turned into the car park and eased to a stop on the far side. The pub stood on a little island, with the canal on one side and the brackish River Colne on the other. It was one of those places with horse brasses and dark oak fittings.

As the barmaid served him a half pint of draft Guinness and put it on a towelling mat on the bar, Garrett looked around. There was no sign of Halford.

He ordered a cheese sandwich and wolfed it down. The clock on the wall above the dartboard told him it was two thirty-five. Still no sign of Halford. A telephone rang somewhere; he heard the barmaid answer it. She came to the bar, looking around.

'Anybody here called Garrett?' she said.

'I'm Garrett,' he told her.

'Wanted on the phone, love,' she said, pointing with her thumb. He went out into the corridor and picked up the telephone.

'Garrett,' he said.

'This is Halford. Outside. In the car park.'

'I'll be right there.'

He hung up and went to the door, which opened inwards. As he hesitated on the threshold, dazzled by the bright sunlight outside, he felt, rather than saw, the black bulk of someone coming at him from behind. His reaction was very fast but still not fast enough. He had half turned toward his assailant when something smashed him down into darkness and then deeper darkness.

★ ★ ★

The steady roar was strangely familiar and yet unexpected. His hands and feet felt numb. He opened his eyes and was immediately blinded by brilliant sunlight. He was sitting in the cockpit of a plane. My plane, he thought, recognizing the accoutrements immediately. He tried to move, but his feet were tied together and his hands were bound in front of him.

The man sitting next to him bared his teeth in the semblance of a smile. There was no hint of friendliness in it.

'You're right,' he said. 'It is your plane.'

'André Dur,' Garrett said. 'Where's Halford?'

'Elsewhere,' Dur said, without elaborating. 'You know Mrs Morris, of course.'

Garrett turned as far to his right as he was able, restricted by his bonds and the flying harness. Dorothy Morris was strapped into the right rear passenger seat, her chin on her chest, her eyes closed.

'What have you done to her?' he rasped.

'Just a psychotropic injection, nothing dangerous,' Dur said urbanely. 'She is . . . less trouble that way.'

'And who's the ape sitting behind me, your friend Georges Barbier?'

'He won't like it if you call him names, Garrett,' Dur said.

'I'll worry about it later,' Garrett

replied. 'You dyed your hair.'

'Small adjustments are the best disguise,' Dur smiled.

'Where are we going?'

'Not far,' Dur told him.

Garrett checked the instrument panel. They were flying at a height of two thousand feet, heading a little north of east. He did not recognize the terrain below.

'How many of them did you actually kill?' he said to the man on his right. Dur ignored the question.

'Let me see if I can guess how you set it up,' Garrett said. 'You read something in one of the tabloids about the Trail of Death. It gave you a beautiful opportunity to get rid of any of the Hayling-Brittain people who wouldn't toe the line anymore, or whose usefulness was over. Am I right?'

Without warning Barbier hit him at the base of the neck with a clenched fist, numbing the bunched muscles there, making his head swim with nausea. 'Enough questions,' the big man growled. 'Shut your mouth.'

Garrett shook his head to clear it and tried to concentrate on discovering where he was and why they were there. Almost as though he had read Garrett's thoughts, Dur banked the plane to port, and Garrett saw the bright broad ribbon of the M11 motorway snaking across the landscape below. Dur was saying something to Stansted air traffic control, but Garrett could not make out the words above the drone of the engine. He concentrated instead upon distances. They would have flown about fifty or sixty miles by now; fully loaded, with max fuel at max economy speed, the Skyhawk's range was slightly less than six hundred miles. He watched, a slight frown puckering his forehead, as the direction needle came round until it was pointing almost due north. If they continued on this bearing, they would overfly East Anglia to their point of no return, three hundred miles out over the North Sea. Where was Dur heading for?

'Georges,' the terrorist said, as if in reply to Garrett's unspoken question. 'Are you ready?'

'Ready,' the big man said.

'*Bon*,' Dur said. He snapped switches on the control panel, engaging the two-axis Navomatic 400 autopilot with which the Skyhawk was fitted. When he was satisfied she was flying automatically, he released his hold on the controls. He took the radio transceiver off its hook and smashed it against the metal cowling of the control panel; it disintegrated in a mess of plastic. He switched off the receiver, then nodded, satisfied. It was now impossible for anyone on the ground to contact them, or vice versa.

'Give me the needle,' he said, holding a hand up over his left shoulder. Barbier slapped the syringe into it like a staff nurse in an operating theatre. Dur reached across, slit the leg of Garrett's trousers with a knife, and put the needle into his thigh, depressing the plunger. Bound firmly hand and foot, there was absolutely nothing Garrett could do. Almost at once, he felt the soft, insidious swirl of impending unconsciousness.

'Have a pleasant flight,' Dur said. He

unfastened the door-catches of the plane, gathered his legs under him and pushed the door open wide before leaping into space. As the door smashed back the big man, Barbier, who had climbed over the seat, stopped it with his boot and again braced it open. He looked at Garrett, smiled, and leapt out. The door banged shut behind him and locked.

The plane droned on, moving slightly as the automatic pilot trimmed and adjusted the controls. Fighting desperately for consciousness, Garrett bucked and strained against the plastic clothes-line with which his legs and arms were bound. The bright sunlight went grey and then darker, and he lapsed into unconsciousness. After a while the Sky-hawk entered the Honington Military Control Zone. On the ground, air traffic controllers at Mildenhall and Lakenheath tried vainly to make contact with the unauthorized intruder. There was no reply. The plane moved on across the bright blue sky.

⋆   ⋆   ⋆

Far below and behind the Skyhawk, two parachutes opened, swaying downward toward Chedburgh, a tiny hamlet on the main road from Haverhill to Bury St Edmunds. André Dur and Georges Barbier landed about a quarter of a mile apart on the abandoned airfield near the village. As he hauled in the billowing canopy, André saw a sleek grey Mercedes 190 driven by Catherine Devieux bumping across the rutted old runway from the entrance on the A143.

There was no sign that anyone had even seen them. He got into the car. Catherine leaned over and kissed him, smiling. She drove down the runway to where Barbier had landed. The big man came lumbering toward them as the car came to a stop, clambered into the rear seat and clapped a meaty hand on André's shoulder.

'Just as a matter of interest,' he said, grinning, jerking a thumb towards the sky, 'where d'you think they'll come down?'

André shrugged. 'Wherever it is, there'll be a hell of a bang,' he said. '*Allons-y*, Catherine!'

In the dream he was in Switzerland, staying with Frau Würmli in the old house on the side of the hill in Herrliberg.

'Charles!' a voice said. 'Charles, wake up!'

He opened his eyes. His mouth felt as if it was stuffed with cotton wool, and there was a slow dark throb of pain inside his skull. It all came back in a rush, the plane, André Dur, all of it. The steady thunder of the engine was unchanged. The side of his face was wet.

'Thank God!' Dorothy Morris said. 'Thank God!'

She started to cry, as if she was exhausted. She was still strapped in her seat, her hands still bound. Garrett realized that somehow she had managed to lift one of the heavy plastic map cases out of the door compartment and get it firmly in her grasp. She had hit him with it again and again. From cheekbone to jaw the skin on the right side of his face was bloody and raw.

He checked his watch. He had been

unconscious for more than an hour. He looked down and saw only sea below them. He ran his eye over the instruments. André Dur had left the plane flying at maximum cruising speed at three-quarters power: around a hundred and thirty miles an hour, not counting any headwinds they might be pushing into. The plane was still heading north. Garrett did some rapid calculations. Dur and his sidekick had bailed out over Stradishall. That was in Suffolk. A hundred and twenty miles north of that point would put the plane out over the North Sea, somewhere between the Dogger Bank and Scarborough in Yorkshire. The fuel gauge showed one tank a quarter full. With no one to switch to the second tank, the plane would very soon have simply fallen out of the sky.

Cold anger touched him. Before today it had been business: all part of the job. This made it personal. A feeling of unutterable weariness seeped through him and he felt his eyelids drooping. Watch that, he told himself;

whatever it was they'd injected him with wasn't out of his system yet. He twisted round in his seat. Dorothy Morris had stopped crying; simple exhaustion and sheer relief had caused the tears.

He frowned. Behind her seat he could see two large drums, twenty-gallon size. Clipped to their spring-loaded caps were glass vials full of liquid with something floating in it that looked like bits of yeast. The device was crude, but almost foolproof: the plane would simply fly on until it ran out of fuel. Wherever it hit the ground — or the sea — the glass vials would shatter, the spring-loaded caps would fly off the petrol drums at the same instant that the phosphorus ignited spontaneously. The resulting fireball would destroy every trace of the plane and anyone in it.

'Dorothy, you'll have to watch me,' he told her. 'I might pass out again. Don't let me go under.'

'All right,' she said. 'All right.'

'Can you get out of your safety harness?' he asked her.

'I don't know,' she said. 'How do you do it?'

'There's a release clasp at waist level, in the centre. Try and hit it. You'll be able to move around.'

'Yes,' she said, and he heard a small clatter.

'Uh,' she said. 'Ah. It's open.'

'You've got to get out of it like a waistcoat,' he said. 'Can you do it?'

'No use,' she said glumly. 'My hands are tied and the straps are inside.'

'Can you lean over in front of me?'

'I'll try.' He felt the warmth of her breath on his neck.

'Dorothy, you've got to get my belt buckle open,' he told her.

'I'll try,' she said.

He felt her weight on his right shoulder.

'Just . . . can't . . . quite . . . ' she said, through gritted teeth. Her fingers clutched at his jacket, six inches short of the belt buckle. Garrett braced his feet hard on the floor of the plane and surged up against the shoulder straps of the harness, putting every ounce of his strength into the movement. Dorothy Morris made a small sound of encouragement, her slender fingers plucking at the buckle, trying to unfasten the belt. He couldn't hold any longer, and slumped down in the seat, perspiration soaking through his shirt.

'Nearly,' she panted. 'Nearly.'

'Again,' he said. 'Ready? Yes? Now.'

He arched his body against the unforgiving harness once more, and she managed to disengage the spike from its hole. The buckle flapped open. She slumped back in her seat, perspiration running down her face, breathing like a sprinter at the end of a race.

'Oh, God, my arms,' she whispered.

'Come on, Dorothy,' Garrett urged her. 'You've done the hard part. All we have to do now is get the damned belt off.'

It took them nearly twenty minutes, but they did it. When the wide black leather belt finally slid clear of the belt loops, she gave a faint sob of relief and collapsed on the seat behind him.

'All right,' he panted. It was relentlessly

hot in the confined space of the cabin, and he was as wet as if someone had thrown a bucket of water over him. 'Now the easy part.'

'Can't we just rest a moment?' she said. 'I can't move my hands.'

'No, Dorothy!' he said. 'You've got to do it now!'

The harshness of his voice made her sit up straight, her eyes flashing with determination.

'Don't shout,' she said. 'What do I do?'

'The buckle is hinged,' he told her. 'Open it carefully.'

Years as a field agent had taught Garrett many lessons. One of the most important was never to be caught without some kind of weapon. Soon after he was seconded to PACT he had the armourer at Lonsdale House make him the special belt he always wore. It was an adaptation of a money belt, with a channel let into the inner layer in which was set a yard-long length of piano wire with flat wooden pegs at each end, a deadly effective garrotte. The round brass buckle split into two halves to reveal the second weapon.

'What is it?' Dorothy Morris said.

'It's a variation on a martial arts weapon called a throwing star,' Garrett said. 'Handle it carefully. It's as sharp as a razor.'

'I've got it.'

'Cut the ropes holding my arms.'

'Wait.'

Her breath was ragged beside his ear. She sawed away for a moment or two at the plastic-covered clothesline and then he heard her grunt with satisfaction. In the same moment he felt the freedom as his bonds slackened. He could lift his bound hands now, and it was the work of only a minute more for her to cut him free.

He used the star to cut her loose, then climbed over to the rear seats. Very carefully he unclipped the two glass vials from the spring-loaded caps on the petrol drums, and told Dorothy to hold them as he got back into the front seat.

'What are they?' she asked.

'They made the plane into a flying

bomb,' he told her. 'These were the detonators.'

He put them carefully into the map case by his right leg. How much of a bump they would take without breaking there was no way of knowing. He switched off the automatic pilot and took the controls. The plane responded immediately to his touch. He banked sharply to port, coming around ninety degrees. Twenty minutes later he looked down and saw the unmistakable outline of Flamborough Head. As he levelled off, Dorothy Morris climbed into the forward passenger seat and strapped herself in. She looked tired, as though she had done a lot of hard physical labour.

'I'm sorry you had to go through all this, Dorothy,' he said. 'I should never have put you at risk.'

'I'm glad you did,' she said, stoutly. 'I feel as if I've done something useful . . . for Ronald.'

'There's something else you can do.'

'What?'

'I want you to try and tell me where they took you.'

'I don't know. A little place somewhere. A cottage.'

'You don't know where it was?'

'They kept me on the seat, face down. I didn't see anything till we got there.'

'All right. When you got there, what did you see?'

'It was in a lane. Very narrow. Open fields opposite. There was a barn. Gravel path. Thatched roof. It was built on the side of a slope.'

'Let's begin at the beginning,' Garrett said. 'And take it step by step. Maybe by the time we get back to Denham we'll have worked it out.'

He did another ninety-degree turn to port and pointed the Skyhawk back the way she had come. Heading back to London would mean he once more had to overfly some restricted zones, setting off yet more alarms in the various air traffic control areas he crossed. The safest and smartest thing to do would be to put down at the nearest landing strip or civil airfield he could find, but the necessary explanations that would inevitably follow would waste valuable time.

The quickest way back to London was the way he had come, and there was only one half-safe way to get there without radio or air traffic assistance: by hedge-hopping about fifty feet above the ground the whole way. He plotted a course and took the Skyhawk down in a steep descent towards Cambridge. From there, he'd play it by ear.

18

In spite of Harry Massiter's precautions, Elaine Harding fooled them all. The way she managed it was evidence in itself that the whole thing had been worked out a long time in advance, and that all she had been waiting for was the right opportunity. It came, by blind chance, just two days after Ian Halford disappeared.

Making one of those impromptu decisions for which he was famous, Arnold Bletchlock decided to fly to Munich for a meeting with August Kautz, chairman of the German industrial corporation that bore his name. He decreed that his secretary should accompany him to Stansted in the big Daimler so that he could dictate en route a non-stop barrage of letters and memoranda which were to be ready for his return the following morning.

They left Amersham at ten-fifteen. By the time the Daimler slid to a stop in front of the terminal building, the company plane, a Lear Jet Model 25 was waiting on the runway, ready to go.

Within ten minutes it was on the runway, awaiting clearance to take off. A few minutes later, it arrowed down the runway and soared up into the cloudless sky. A small smile on her face, Elaine Harding told the driver to go back to Amersham. Although she had been aware of it the whole time, she affected not to see the Ford Sierra which had tailed the Daimler from London turning to follow it back.

She was back at the office a little after midday. At a few minutes past two, her telephone rang. It was Bletchlock, and he was in a foul mood. Three vital computer discs were missing from the contract package which had been his main reason for fixing the meeting with Kautz.

'Listen to me, girl: I'm sending the Lear back to Stansted. It should get in at three-thirty or thereabouts,' Bletchlock rumbled. 'Get on the plane, bring the discs by hand, understand?'

'No problem,' Elaine said.

'Good,' Bletchlock said. 'I'll have a car waiting for you at Munich airport.'

Elaine Harding put down the telephone. It was no accident at all that the floppy discs had been omitted from the contract package; she had seen to that personally. She called Transportation and told Dave to bring the Daimler round to the front door. He drove her first to her apartment to pick up a change of clothes, and then out to the airport.

The DI5 watchers were aware of all these developments, of course; Tinkerbell had taken good care of all Elaine Harding's telephones, and the men who were keeping an eye on her were pros. Arrangements to have her shadowed by agents of the German security service, working in tandem with Five's resident in Munich, were being put in hand almost before she hung up. When she climbed into the Lear at Stansted and winged off into the sky the DI5 watchers returned to London to await news of her movements from the German office for the Protection of the Constitution — *Bund für Verfassungsschutz* — who would keep Harding under surveillance from the moment she landed.

They lost her.

During the one-and-a-half-hour flight, Elaine Harding so completely altered her appearance that when she came through customs and into the arrivals hall, nobody recognized her. Leaving London, she had been wearing a dark blue business suit and a white silk blouse, her dark hair tied back with a bright red bow. When she landed at Munich-Riem, she was wearing a black tank-top beneath a blue cotton blazer, ill-fitting blue jeans, and a well-used pair of Gola trainers. Instead of coming straight through, Harding loitered in the luggage reclaim area until the baggage for a charter flight from Palma arrived, then joined the throng of noisy, tanned holidaymakers emerging from the customs hall. Her dark hair concealed beneath a blonde wig, the bright blue eyes hidden behind sunglasses, she looked like just another *Ferienfräulein*, and the watchers posted in the arrivals area didn't even give her a second glance.

Instead of heading for the exit, Elaine

Harding took the stairs to the departures area on the lower level. She went across to the Lufthansa desk and purchased a one-way ticket to Zurich. The plane touched down at Zurich-Kloten at seven-forty. Elaine Harding got off it and disappeared.

★　★　★

Garrett sat in on the debriefing conducted by the PACT retrace experts as they carefully took Dorothy Morris through her memories of her face-down journey in the back of the Volvo. Did anyone speak? Did they say anything about what had happened, about their destination? Did they drive fast or slow? Did the driver make a lot of turns? Which direction? Did he stop often, sound his horn? What sort of sound did the car make on the road? How long did the whole journey take? The answers to these questions could tell a trained operative a very great deal about a probable route.

They went over it all several times, asking different questions, adding others.

When they were finished, everything was given to the field operatives. Starting from the bank in Heathfield they would try every combination of roads and speeds until they found a pattern that matched her memory: a roundabout, a level crossing, and a gravelled drive that led them to a thatched cottage set among conifers and horse chestnut trees. Retracing was anything but an exact science, and there was no guarantee they would solve the puzzle. In the absence of other leads, it was their best chance. While they did it, there was nothing Garrett could do but wait.

He made a rueful face as he recalled the events which followed his unauthorized landing at Denham. A squad of Thames valley police was waiting on the ground to arrest him for about sixty-seven different air traffic violations. They looked positively downcast when they learned they were not going to be allowed to lay a finger on him.

Garrett's inquisition did not end there. When he got back to Lonsdale House, Nicholas Bleke was waiting for him. Like

Queen Victoria, he was not amused.

'Have you any conception of the amount of trouble I've had to go to in order to stop the ministry from revoking your licence and throwing you into jail?' he asked, angrily. 'You damned nearly started World War Three.'

'I'm sorry,' Garrett said. 'But not very.'

'Sometimes you cut too many corners, Charles,' Bleke grumbled. 'But we won't waste any more time on that. Now, d'you think we've got any chance of locating this maniac we're after?'

'I'm hoping the retracers will come up with something.'

'It's a damned long shot.'

'It's the only one we've got,' Garrett answered. 'Dur's been in the clear for more than twelve hours. He could be anywhere by now.'

'With a shoot-ready Cosmos missile. Where do you think he plans to use it?'

'Dur's cell is dedicated to destroying American targets. What better target could they have than a nuclear submarine? It would be the ultimate ecological disaster, Chernobyl on the high seas. And the Americans would be responsible. Look at the way the world press reacted when that Russian sub sank off Bear Island. If one of the damned things actually blew up . . . ' He left the rest unsaid.

'If we assume they're after a nuclear sub, they have to go where the subs are. That means either Holy Loch or Faslane.'

'Agreed. But that doesn't help us much. Nuclear subs coming out of Holy Loch or Faslane usually run south through the Irish Sea. Other times they take the North Channel out into the Atlantic. Dur's got a dozen options.'

'All right, all right,' Bleke growled. 'I get the picture. Have you alerted the Royal Naval Submarine Establishment?'

'They're on Alpha Bikini Black. No departures without our authorization. But they have a problem with incoming vessels.'

'What's that?'

'Silent running is standard. The subs don't break radio silence until they're within a few miles of Faslane.'

'How do they know where they are?'

'They track them on something called

SUBSATINFEX, the submarine satellite information exchange, but they have to be at periscope depth. When they're submerged, nobody knows their exact location. In an emergency they can send a signal, of course, but we'd have to give them pretty concrete reasons for turning a homeward-bound sub away.'

'What about the Americans? Have you spoken to them?'

'I got the feeling they think we're exaggerating the problem. Of course, they don't know about Cosmos, and I can't tell them.'

'We may have to,' Bleke said.

'The trouble is, we don't know where Dur is, or when he plans to strike.'

'It had better not stay that way, Charles.'

'I don't plan to let it.'

'Good,' Bleke said. 'Call me as soon as you have anything.'

★   ★   ★

The retrace teams found the house at four that afternoon. It was called Tumbledown Cottage, and it was located in a village called Netherham, about five miles south of Hurst Green, just off the Hastings road.

'Mrs Morris has confirmed it's the right place?'

'She's here now. It looks good. The road route more or less fits as well.'

'What have you found?'

'They're vacuuming right now. Nothing so far. The place looks pretty sterile.'

'Give me the number there,' Garrett said. 'Call me if you come up with anything else.' He hung up and immediately dialled the Lonsdale operator. When she answered he gave her his personal clearance code. She sounded alert and intelligent.

'I want an immediate priority trace on all long-distance calls made in the last seven days from this number,' he told her, and repeated the Hurst Green number the retrace team in Netherham had given him. He drummed his fingers on the desk while she contacted the GPO security switchboard in Ebury Street. *Come on*, he urged her silently.

'Sir?'

'Go ahead.'

'Tinkerbell says four long-distance calls were made from that number during the last — '

'Never mind that,' Garrett interrupted. 'Just give me the details of the inland call.'

'How — ?' The operator checked herself; she knew better than to ask questions. 'The number was oh three nine one seven eight eight eight nine three. That's in Fleetwood, Lancashire.'

Fleetwood. The largest fishing port on the west coast of England. Boats in profusion, expert knowledge of the sea lanes plied by the nuclear submarines, all there for the asking.

'I need a name and address for that number,' he said. 'How soon can they — ?'

'I anticipated you'd want that information, sir,' the Lonsdale operator said crisply. A small smile touched Garrett's lips; let her have her moment of triumph. 'The subscriber is Daniel Ackerley, 37 Sylvia Street. Occupation, trawlerman, retired.'

'And they said you were just a pretty

face,' Garrett said. 'Thank you, Lonsdale.'

Now he dialled Tony Dodgson's personal number. The cool voice of Joanna McCallum replied.

'This is Charles Garrett. Is Tony there?'

'No, sir. He's at a conference.'

'Then you'll have to do, McCallum,' Garrett told her. 'I want an incident check and I want it yesterday.'

'Details?' The casual tone had disappeared; she was all business.

'Location: Fleetwood, Lancashire. I want you to check to see if there has been any report of the theft of any kind of boat, probably a fishing boat, within the last twenty-four hours.'

'I'll get back to you,' she promised.

He put down the phone and called Denham airfield and asked them to get the Skyhawk ready. Tony Moynahan, the dispatcher, promised to file his flight plan — destination Blackpool municipal airport, most direct route — to save him time when he got there. As Garrett hung up the phone rang again.

'McCallum here, sir,' Dodgson's assistant said. 'No incident of the type you inquired about has been reported.'

It will, McCallum, he thought grimly, it will. He thanked her and was about to hang up when a stray thought struck him.

'By the way, how was dinner?'

There was a moment's silence. 'Ahah,' she said.

'Ahah, what?'

'I wondered what put it into his head. It was you, wasn't it?'

'Me?' Garrett said. 'Why would I do a thing like that?'

'Just what I was wondering,' she said, and there was a smile in her voice. 'You don't look much like Cupid.'

'Master of disguise,' he said. 'Fools everyone. Thanks again, McCallum.'

'Hey!'

'What?'

'Thank you,' she said softly, and hung up.

He made two more calls, then used the intercom to call Bleke's office. Liz James put him through, and he heard Bleke's familiar bark.

'It's Fleetwood,' Garrett told him.

'You're sure?'

Garrett told him about the phone trace from the house in Netherham. 'Trawlers out of Fleetwood fish in the Irish Sea, north of the Isle of Man or between it and the Irish coast. There's a narrow deep-water fault channel there, the Beaufort Dyke. It's used as the main route to the Atlantic by the subs. They call it the Rat Run. All Dur has to do is hijack a boat, put Cosmos on board, and wait until a target comes along.'

'Any sighting?'

'I've contacted Harry Massiter. Five will have a team of watchers in place at Ackerley's house within the hour.'

'Very well,' Bleke said. 'I'll pass the word to Faslane and Holy Loch. What alert state did you say they're at?'

'Alpha Bikini Black, terrorist attack expected.'

'I'll move them up a notch. You'd better call in Special Branch, too.'

'A local squad is on standby; they'll move when Massiter's people get there.'

'Do you want the SAS or the Special Boat Service in on this?'

'In readiness, perhaps.'

'I'll see to it. You'll go to Fleetwood right away?'

'I'll fly to Blackpool. The local police can pick me up there.'

'Keep in touch,' Bleke said.

★   ★   ★

Harry Jackson, master of the trawler *Boy Christian*, lived in a neat town house on a small estate about half a mile from the centre of Fleetwood. He was young for a skipper, only thirty-nine, and things were going well.

Most lunchtimes when he was not at sea — one day in three — Harry walked the half mile to his local, the Hope and Anchor, and had a couple of pints before going home for his meal. If he wasn't sailing that night he'd have tea with Jessie and the kids; if he was, it would be a bacon sandwich and a cup of tea before climbing into his Ford Capri to drive down to the East Dock.

He liked to have plenty of time to get the boat ready for sea. She was his pride and joy; it had taken him the best part of

316

six years to get her fitted out the way he wanted. She had the best navigational and sonar — echo-sounding — equipment he could afford and a really good Decca radar system. These days you were competing with Irish and European boats, not to mention Russian factory ships that sailed in and sucked the fish off the sea-bed like some gigantic vacuum cleaner. It helped to have a 'nose' for where the fish might be, but the only reliable way to outmanoeuvre the competition was to have all the right gear.

Boy Christian was named after the eldest of his three sons. Chris was nine now, James seven, Michael a year younger. He sometimes wondered if any of them would want to go to sea. It would be nice to teach them all the tricks of the trade he'd learned. And the little superstitions, like tying a scrap of a new baby's christening shawl to a bush near the sea to guard him from drowning. But Jessie was dead against any of the lads becoming trawlermen. She wanted them to go to university. He wondered what his own father, a trawlerman like his father before him, would have said if he thought his grandchildren might all go to university.

Wrapped up in his thoughts, Harry was surprised when the two strangers stepped out in front of him as he walked along Poulton Road. They obviously weren't local men. Probably a couple of visitors, he thought, who'd wandered a bit off the beaten path and got lost.

'Need some help, then?' he said, smiling.

'Get in the car,' the one on the right said. He was a big fellow with a broken nose; the other one was slimmer, with dark brown hair and very bright blue eyes. Jesus, Harry thought, his heart leaping in his chest, he's got a fucking gun! He looked wildly about, but there was no one in sight. There was a grey Mercedes at the kerb, the rear door open.

'Lissen, what's this all ab — ' he began. The big man made an impatient sound and hit him on the side of the head with the pistol. Stunned, Harry reeled sideways. Rough hands bundled him into the car. He shook his head, hearing the doors slam. There was one of them one each side of him. Another one driving. He shook his head.

"'ere,' he said. 'You can't — '

'Sit still, Harry,' the man said. 'We're taking you home.'

Harry Jackson shook his head again, his brain still fuddled from the wicked blow; he could feel the sly trickle of blood down his face.

The car slid to a stop outside his house. The big man — Georges Barbier — handed Harry a pair of field-glasses.

'Take a look, Harry,' he said. 'Upstairs.'

The front bedroom had a nice big picture window. They'd had uPVC double glazing fitted earlier in the year. As he watched, the curtains parted and he saw Jessie at the window. She looked strange, stiff; her face was tight and tense. Then one by one, the three boys appeared. Michael was rubbing his eyes, as if he had been crying. Behind them, Harry could see the figure of a woman with dark hair. She had some sort of submachine gun in her hands. The muzzle was almost touching Michael's head. Before he could speak, the Mercedes slid away, leaving the house behind.

'Who's that woman?' Harry shouted. 'What's she doing with my family?'

'Be quiet, Harry,' the younger man — André Dur — said. 'We don't want to hurt you if we don't have to.'

Although he did not raise his voice, there was no mistaking the menace in it. Fear drowned Harry's anger. His legs felt loose, weak. A strange sense of unreality held him in thrall. His mind was a stunned blank. This just couldn't be happening. It couldn't be!

The driver of the Mercedes stopped opposite the Avesco garage on Copse Road. Harry could see the girl attendant at the cash desk inside. Occasionally a car went by, tyres burring on the cobblestones. Nobody took any notice of the Mercedes. If they killed him here no one would even know.

'What do you people want from me?'

'We want your boat, Harry,' André Dur said.

'My boat? What you want my boat for?'

'Never mind what for. Just do exactly

what we tell you, and everything will be fine. Give us the slightest trouble, I call my lady friend. And your wife and kids are dead, Harry. You understand me?'

'You — you wouldn't . . . '

'You do what we tell you and they'll be fine.' He leaned forward and tapped the driver on the shoulder. 'All right Lucky, let's get down to the dock.'

★ ★ ★

The docks were deserted; no one saw them board the trawler. Immediately they were aboard, Delormes got to work installing the oscilloscope. The other four swung the lifting tackle up to the dock level and wrestled the short, coffin-like crate out of the back of the stolen delivery truck in which Paul Gérard had brought it there. Working with great care, they manoeuvred the crate down to the deck of the trawler. Then they climbed back down to the boat, and helped Gérard remove the top of the crate.

They stared down at the missile. It was about seven feet long, as thick as a man's body, sleek and deadly, a masterpiece of miniaturization.

'Like a shark,' Delaguerre said.

'You've done a great job, Paul,' André said. 'Great.'

'Still quite a bit more to do,' Gérard said briskly, the watery eyes shining behind the granny glasses. 'I'd better get on with it.'

At about four, Delormes announced he was ready to do the underwater work on the hull of the trawler. André and Lucky Luke donned the wetsuits Delaguerre had bought at the scuba shop in Liverpool, and slid off the Dayglo yellow inflatable that had been purchased at the same time, into the murky water of the dock. The work was awkward and arduous; Delormes balanced precariously in the inflatable, handing the two men components, clucking instructions at them as they worked. It took them more than two hours to fit the scanners at bow and stern, and by the time they were finished they were exhausted. They crawled back aboard the trawler and gulped down hot coffee laced with whisky from the big

Thermos flasks they had brought aboard.

At about six-thirty, Delormes announced he was finished and invited them to come up to the bridge and inspect his work.

'What would be nice would be to have a computer like the big boys,' he grinned, sweating as he finished connecting the wiring along the steel walls. 'You know, they've got processing architecture now that can strip away ambient and natural sea noise to isolate the slightest man-made sound.'

'What we're looking for is four hundred feet long and the height of a three-storey building,' André told him. 'It travels at around thirty knots and displaces more than eight thousand tonnes. It shouldn't be too difficult to hear.'

Delormes smiled. 'It isn't a question of whether we hear her or not, André,' he said. 'It's more a question of how far away you want to be when the balloon goes up.'

'Amen to that,' Lucky Luke growled. 'How you doing down there, professor?'

Paul Gérard looked up and grinned, making a thumbsup sign. André Dur checked his watch. While they had been working, Harry Jackson had been locked in the midships cabin; it was time to get him ready. André swung open the door and stepped in over the coaming. Jackson was sitting on a chair at the far end. The crew quarters were a long way from luxurious; the cabin contained only a couple of battered old armchairs, four bunks and the poky little galley with its Primus stove and battered crockery. Stained and peeling centrefolds from *Playboy* decorated the flaking steel walls. It stank of cigarette smoke and male sweat.

'What time do your crew start arriving?' André asked the skipper.

Harry Jackson shrugged. 'Any time from eight o'clock on.'

'How many of them?'

'Five,' Harry replied. 'Six if you count me.'

'When they come aboard, keep them out of here, Harry. Understand?'

'They'll want to make tea. Stow their gear.'

André Dur reached forward and grabbed Harry Jackson's head between his hands, pulling him forward so that their faces were only inches apart. 'You're not listening, Harry,' he hissed. 'Watch my lips. Nobody in here, under any circumstances. Got it?'

Harry nodded.

★　★　★

High tide was at 12.49 a.m., and by ten-thirty the scruffy East Side Wyre Dock was ablaze with lights and movement. Trawlermen full of Fleetwood Arms beer shouted obscene greetings to each other, keeping one eye on the deckies swinging equipment and nets aboard, the other on the clock. Each boat was allocated its slot by the harbourmaster, and woe betide the skipper who missed his: everyone else would move up, leaving him last in the queue, which meant that by the time he got out to the fishing grounds, all the best locations would be staked out. No fish equalled no profits, and no profits equalled a disgruntled crew who'd damned soon find themselves another boat. You couldn't keep men if the money didn't come in regularly.

Jackson's crew were all on board by ten. There had been a couple of grumbles — no more than niggles, really — when he told them they couldn't use the crew cabin, but that was all. Once or twice, he found himself wondering what the hijackers had taken in there, but he decided in the end he really didn't want to know. He went about the business of readying the boat for sea, trying to act as naturally as he could. If any of the crew noticed how edgy he was, nobody said anything.

The twenty-minute hooter sounded at twelve twenty-nine, and the activity on the wharfs speeded up. Last-minute adjustments to tackle and equipment were made as crew got into their seagoing clothes and made ready to cast off. There were six hours or so of sailing ahead of them before the work really began, but there was still plenty to be done before they put out to sea. At twelve thirty-nine the ten-minute warning was sounded, and the roar of engines being started up drowned all other noise in the docks. Above, the ceaselessly circling gulls dipped and swooped in and out of the light, crying like souls in Hell. A pale new moon slid behind shifting cloud.

One by one, the trawlers moved toward the river, line astern and high in the water, turning north to follow the lighted buoys down the dredged channel leading to open water. The lighthouse at the estuary winked as they went past the end of the pier on the seafront and out over the shallow bay. Shouts echoed over the oily water as each boat set course for the fishing grounds, disappearing into the darkness until only their navigation lights were visible. On the radar in the harbourmaster's office they looked like a cluster of fireflies moving slowly up the screen.

The *Boy Christian* was well out to sea when the men with the guns appeared. Dave Hughes was the first to see them; he was mending a torn net when the door of the midships crew-room banged open and four men stepped out. They all wore black ski-masks and carried submachine guns. He could hardly believe his eyes.

'Flat on the deck!' one of them

snapped harshly. 'Hands behind your head. Do it!'

Hughes fell face-down on the nets he had been mending, his hands linked behind his wool-capped head. He risked a peep over his shoulder; one of the men was standing over him. The muzzle of the submachine gun looked like a cannon.

'Who . . . what's going on?' he asked, hoarsely.

'Shut up!' his captor snapped. He looked tough and capable, and Dave Hughes didn't argue. He watched as Harry Jackson and his mate, Joe Cleary, were hustled off the bridge. Another man herded the other three crewmen, Pete Naylor, Joe Storms, and Pete Bishop, astern. They moved like automatons: the enormity of what was happening was just beginning to dawn on them.

Georges Barbier stalked over. 'Move!' he said, and made an imperative gesture with the machine pistol. The door of the crew quarters was flung open with a metallic bang and the six seamen were hustled inside. Barbier swung the door closed and they heard the heavy metal bolts being slammed into place.

'What the fuck is going on, Harry?' Joe Cleary hissed at his skipper. 'Who are these people?'

Harry Jackson said nothing. They had told him to keep his mouth shut, and he wasn't going to open it, not for Joe Cleary or anybody else, until he was absolutely certain that Jessie and the boys were safe. They could keep the fucking boat, they could do anything they liked. All he wanted was his wife and sons to be all right.

'Bastards,' Dave Hughes said again into the darkness. He said it louder this time, putting more heat into the word; it made him feel better. Now the crewmen heard the sound of the *Boy Christian*'s engine deepen; they felt her begin to move faster through the long swells of the Irish Sea. Up on the bridge, André Dur looked at the bright pinpoints of light on the radar screen that were the other boats of the fishing fleet. There were not as many now, nor were they clustered so closely together. He knew at least half a dozen of them would be heading for the same area;

329

that would be enough. He watched as Henri Delaguerre set their course a few degrees north of west, taking them south of the Isle of Man, and from there another forty or so miles to the deep geological fault known as the Rat Run.

19

By the time the wheels of Garrett's Skyhawk touched the runway at Squire's Gate, Blackpool's municipal airport, a few minutes after 8 a.m., a massive security operation — codename PREVENT — was in motion. The harbour-master's office on the third floor of the redbrick dock and harbour board building in the East Dock was already a hive of activity, with electricians stringing cables and lights, radio technicians and Telecom engineers installing direct links with the British Royal Naval Submarine Establishment at Faslane, the United States Navy's COMSUBSUK — officer commanding submarines in the UK — at Holy Loch, the VLF submarine communications station at Criggion in Shropshire, the commander of SO.12, Special Branch, in the office of the chief constable of Lancashire at Lancaster, liaising with its sister organization SO.13 — the anti-terrorist branch — at Scotland

Yard, and the Search and Rescue unit of the Royal Air Force at Valley in Anglesey.

Commander Henry Fryer, head of the SO.13 unit assigned to this operation, was waiting at Squire's Gate in an unmarked car. As the police driver whisked them the ten miles up the coast to Fleetwood, Fryer briefed Garrett on the Danny Ackerley surveillance. It didn't take long: Ackerley had made no phone calls, kept no rendezvous.

'My guess would be he's already done whatever it was they needed him for,' Fryer opined.

'No report of a boat being stolen?'

'No.'

Garrett frowned. Could he have been completely wrong? No, dammit, he could not. He looked out of the window. The sea was bright and blue; it was going to be another beautiful day. He made a decision.

'Go straight to Sylvia Street,' he told the driver. 'Let's give Danny Ackerley a surprise.'

'You're going to blow the surveillance?' Fryer asked. He was a short, tubby man with plump cheeks and a salt-and-pepper moustache. He looked more like the chief clerk in a shipping office than an anti-terrorist officer.

'We're running a poor second all the way with these people, Commander,' Garrett said tersely. 'My bet is they've hijacked a boat and they're already on the water.'

'How could they have done that and not been seen?'

'I don't know,' Garrett said. 'But I know a man who does. And his name's Danny Ackerley.'

The police driver turned right into an avenue that led to the main road, and from there to the docks. Another right turn brought them into Sylvia Street. A seven-year-old boy was doing wheelies on a BMX bike on the sidewalk outside number thirty-seven. He watched Garrett and Fryer get out of the car with the unafraid curiosity of the very young.

Garrett banged on the door; there was neither bell nor knocker. No answer. He banged again, harder. This time he heard footsteps, the sound of someone coming down stairs, a querulous male voice wondering aloud who the bloody hell was banging on the door at this time of the morning.

The door swung open. Bleary-eyed and unshaven, Danny Ackerley wore a collarless shirt, work pants with the belt unfastened, and carpet slippers. He looked at Garrett uncomprehendingly.

'What's t'racket about, eh?' he asked pettishly. 'What the bloody 'ell's all t'racket?'

'Inside,' Garrett said. He grabbed Danny's arm and frogmarched him in. Fryer followed, leaving the front door open. The house had originally been a two-up, two-down, but the ground-floor rooms had been knocked into one. The newest piece of furniture in it was a television set. Apart from two greasy armchairs, there was a coffee table with a tile inlay, a rickety-looking china cabinet with a broken glass front, and an electric convector heater set into the tiled fireplace. The carpet was soiled and frayed; flies buzzed against the windows.

'Nice place you've got here,' Fryer

observed, wrinkling his nose, as Garrett shoved the struggling Ackerley into one of the armchairs. Danny started to get back up, putting an indignant expression on his foxy face.

'Lissen, 'oo the 'ell d'ye think you are, bargin' in — ?'

'Don't waste our time, Danny,' Garrett snapped. He shoved Danny back into the chair and laid photographs of André Dur and Georges Barbier on the coffee table in front of him. 'I want these two men. Where are they?'

Ackerley's sallow face changed, the rheumy eyes suddenly shifty. He fumbled in his pocket for a pack of cigarettes and lit one with a shaking hand, sucking in smoke greedily.

'Who are you?' Danny whispered, his eyelids fluttering, his voice cracking with fear. 'Police or something?'

'Something.' Garrett said. 'Now: talk!'

'He told me he was writing a book,' Ackerley said querulously. 'He needed to know about the boats.'

'But one boat in particular?'

'Aye. Harry Jackson's. The *Boy Christian*.'

'Quick, now, Danny — where does this Jackson live?'

'Rossall Avenue. It's off the Poulton Road.'

Garrett's eyes met Fryer's. The detective hurried out; through the window Garrett could see him using the carphone. So could Danny Ackerley. His fingers plucked at the worn moquette on the arm of his chair. His eyes were brimming with unease.

'He told you he was writing a book,' Garrett prompted.

'It was on the docks. He bought me a drink. I didn't know he was up to something.'

Once he started, it gushed out of him like water from a tap. Garrett listened, interpolating the occasional query. He could have guessed most of it. The technique was straight out of the handbook: find a lonely old man, buy him drinks, make him feel valued. Exploit his local knowledge to get to know about the skippers of the different boats, where they lived, their family, their friends. He looked up as Fryer came back in. The detective made a gesture. Garrett followed him into the hall.

'Something odd. I sent someone to check on Jackson's wife, Jessie. She insists everything is kosher. But the neighbours say the kids didn't go to school yesterday afternoon, and she didn't go out either. Jackson hasn't been seen since yesterday lunchtime.'

'You think she's had the frighteners put on her?'

'Could be.'

'By whom?'

'One of the gang. One who stayed behind. A woman, maybe. We'll see what we can find out.'

'What about the boat?'

'Sailed with the fishing fleet just before one a.m.'

Garrett frowned. 'And Jackson?'

'Assistant harbourmaster remembers seeing him on the bridge. I've told him to get the boat on ship-to-shore. What about him?' Fryer jerked a thumb at Danny Ackerley.

'He rented a place for them to use as a safe house; it's across the river at Preesall Park.'

'I'll get a forensic team out there right

away. What do you want to do with our friend?'

'Hand him over to Special Branch. Local slammer. I'll whistle up a team of dredgers. He's going to be looking at photographs until his eyes drop out.'

Dredgers — skilled PACT debriefing experts — would take Ackerley one by one through all the surveillance photographs of known associates of André Dur. Eventually, they would not only have the names of those involved in this operation, but know from their dossiers what kind of men they would be up against in the event of a confrontation.

'There's a car on the way,' Fryer told him. The sergeant driver appeared in the doorway. 'What?'

'Harbourmaster's on the phone, sir,' he said. 'Says he wants you at the dock immediately.'

They ran out of the house and Garrett snatched up the carphone.

'Harbourmaster, this is Garrett,' he said. 'What is it?'

'We made radio contact with Jackson's boat,' a dour Lancastrian voice replied.

'He's been hijacked.'

'Five minutes,' Garrett said.

They made it in four.

★ ★ ★

'*Boy Christian, Boy Christian*, this is Fleetwood harbourmaster. Respond, please.'

The litany had been repeated every five minutes for the past twenty-five; if the men on board Jackson's boat could hear it, they were making no effort to reply. Garrett went across to the harbourmaster's desk at the left-hand end of the console facing the picture window looking out across the River Wyre. Walter Bailey was a man of nearly fifty, with iron-grey hair and pale grey eyes with deep sunsquint wrinkles around them.

'Anything yet?'

Bailey shook his head.

'How many boats went out yesterday?' Garrett asked.

'From both docks? Se'nty fower.'

'Seventy-four. Do they all head for the same fishing grounds?'

'Course not,' said the harbourmaster,

scornfully. 'They're all over the bloody place by now.'

'Can you pick them up on your radar?'

Bailey smiled the patient smile of a man dealing with an idiot. 'Nice day, sun shining, no wind, we might — I says might — be able to pick up something forty miles out. Let the wind or the weather change and we wouldn't see it at six. We use radar to keep boats from bangin' into each other in the harbour, not to work bloody miracles.'

'The people in Jackson's boat will have gone out in the Rat Run. You know where that is?'

Bailey grinned, showing fine teeth. 'Be 'ard put to work round 'ere and not know that,' he said. 'Trouble we've 'ad 'th them nuclear subs.'

'Trouble?'

'Don't you read the papers, mate?' asked Fred Simpson, the fat man sitting next to him. Twinkling brown eyes like glass marbles pushed into pink dough regarded Garrett benignly. 'Submarines run into the fishin' nets, see, drags boats down and sinks 'em, then keeps on goin', see, like soddin' 'it-an'-run drivers. Never even stop to pick up survivors, they don't.'

Garrett remembered now that there had been questions in the House about the incidents involving nuclear subs and fishing boats.

'Have any boats been lost this year?'

'Aye, one. They said she had a collision. One of they Yank subs, the *Will Rogers*,' Simpson put in.

'I thought the Navy had agreed to warn the fishermen if a sub was coming out or going in?'

'Ar, up there round Holy Loch, they did. Not down here, though. Anything happens down here, the sailor boys don't want to know.'

The radio operator was still reciting his call to the fugitive ship. As he switched to receive, the empty hiss mocked his efforts.

'*Boy Christian, Boy Christian*, this is Fleetwood harbourmaster. Respond, please.'

'Fleetwood harbourmaster, this is *Boy Christian*. Are you receiving me?' The voice sounded harsh and metallic on the big speakers above the radar console.

Bailey strode across to the radio desk and grabbed the mike.

'Get a fix on this transmission!' he snapped at the technicians standing watching. 'Move, damn you!'

' . . . are you receiving me?' the speaker repeated.

'Receiving you loud and clear, *Boy Christian*. Identify yourself, please.'

'You know who I am. Listen carefully, because I will say this only once. We have Jackson and his crew as hostages. Six men. If any attempt is made to approach this vessel — *any* attempt, either by sea or air — they will be executed. Is that clear?'

'Understood, *Boy Christian*,' Bailey said. 'Now hear this: all nuclear submarine movement has been frozen. You can stay out there until Kingdom Come and you still won't have a target.'

'Do you take us for fools?' Dur sneered. 'We know the movements of those subs as well as you do. Probably better.'

Bailey turned to look at the technicians who were trying to get a fix on the radio

342

signal. *Keep him talking*, the technician at the console signalled.

'What about Jackson and his crew? How do we know they're safe?'

'You have my word for it,' André Dur said. 'Just remember what I told you: make sure nothing overflies us. If we so much as smell anything wrong, we will start killing the hostages.'

'Let me speak to one of them!' Garrett said. The speakers hissed emptily: Dur had switched off his transmitter. Garrett went across to the technicians at the big console.

'Well?'

The foreman shook his head glumly. 'We didn't have long enough,' he said. 'Another minute would have done it.'

'The men on the boat knew that too,' Garrett told him. 'Did you get anything at all?'

The technician stuck out his lower lip and shrugged. 'Not much.'

'Show me.'

Although the equipment used these days was infinitely more sophisticated, the technique for locating a radio transmitter remained pretty much the same as it had always been: directional trackers at different locations pinpointed the direction from which a transmission was reaching them. Where all the lines intersected was the location of the sender.

'It's only a rough guess, you understand,' the technician said, 'but it looks as if he's somewhere around . . . here' — he pointed to the map — 'about twenty, twenty-five miles east of Dundrum Bay.'

'Where the Mountains of Mourne sweep down to the sea,' Garrett said, reflectively. 'Small world, isn't it?'

'Sir?' the technician asked, puzzled.

Garrett shook his head. 'Sorry,' he said. 'Just thinking aloud.'

Sean Hennessy. Would he ever forget that final confrontation? Would that last astonished look on the terrorist's face ever fade from his memory?

A technician in white overalls appeared at Garrett's elbow. 'We've got your line to Faslane open, sir,' he said. Garrett went across to the co-ordinator's desk. By the time the various officers Nicholas Bleke had drafted in as a crisis management team arrived, the engineers would have the whole system up and running; right now it looked like a huge pile of multicoloured spaghetti. He glanced at the clock: ten-thirty. The crisis management team ought to be here any moment.

'Which line?' he asked the engineer.

'On your left,' the man said. 'Direct link to the RNSE operations room.'

'Faslane, this is Fleetwood,' Garrett said. 'Have you been briefed on PREVENT?'

'We've been on secondary alert since midnight, Fleetwood,' came the patient reply. 'What news do you have for us?'

'We have identification of the target vessel. She is the Fleetwood trawler *Boy Christian*, a hundred and twenty footer, blue hull, blue and white superstructure. Our estimate is she's somewhere between twenty and twenty-five miles east of Dundrum Bay. I want a TR-1 flight scrambled out of RAF Alconbury immediately.'

The Lockheed TR-1 tactical reconnaissance aircraft was a descendant of the more famous U-2R of earlier days, but infinitely more sophisticated. Equipped with astro-inertial navigation, phased array radar, UHF relay, data-link systems and sensor packages, the big bird could fly at a height of over 88,000 feet — far too high to be seen by the naked eye or detected by ground-based surveillance.

'I want high-definition photographs of the area that trawler is in, Faslane, and I want them yesterday, understood?'

'Understood, Fleetwood,' came the crisp answer. 'But wouldn't it be easier and quicker to get RAF St Mawgan to divert an AEW over the target area.'

'Negative,' Garrett said. 'An airborne early warning plane would be visible to the naked eye or radar. The hijackers have six hostages. They've threatened to kill them if we approach or overfly the trawler.'

'Understood, Fleetwood,' Faslane said. 'We'll notify Alconbury immediately.'

'What about sub movements? Have you frozen?'

'Sorry, Fleetwood,' was the flat reply. 'Can't tell you that. You'll have to wait till our liaison officer and his opposite number from COMSUBSUK are in place down there.'

'For God's sake, at least tell me if there's anything coming up the Rat Run in the next few hours!' Garrett snapped.

'I repeat, Fleetwood, I can't transmit that information until this channel is secured.'

'Get real, Faslane, haven't you heard that the Cold War is over?' Garrett growled exasperatedly. 'Who the hell are you keeping this secret from?'

'Some things change, Fleetwood,' Faslane replied unperturbedly, 'and some things don't. We still listen to Them. They still listen to us. Got it?'

'Then let me ask you something you can answer, Faslane,' Garrett said. 'Have you got an SDV up there?'

'Affirmative. Why do you ask?'

'Put it on standby,' Garrett told him. A swimmer delivery vehicle was, to all intents and purposes, a miniature submarine, not unlike the human torpedoes of World War Two, although usually these days employed without the explosive warhead. 'With something that can airlift it. Have you got a Chinook, or something like that?'

'Affirmative. But I'll need authorization — '

'You'll get it, Faslane,' Garrett gritted. 'Get back to me when that reconnaissance plane is in the air.'

'Garrett?' It was Walter Bailey, holding up a phone and pointing to it. 'Henry Fryer. Your VIPs have arrived.'

'Where are they?'

Bailey spoke into the phone, looked up again. 'Be here in ten minutes,' he reported, and hung up.

'Are we ready for them, chief?' Garrett asked the head technician. He had the harried look of a man who knows he is always going to be asked questions to which there is no adequate answer.

'Ready as we'll ever be,' he said, waving a hand.

The big third floor dock office was a simple rectangle, with the harbour-master's console desk facing north, its windows overlooking the estuary of the River Wyre. There were five seats: one for Bailey, one for Fred Simpson, another

348

for Charlie Dawes, the radar operator, a fourth for Mike, the radio operator, and a fifth for the fleet manager. Behind these, in a rough 'H', the ministry technicians had set up three more consoles. On the west side were the consoles with direct links to, respectively, SUBSATINFEX, to COMSUBSUK at Holy Loch, and to RNSE at Faslane. At the centre console would be the PREVENT co-ordinator, and opposite him the Ministry of Defence liaison officer. To the co-ordinator's left, on the eastern side of the room, were three more consoles, one for the use of the police co-ordinators, Special Branch and Lancashire Constabulary, one for Fryer of SO.13 and the third linked directly to RAF Search and Rescue at Valley.

Five minutes later, the VIP cars swept around the dock and eased to a stop in front of the harbourmaster's control office. The swing doors banged open and a phalanx of men in uniforms, led — to Garrett's surprise — by Nicholas Bleke suddenly filled the room with noise and activity. Several of them wore the black with silver trim of senior police officers, two the dark blue and gold braid of the Royal Navy, another the lighter blue of the Royal Air Force. Alongside Bleke stood a tall Army officer in tailored khaki, the red band of Military Intelligence on his cap. He spoke quietly to Fryer, who nodded and directed the various officers to their stations. While they inspected their respective facilities, Bleke came across to Garrett.

'Surprised to see you, chief,' Garrett said.

'Decided I'd better be here or hereabouts,' Bleke said, his voice crisp and decisive. 'What's the situation?'

Garrett told him in terse monosyllables, ending with a question.

'No,' Bleke replied. 'With the exception of Kennedy — he's the Army officer, Ministry of Defence liaison — none of them knows about Cosmos.'

'We'll have to tell them,' Garrett said. 'They'll need to know what we're up against.'

Bleke put a hand on Garrett's shoulder. 'As and when, Charles, as and when.' He walked to the centre of the room and rapped on the top of the desk with a pencil.

'Gentlemen,' he said loudly. The officers looked up expectantly. 'This is Charles Garrett, my executive officer. Next to myself he has complete authority here.' There were one or two murmurs of acknowledgement, but nothing more. 'Very well. Let's get started. Captain Lavery, get on to Faslane and find out if that reconnaissance plane is in the air yet. And check if they've frozen sub movements as we asked them. Captain Kieling, maybe you could do likewise with your people at Holy Loch.'

'Aye, aye, sir,' said Kieling. He was thin and blond, with prominent cheekbones and an angular jaw. He picked up his link and started talking. Peter Lavery, the Royal Navy officer acting as RNSE liaison, followed suit.

'Group Captain Hodge,' Garrett said. 'Tell your people I need a helicopter up here. Civil markings, not military.'

The young Royal Air Force officer picked up his unit and spoke rapidly into it. Bleke beckoned Garrett across.

'This trawler. What kind of equipment has it got?'

'Top-quality radar and sonar,' Garrett said. 'Of course, Dur may have taken extra equipment on board, an oscilloscope or even an MAD.'

'A what?'

'Magnetic anomaly detector. If a huge lump of metal — a submarine — is around, it disturbs the Earth's magnetic field. An MAD can detect that disturbance. It's pretty short-range stuff, five or six hundred yards to right and left, but it would be enough.'

'They'd have no trouble locating a submarine if one came within range?'

'None at all.'

'How would they launch Cosmos?'

'A guess? Probably from a towed drogue. Same principle as a minesweeper. Run a cable to her, with a switch to arm her and set her running simultaneously.'

Bleke stalked over to the big map on the wall, his mouth clamped shut. He shook his head exasperatedly. 'Damn them,' he said, as much to himself as to Garrett.

'RAF Valley reports helicopter en route,

sir,' Group Captain Hodge reported. 'ETA forty minutes.'

'What are they sending us?'

'Westland Wasp, HAS Mark One five-seater, sir.'

'Civil markings?'

'As you stipulated, sir.'

'Thank you, Group Captain,' Bleke said. 'Any news from COMSUBSUK, Captain Kieling?'

'Just coming through, sir. I'll put it on the PA.'

The big speakers hummed with static. A bored-sounding American voice filled the room. 'PREVENT, this is COMSUB-SUK. COMSUBSUK confirms there will be nil US movement in your target area tomorrow.'

'Sir!' It was Lavery, the young Royal Navy liaison officer sitting next to Kieling. 'Priority signal from Faslane!'

Bleke nodded. 'Let's hear it, Captain.'

'PREVENT, this is Faslane. VIPAR priority. We have a sub coming in.'

'Location?' Lavery asked.

'Fastnet. Approximately fifty miles south west of Old Head of Kinsale.'

Bleke picked up the microphone. 'Faslane this is PREVENT Leader. Can you signal her to stay away?'

'Already done, PREVENT Leader,' the speaker snapped back impatiently. 'That's not the problem.'

'Go ahead, Faslane.'

'There's a bandit — sorry, sir, force of habit — there's a Russian submarine moving north ahead of her into the Rat Run, trailing her from the front. We haven't got a proper fix on her yet, but she looks like a boomer.'

'Boomer?'

'Sorry, sir. Typhoon — or Mike-class nuclear bombardment submarine. Captain Lavery can brief you.'

'No way of contacting her?'

'We've tried, sir. She doesn't respond.'

'All right. Get on to Admiralty. Highest priority. Tell them to contact Russian Fleet Headquarters in Murmansk or wherever the hell it is. Tell them to divert that fish.'

'Affirmative, Fleetwood.'

'How long have we got?'

'We estimate she'll be inside target area

in less than six hours.'

'Stand by, Faslane,' Bleke said. He put down the mike and turned toward Captain Lavery. 'You'd better brief us, Peter,' he said.

'The Typhoons are the biggest fish in the sea, General,' Lavery said. 'Nearly five hundred feet long, over seventy-five in the beam. They displace around twenty-five thousand tonnes, so they're a good third larger than the biggest American boats.'

The Typhoon-class submarine carried twenty SS-N-20 solid-fuel rockets with a five-thousand-mile range, which had enabled it to fix on targets in Canada, the United States or Asia from its Barents or White Sea bases, he told them.

'She might even be carrying the newer liquid-fuelled SS-N-24 missiles; each one of those babies is capable of delivering ten independent warheads to within half a mile of a target.'

The Mike class was smaller, but only relatively speaking. Four hundred feet long, they carried sixteen SS-N-16 or -21 missiles; also Starfish and Stallion anti-submarine missiles with nuclear tips.

Fitted with titanium and liquid-metal cooled reactors fuelled by uranium 235 or plutonium, these vessels could dive deeper and travel faster than anything the Royal Navy or the United States Navy had in service.

'Crew?'

'Ninety-five on the Mikes. More on the Typhoons.'

Bleke's face was impassive, but everyone in the room knew what he was thinking. If the terrorists attacked the Russian submarine, the result would be a nuclear disaster that would make Chernobyl look like a Christmas cracker.

'Charles,' Bleke said. 'Lay it out for us.'

'Gentlemen,' Garrett said, his voice as level as if he were discussing what to have for dinner. 'In order for you to fully understand how grave the situation is, I have to tell you that the men aboard that fishing boat have stolen a secret weapon. It is called Cosmos. It is capable of independently locating and destroying any submarine that comes within a three-mile range.'

The naval officers exchanged glances.

Brigadier Kennedy's face set in instant disapproval. No one spoke; the atmosphere in the room was electric.

'These people have stationed themselves over the Rat Run in order to attack the first British or American submarine that comes along,' Garrett continued. 'Instead, we have a Russian vessel moving into harm's way. Unless we can find some way of contacting them, we cannot warn them of the danger. The terrorists have switched off their radio, so we can't contact them either. Comments and suggestions, please.'

'What about if we whistled up a Harrier strike, sir?' asked Group Captain Chris Hodge. 'Blow the beggars out of the water?'

'What about the hostages, Group Captain?' Bleke said.

'We're staring a major nuclear disaster in the face, General,' Hodge replied. 'I'd have thought in the circumstances half a dozen casualties would be an acceptable loss.'

'I agree,' Kennedy said forcefully. 'We can't risk the possibility that Cosmos might be used against a Russian vessel. A pre-emptive strike is the obvious solution.'

'Bastards!'

The word was quietly spoken, but everybody in the room heard it. Brigadier Kennedy's ears went bright pink. The speaker was the harbourmaster, Walter Bailey, who swung down from his seat at the console and headed for the exit, shoving aside DCI Martin Finey, the Special Branch co-ordinator. No one tried to stop him. Nobody spoke. As he reached the door, Bailey turned around to glare at all of them.

'Cold-blooded bastards!' he shouted. 'You don't give shit for anyone, do ye? Those are real men out there on that boat, you know, not fucking statistics!'

He slammed out of the room and the swing doors flapped in his wake. Bleke looked at Garrett; the big man shrugged. Walter Bailey was perfectly right, of course. But so was Kennedy. He looked at the clock. Twelve forty-two. Call it three hundred and eighteen minutes to crisis. The minute finger clicked up a notch. Three hundred and seventeen.

20

Scrambled out of Alconbury, a few miles northeast of Huntingdon, flying over four hundred and thirty miles an hour at seventy thousand feet, the Lockheed TR-1 of United States Air Force Europe's Ninth Strategic Reconnaissance Wing was on station above the designated surveillance area by 1330 hours. Fitted with two crosstrack F95 Mark 10 infra-red linescan cameras and an optical camera combination linked to a NAV-WASS digital computer for latitude, longitude, height, speed and attitude information, the big bird had completed its mission and was on its way back to base within fifteen minutes.

The Ninth SRW was doing its superb best, but time was running out. As the minutes ticked away, the faint outlines of an alternative resolution to the problem began to take shape in Garrett's mind. The question was, could it be pulled together in time? He went across to Bleke's console.

'I think there might be another way of stopping Dur,' he said. 'Do I have your okay to explore it?'

'What do you have in mind?'

'I've been thinking about what Hodge said.' Garrett said. 'Sanctioned termination. Take out Cosmos before they can launch it.'

'What do you need?'

'Builder's drawings of the trawler. And a free hand with COMSUBSUK and RNSE Faslane.'

'Take them as read,' Bleke said crisply. 'What else will you need?'

'A lot of luck,' Garrett said.

He went across to Captain Kieling, the COMSUBSUK liaison officer, and told him what he wanted. Next he explained RNSE's role in his scenario to Captain Lavery. That done, he called Lonsdale House, who patched him through to Eric Mackenzie at Hayling-Brittain. It was ten or fifteen minutes before he finished talking. He looked up at the clock. Two-fifteen. Over by the door, Commander Fryer lifted a hand. Garrett went over to him.

'Just got a report on the Preesall Park house,' Fryer told him. 'It's pretty clear the missile was assembled there.'

'That all?'

'We've also got a corpse,' Fryer said. 'Shot once in the back of the head and buried in the garden.'

'Halford,' Garrett said.

'You don't sound surprised.'

'It always figured that Dur would kill him once they had what they wanted,' the big man shrugged. 'He could only become a liability. Was there anything else of interest?'

'Your people got some names out of Danny Ackerley,' Fryer replied. The PACT dredgers had gone through André Dur's AKA dossier page by page with him, and Danny had picked out four of the terrorists from their photographs: Jacques Delormes, a former sonar officer in the French Navy; Paul Gérard, a one-time rocket assembly scientist; Henri Delaguerre, ex-charter captain and drug smuggler; a convicted terrorist and murderer named Laurent Schaimes; and a woman, Catherine Devieux, the former mistress of Action Directe's armourer, Pierre Warter.

'It fits the scenario,' Garrett said. 'The woman holds Jackson's wife and children hostage so Jackson will do exactly what Dur tells him. As soon as they're at sea, she lets Jessie and the children go. Probably told her to keep her mouth shut or they might just disappear on their way home from school.'

'My thoughts precisely,' Fryer said. 'I've asked Five for a watch on all airports and exit points. The odds are she's on her way to a prearranged rendezvous.'

Like the beautiful Elaine Harding, Garrett thought. How ironic it would be if she was waiting at some expensive European watering hole for Ian Halford to turn up with the account number she needed to get at the money.

Fryer nodded. 'Anything else?'

'Pass the word to Five that we don't want Dur's girlfriend taken. Let her run. If Dur gives us the slip for any reason, we'll need to know where she's going.'

'I'll keep you posted,' Fryer said.

Garrett looked at the clock again. Two twenty-five. The reconnaissance plane would have landed at Alconbury by now, and things would be happening very fast. Normal NATO rules demanded release of a field intelligence report of the processed film within forty-five minutes of engine-stop; because the PREVENT mission had maximum precedence, the USAFE reconnaissance unit had it through the automatic processing shelter and duplicated in half the usual time.

Locating and photographing the *Boy Christian* in so short a time was a remarkable achievement; but three hours were still three hours: two hundred and ten minutes to crisis.

'Well, Charles?' Bleke said. 'What do you think?'

'The photoanalysts at Laconbury were right, sir,' Garrett said. He tapped the hugely magnified colour photographs that were spread on the console in front of Bleke. 'That's her, all right. You can see the blue superstructure. That dark sliver out behind her is probably the paravane carrying the missile.'

'General.' It was Lavery, the Faslane co-ordinator. His tone was urgent. 'Faslane reports our bandit is now passing Ross-lare.'

'COMSUBSUK confirms, General,' Kieling echoed.

'Still moving north?'

'North, aye,' the American confirmed.

'No word from the Admiralty?'

'Nothing yet, sir.'

'I hate to admit this, but I'm beginning to think Kennedy is right,' Bleke said in an undertone. 'We may have to bite the bullet.'

'We've still got time,' Garrett said. 'Let me try my way first.'

'What's your readiness state?'

'Everything is on line. All we need is a go.'

'Let's try it out on the team, then,' Bleke said briskly. He picked up a glass paperweight and banged it on the desk. 'Gentlemen, your attention, please.'

Conversation ceased; the team of officers looked up from their consoles around the room.

'We're running out of time,' Bleke told

them. 'It's three hours from crisis, but we're no nearer a solution. Before we take irrevocable action, Garrett has an alternative scenario he would like you to consider. I want you to listen to it and to criticize any aspect of it about which you are uneasy. Go ahead, Charles.'

'There is a way of stopping the Cosmos launch without getting the hostages killed,' Garrett said. 'A one-man strike to sabotage the missile before Dur can fire it.'

'A one-man strike?' The speaker was Brigadier Kennedy, the ministry liaison officer. 'A suicide mission, you mean.'

'I won't pretend there isn't a high risk factor, but I'd give it at least a sixty per cent chance of success,' Garrett said. 'We've got the location of the *Boy Christian*. She won't move until Dur launches Cosmos. That gives us a chance to neutralize the missile. COMSUBSUK has positioned the submarine *George Washington* twenty miles southwest of the Calf of Man. A two-man SDV has been airlifted down to her from Faslane. A qualified operator and all the requisite sub-aqua equipment are ready. All that's necessary is for Group Captain Hodge to fly me out to the sub. She can take us to within range of the *Boy Christian*. We can launch from there and go the rest of the way underwater.'

'May I ask another question?' It was Kennedy's brittle voice again. 'You're not a missile engineer, Garrett. How do you propose to neutralize the missile?'

'I've spoken at length to Eric Mackenzie, the chief designer of the weapon at Hayling-Brittain,' Garrett said. 'Dur has to put Cosmos in the water to launch her. If she's in the water, we can get to her. From the photographic evidence, it looks as if Dur is planning to launch the missile from a paravane, a sort of maritime drogue. Mackenzie also says it's highly unlikely they've got the equipment they'd need to launch her by remote control, which means there will have to be an umbilicus from the trawler to the missile. If I can get near enough to cut it — '

'Won't they spot you on radar or sonar?'

'The SDV has special carbon fibre non-reflective tile cladding similar to the material they use on Stealth bombers. And she's very small. If by any chance they do spot her, the odds are they'll think she's a dolphin or a shark. They're looking for something much bigger.'

'But if you attack the boat, they'll kill the hostages,' Kennedy protested.

'They're going to kill the hostages anyway, General,' Garrett said flatly. 'What else can they do with them?'

Bleke looked at Garrett reflectively for a moment, then nodded. He turned to face the other officers.

'Comments, gentlemen?'

'I must say I am strongly opposed to sanctioning this ... escapade,' Kennedy said. 'In my opinion, as I said before, it's nothing less than a suicide mission.'

'Thank you, Brigadier,' Bleke said gravely. 'Kieling?'

'COMSUBSUK says go for it, sir.'

'What about RNSE?'

'Admiral Redcar wishes me to advise the General that he considers the mission worth undertaking, sir,' Lavery said. Bleke smiled. Charlie Redcar was an old friend.

'You'd appear to be outnumbered, Bill,' he said. Brigadier Kennedy shrugged and stared at his console, his body stiff with disapproval, his expression that of a man who has been overruled by fools. Bleke looked at the clock. A hundred and eighty minutes to crisis. Even if Garrett could pull it off, it was going to be damned close.

'General.' It was Lavery, his voice again urgent. 'Admiralty.'

'Go ahead, London.'

'Fleetwood, we've accessed SOVSUB-COM Murmansk. The sub is the *Boris Godunov*, Typhoon class, heading for base.'

'Have they contacted her?'

'Negative, Fleetwood. They can't talk to her. The sub had an onboard fire. Her radio transmission equipment was destroyed. The captain can neither send or receive. SOP in such circumstances is always the same. The captain is going exactly by the book. He's taking the boat home by the shortest route.'

'Then what the hell is he doing in the Irish Sea?'

'He was already there when they had the fire.'

'You've advised Murmansk that we have a problem?'

'We told them the bare facts.'

'And?'

'They said, and I quote, that they appear to have no option but to leave the resolution of the matter in your hands, Fleetwood.'

'That's nice of them. Anything else?'

'Negative, Fleetwood. Good luck.'

'We'll need it,' Bleke said. 'Thank you, London.'

He looked around the room.

'That's it, then, gentlemen,' he said. 'Garrett goes.'

'And if he fails?' Brigadier Kennedy asked.

'I'll be in the target area within an hour, General,' Garrett said, noticing Bleke's sombre expression. 'You'll still have plenty of time to launch a pre-emptive air strike if I can't cut the mustard.'

Bleke put a hand on Garrett's shoulder. 'Godspeed, lad,' he said.

* ★ ★

Lieutenant (j.g.) Bobby McCubbin, the officer selected to drive the Swimmer Delivery Vehicle, was a stocky young man of middle height, with a broad-planed face and a ready smile. He looked strong and capable in the black rubber wetsuit, twin scuba tanks strapped to his back.

'You ever ride in one of these contraptions before, sir?' he asked Garrett. They were standing on the slatted foredeck of the huge submarine, surfaced southwest of the Calf of Man, the rocky island off the southern tip of the Isle of Man. Further southwest, just below the horizon, was the target zone in which the *Boy Christian* had been located by the TR-1 from Laconbury. The SDV in which they were about to start their journey was standing on the cradle in which she had been carried out to the *George Washington* by a huge Boeing-Vertol CH-47B Chinook helicopter from Faslane. She looked like a cross between a torpedo and a bobsleigh, Garrett thought, with cockpits fore and aft.

370

'Can't say I have,' Garrett admitted. 'What's the plan?'

'You sit up front and I'll drive,' McCubbin grinned. 'We'll run along on the surface at about fifteen knots until we get within visual range, then go in maybe thirty-five feet down.'

'That fast?'

'She'll do a little better if we push her.'

'Sounds good,' Garrett said. 'Where are you from, Lieutenant?'

'El Paso, Texas,' McCubbin replied. 'Home of the Scud-Busters.'

'Been in the Navy long?'

'Marines, sir,' the American replied. 'Delta Force.'

The Delta Force unit, a direct descendant of the Green Berets, was the tough American equivalent of Britain's Special Air Services regiment. The Navy had given him a good backup man.

'You men ready down there?'

Amplified by the loud-hailer, the voice sounded metallic and flat. The two men looked up toward the command platform on top of the sail — what old-time submariners still called the conning tower

371

— over thirty feet above them. Looking down at them was Captain Jack Carlson, commanding the submarine.

'Ready, aye, sir!' McCubbin yelled.

'Stand by to submerge!' Carlson called. 'Three minutes, repeat, three minutes to klaxon. Good luck!'

McCubbin threw him a casual salute, turned to Garrett and pointed up at the cockpit.

'Up you go, sir,' he said.

'Stop calling me, sir. Charles will do fine.'

'Okay, Charles,' McCubbin said. 'All you need to know is, a flashing amber light means get ready either to dive or surface. A red light means we're going down, a green light means we're going up. Got it?'

'I think I can remember that.'

'Sorry,' McCubbin grinned. 'I've had to teach a lot of dumb rookies. One more thing: what depth are you cleared for?'

'Scuba? A hundred and fifty feet.'

'We won't go anywhere near that,' McCubbin said. 'Okay, all aboard. Let's get ready to put this fish into the water.'

Garrett clambered up the steel ladder fitted into the frame and got into the cockpit, strapping himself into the rubber webbing harness. McCubbin climbed up to the rear cockpit, and after a few more moments Garrett felt the enormous throb of the submarine's nuclear plant. A long wave washed along the foredeck as her nose started to dip beneath the water.

'Here we go!' McCubbin sang out, and the engine of the SDV fired, settling into a powerful hum as the *George Washington* sank beneath them. McCubbin made a sweeping turn to starboard as the huge sail sliced through the swell like a great metal shark, and then all at once the little SDV was alone on the ocean, her blunt nose smacking into the long swells as McCubbin ran her away from the vast undertow of the disappearing submarine.

The *George Washington* would turn back now, going deep and staying silent, using the lee of the Isle of Man to shield her from detection by the terrorist trawler. There she would wait for Garrett's signal or for the air strike that would follow in the event of his failure.

The two men in the miniature submarine pushed steadily southwestward across the sunlit sea. Garrett checked his watch. Sixty-eight minutes to crisis. He distributed his weaponry in the pouches and pockets on the heavy belt around his midriff, and checked the strap on his depth gauge. He was as ready as he would ever be. An amber light flashed on the fascia in front of him: the signal to prepare to submerge. He clamped the breathing mask on to his face, positioned the mouthpiece comfortably, waited. The amber light changed to red. He switched on his oxygen tank as he felt the attitude of the SDV change. Then they were beneath the water, rushing through a phosphorescent world of yellow-green, lighter above their heads, almost black beside and below them.

Garrett's whole mind was concentrated now on what lay ahead. The luminous dial on the depth gauge on his wrist told him they were moving on an even keel about forty feet below the surface. The amber light on the console in front of him began to flash, then changed to green;

McCubbin was taking her up. They rose very slowly, inches at a time, the light becoming steadily stronger. As the curved top of the sloping transparent watershield in front of him broke the surface, the upward movement stopped. The top of his head just out of the water, Garrett swivelled right and left to orientate himself. Ahead of them and slightly to their left was the rusty hull of a trawler. It was the *Boy Christian*, wallowing at anchor.

McCubbin took the SDV down again, and Garrett gave him a thumbs-up sign. They had agreed on radio silence from the outset: they had no way of knowing what kind of monitoring equipment the terrorists might have on board, but he still wanted McCubbin to know he admired the way he had so accurately piloted the little sub to their destination. Now they ran below the trawler. If the men aboard were going to spot them on sonar, Garrett thought, it would be now.

He felt the engine slacken, and looked up. The black bulk of the boat was directly above them, blocking out the light. He released the harness and raised himself far enough to be able to see the pale blur of McCubbin's face in the rear cockpit. He pointed upwards three times. McCubbin responded with a thumb-and-forefinger circle, okay, go ahead. As Garrett kicked free of the boat, the American gave the engine a little blip and took the SDV up ten feet or so. She was now directly beneath the hull of the trawler, completely invisible to anyone on board or any surveillance equipment they might be using.

Garrett swam in a long rising line away from the trawler, staying below the surface until he was sure he was a good twenty yards astern of her. He allowed his head to break surface for a moment, just long enough to orient himself. The *Boy Christian* was riding high in the water; he could see no one on deck. A long cable stretched out from her stern, dipping into the water off to Garrett's right. He turned around, and now he could see the long, cigar-shaped paravane with its red flag, perhaps sixty feet away. He dived beneath the surface and swam toward it.

The paravane was about eight feet long, an aluminium canister with an aerodynamic shape. He swam closer until he could see the cradle assembly, professionally constructed from angle-iron and steel tubing. The stubby shape of the Cosmos missile was clearly visible below the surface, its blunt nose pointing away from the trawler. Simple, he thought. As soon as the target was within range, they would get under way, paying out cable until the paravane was a long way behind them. Once the missile was activated, they would make their best possible speed away from the explosion zone ten miles to their rear.

He eeled beneath the cradle. Inch by inch he moved down the slick anodized casing, searching for the input socket for the electrical cable which would carry the impulse to activate the missile. Mackenzie had told him to look for it about two feet back from the nose. Eventually, he found the small circular indentation which the engineer had described. He trod water, staring at it.

There was no cable.

Garrett stifled a curse. Somehow or other Gérard, the renegade rocket engineer, had worked out a way to activate the missile by remote control! He eeled back to the missile and stared at its silver skin. It would take an expert with specialist tools and knowledge, working in laboratory conditions, at least fifteen minutes to remove any of the flush-fitted inspection covers that allowed access to the machinery of Cosmos. Working underwater, it would take him at least twice that long. There just wasn't time.

From the pouch on his belt he pulled out the two-pound wodge of plastic explosive and packed two large lumps of it into the metal carrier housing the missile. Into each he inserted a slim metal detonator. The remaining half-pound or so of C4 he packed into the C-pin hasp fastening the cable to the carrier, then pushed in the third and final detonator. That done, he swam down beneath the hull of the trawler, homing in on the pinpoint of light that identified McCubbin's location.

The American's face was hardly visible

in the gloom; Garrett switched on his torch so that they could see each other. Behind the glass mask, McCubbin's eyebrows were raised in anticipation. He made a thumbs-up, meaning all okay? Garrett shook his head, no, and reached into the SDV for the message slate.

NO CABLE, he printed. UNABLE NEUTRALIZE MISSILE. C4 IN PLACE.

McCubbin took the slate. DETONATE AND LET'S GET OUT OF HERE, he wrote.

GOING TRY RESCUE HOSTAGES, Garrett scribbled.

McCubbin's eyebrows met in a frown. He gestured at his watch. Garrett nodded. The Russian submarine would very soon be within range of the trawler's sonar. He pointed up at the hull above them.

FIFTEEN MINUTES, he wrote on the slate. IF NOT BACK BY 1800 SIGNAL BLEKE LAUNCH AIR STRIKE.

McCubbin shrugged and gave the thumbs-up signal again. Garrett slid out of the scuba harness; he inhaled good lungfuls of oxygen prior to taking off the mask and removing the mouthpiece. He put the tanks into the SDV, gave a powerful kick, and surged up away from the SDV and around the barrel bottom of the trawler's hull, surfacing below the stern. He kicked off the webbed flippers as he reached up to grab the paravane cable, going carefully up it hand over hand until his nose was level with the bulwark.

He thought he could hear voices, but there was no one in sight. He eeled over the side of the boat and flattened himself against the steel wall of the crew quarters. There were two doors: one opening on to the stern fantail, the other about twenty feet up the deck. He eased toward the nearer one and tried the handle. It was locked, probably from the inside. He came back around the corner of the cabin, slithering along the steel wall toward the forward door at the foot of the stairway leading up to the bridge. As he did the door opened outward, between him and whoever was on the other side. The man stepped over the coaming and on to the deck, turning to close the steel door. Garrett recognized him immediately from the AKA dossier photographs as Jacques Delormes.

Delormes saw him and froze, his eyes wide with shock. His hand darted for his hip pocket but Garrett was already moving, the edge of his right hand whipping like a swordstroke, smashing into Delorme's Adam's apple and paralysing his vocal chords. He reeled backwards and dropped to his knees, eyes bulging, fighting to draw breath. Garrett hit him above the ear with the barrel of the ASP Smith & Wesson and the big man folded to the deck like a dropped marionette.

Almost without breaking his stride, Garrett grabbed the handle of the cabin door, opened it, and lifted the inert body over the coaming and into the crew quarters. He closed the door and turned to see six astonished faces staring at him. The crew of the *Boy Christian* were sitting in a rough semicircle on the floor, hands and feet bound.

'Who the fuckinell are you?' one of them gasped.

'Quiet!' Garrett hissed. 'Keep your voices down. Now — which of you is Harry Jackson?'

'I am,' Harry Jackson whispered. 'What's going on, mate?'

'Is there anyone in the engine room?'

'That feller there just came out of it,' Jackson told him. 'There's no one else down there.'

Garrett went across to him and sliced through the ropes binding his feet and arms. Then he handed the broad-bladed commando knife to Jackson and told him to cut his crewmen loose.

'How many on board besides this one?' he asked as Jackson went to work.

'Five more,' Jackson said. 'Who are you, anyway?'

'There's no time for that now,' Garrett told him impatiently. He gestured at the prone body of Delormes. 'Use some of that rope to tie him up. Can any of you men use a gun?'

'I can.' The speaker was a thin, lanky man with a deeply lined face on which a lopsided grin was pasted. 'I was in the Army.'

'What's your name?'

'Joe Storms.'

'Seen one of these before?' He handed Storms the other pistol he had brought with him. The crewmen looked at it as if it might bite.

'Aye,' Storms said, hefting the weapon in a horny hand. 'The old Colt .45 M1911 Automatic. Yank officers used to have them.'

'This is the Combat Commander model,' Garrett said. 'Kicks like a mule, but anyone you hit with it will fall down.'

Storms nodded tensely.

'Here's what I want you to do, Joe. Go astern, climb up on the roof of this cabin. There are two or three gas cylinders up there. I want you to lift one over the rail, drop it down on to the deck on this side, starboard. Can you do that?'

'Aye.'

'Someone will come out to see what the hell is going on. It may be one man, it may be two. The minute they show their faces, start shooting.'

'You mean . . . to kill?'

'Just keep pulling the trigger,' Garrett

said. 'Here's an extra clip of ammo. You've got eighteen shots. Don't worry about aiming, just turn loose and keep shooting, okay?'

'And what about the rest of us?' Jackson said. 'Do we just sit on our backsides and do nothing?'

'They'll be using real bullets out there, Harry,' Garrett told him unsympathetically. 'Keep your head down till the shooting stops. And that's an order. You ready, Joe?'

Storms nodded. He was sweating and breathing heavily, but there was a determined look in his eyes that told Garrett the older man was going to be all right. He eased the door open a crack, checked outside. There was no one in sight. He opened the door and stepped out; Storms followed. Garrett led the way astern. Joe climbed the five-rung ladder to the roof of the crew cabin. Garrett nodded and gave him a thumbs-up sign. Joe stuck the Colt into the waistband of his pants, lifted one of the eighteen-kilo gas cylinders over the rail and dropped it on to the deck. It landed on the wood with a thick, heavy sound and then as the ship moved on the long swell, it rolled against the metal cabin wall with a metallic clang.

Someone on the bridge shouted something. The gas cylinder made another huge clang as it rolled across the deck and hit the steel bulwark of the trawler. The flattened bark of the Colt was followed by a scream of fear or pain. Storms fired again, again, again, again; and then there was another metallic sound, the vicious *brrrrrrraaapppp* of an automatic weapon. By this time Garrett was at the door on the port side of the bridge. He wrenched it open, threw in the stun grenade and went in behind it shooting.

The three men inside the cramped bridge cabin never had a chance. That was the way they had taught Garrett in the 'killing house' at the SAS training centre in Hereford. No hesitation, no compromises. You were there to kill. Four seconds after he went in all three of them were dead. Garrett hardly paused in his forward momentum, going over the sprawled bodies and out of the door on the starboard side of the trawler.

At the foot of the steps a dead man was sprawled face down in a spreading pool of blood. The body of Joe Storms, also dead, was slumped in a sitting position in the metal angle formed by the bulkhead of the bridge and the side of the funnel. The door of the crew quarters was open. He inched forward warily.

'Garrett!' a harsh voice yelled from inside. 'It's over! Put down your gun or we kill the crew now. You hear me?'

We, Garrett thought. Dur and one other. Which one? 'All right!' he shouted. 'I'm putting my gun down. On the deck.'

'I'm watching you through the window,' Dur warned him. 'Kick it away from you. Toward the stern.'

Garrett kicked the gun away. It spun across the deck and hit the twin capstans with a metallic clunk.

'Lie face-down on the deck, hands behind your head!' Dur yelled. 'Do it fast, damn you!'

Garrett stretched out on the deck in the position he had been told to assume. Behind him he heard them coming out of

386

the crew cabin, and then they were standing looking down at him.

'Bastard!' the man with Dur said, and kicked him savagely in the ribs. Garrett hunched up with pain, and the man kicked him again.

'Let me kill the sonofabitch, André,' he panted. 'Let me kill the bastard right here.'

'Not yet, Lucky,' Dur said. 'Not yet. Get up, Garrett. Stand with your back against the cabin wall.'

Garrett got to his feet and did as he was bidden. The whole of his right side was throbbing with pain where Schaimes had kicked him.

'You're harder to kill than I expected, Garrett.' Dur grated, his handsome face a tight mask of anger. 'How did you get here?' He stuck the barrel of his machine pistol into Garrett's belly, eyes alight with the lust to kill. 'Talk, you bastard, or I'll cut you in two!'

'He brought me,' Garrett said, gesturing with his chin. Crouched in the classic shooting stance beside the bridge companionway, a short-barrelled .357 Magnum

Sterling revolver in his hands, was Bob McCubbin.

'Freeze!' he yelled.

Lucky Luke Schaimes whirled like a cat, but he was a good second too late. McCubbin's first shot hit him just above the heart on the right-hand side of his chest, and the second high on the right side of his forehead. McCubbin's third shot hit André Dur between belt and breast, drawing a shout of agony from the terrorist as it ripped through his body. McCubbin's fourth shot was too hasty, and merely clipped Dur's temple, knocking him to his knees.

Before McCubbin could fire again, Dur squeezed the trigger of the Uzi, spraying shots wildly. They screamed and ricocheted off the steel upperworks, scouring huge gouges out of the paintwork. One of them hit McCubbin high on his left thigh, and he collapsed on the deck with a shout of pain. As McCubbin fell, Garrett lashed out with his right foot, trying to kick the Uzi out of Dur's hands. With a roar of rage the terrorist surged to his feet and blindly struck out at Garrett with it.

Half-stunned, Garrett reeled against the steel wall of the crew cabin, bracing himself for the shock of the bullets as André Dur swung the Uzi round to kill him.

In that same microsecond McCubbin, his face twisted in pain, levered himself upright, fired again at Dur, then passed out. Garrett heard the meaty smack of the bullet as it hit the terrorist. He dropped the Uzi and reeled toward the stern of the trawler, hunched over in agony, a gouting track of blood marking his passage across the six or eight yards of deck. Pawing blood from his eyes, Garrett lurched after him, snatching up the Uzi from the scuppers where it had lodged. Dur was standing facing him in the stern, his eyes glazed with agony. What the hell was keeping him up? Garrett thought angrily. Dur was fumbling in his pocket, trying to get something out, but he had no control over his hands. Garrett knew what it was. He raised the Uzi and steadied himself. André Dur spat blood at his feet as Garrett pulled the trigger.

Nothing happened; the magazine was empty.

André Dur made a sound that would have been a triumphant laugh; it came out as a strangled cackle.

'*L'audace!*' he croaked, '*toujours l'audace!*'

He turned round and fell forward over the stern and into the sea, flailing clumsily at the water, moving away from the trawler, his head bobbing between the waves. Garrett ran to the rail. The terrorist was already about fifty yards astern of the trawler. It was astonishing. The man had been dead on his feet, yet he was still out there, still moving, swimming toward the paravane. And he still had the remote control device in his pocket. Slowly, almost reluctantly, Garrett reached into the pouch on his belt and took out the miniaturized radio transmitter that would detonate the explosives he had placed.

His face like stone, he threw the switch.

21

Across Christ Church Meadow the buildings of Oxford shimmered in the afternoon sun. Ducks foraged busily on the river, cheeping chicks behind them. Earlier, they had seen a heron.

'I'm glad we did this,' Garrett said. 'And I'm even gladder you finally met my parents.'

'I like them,' Jessica said. 'They don't expect one to . . . perform.'

'My father says you're a bobby-dazzler,' he told her.

Jessica laughed in surprise. 'A what?'

'A bobby-dazzler. Something special. And he's right.'

She hugged his arm. 'It's nice to have you all to myself,' she said. 'No London, no . . . any of it.'

He was always aware of how she felt about what he did, about his unswerving loyalty to Nicholas Bleke. She saw it as an exchange for unlimited protection, and that sometimes raised a barrier between them. Jessica knew that when the occasion demanded he killed for his country; that made it difficult for her to commit herself fully to the love he knew she felt. His commitment to her was unconditional, but that did not diminish his commitment to what he did. Those were ghosts both of them had to exorcise; but they were not here, not now.

He had told her only a little, and that in the most general terms, about the events in which he had been involved. Nothing of what had happened at Fleetwood or on the Irish Sea had appeared in the newspapers, and nothing ever would. To all official intents and purposes, Operation PREVENT had never taken place, André Dur and the terrorists who died with him on the *Boy Christian* had never existed. A liberal compensation package had been worked out for the widowed mother of the dead Joe Storms. The rest of the rescued trawlermen, happy to be safely home, had signed the Official Secrets Act within an hour of landing. No loose ends: that was the way Nicholas Bleke liked it.

'Let's walk into town,' Garrett said. 'I want you to see Magdalen Tower.'

They crossed Folly Bridge and walked up towards Pembroke College.

' "Sweet city with her dreaming spires",' Jessica said.

'Who said that?'

'Matthew Arnold, I think. But it must have been before all these grockles got here. Come on, let's cross over.'

The sidewalks were jammed with pedestrians, youngsters in shorts and T-shirts, men in open-necked shirts with summer-frocked wives pushing baby buggies, older visitors clutching maps. They walked through the cool, silent Memorial Garden, and along Merton Street. Their footsteps echoed off the old stone walls.

In the busy High Street a raucous crowd of shaven-headed young men in ill-fitting T-shirts and cheap, gaudy cotton Bermuda shorts was milling about in front of Magdalen College. Somebody had a ghetto-blaster; the heavy thump of rock music cut through the softer sounds of the afternoon.

'City of dreaming spires,' Garrett said tightly.

'Charles,' Jessica said, gently touching his arm.

'All right,' he replied, letting his breath out slowly. 'All right.'

It had been his idea to come to Oxford for the day, to walk along the banks of the Isis to St Edmund Hall, his old college. As they walked, he told her how, in his first year, he had walked to this spot in the darkness preceding dawn to attend the Carolling of the May.

'Sounds positively pagan,' Jessica mused.

It was certainly an ancient custom. The first day of May was celebrated with a salute from the choir of Magdalen College. In the pre-dawn chill, young men from the college and boys from the school attached to it, dressed in white surplices and ruffs, had climbed the steep narrow stairway to the top of Magdalen Tower like a living enactment of the Holman Hunt painting. As dawn broke the choir would burst into joyful song.

'It must have been lovely,' Jessica said.

'It was all of that,' Garrett nodded. 'If

you weren't up early enough to follow the choir up to the top of the tower, you waited in the street. You had to strain to hear the music. Now . . . '

He shrugged. In 1976, seven years after he came up to St Edmund Hall, the pollution-raddled Magdalen Tower had been completely rebuilt; it was now a replica, younger in fact than Disneyland.

'All part of the theme-parking of Britain,' he said. 'Lager louts on the streets instead of dew-wet students. And the choir replaced by an electronic relay.'

As he spoke, the crowd of youths across the street raised a ragged, drunken cheer. The one with the ghetto-blaster turned up the volume, the tinny thud of the heavy metal rock drowning out the lighter sounds of the summer afternoon. Then, as if at a signal, they swept up the High Street *en masse*, capering and shouting, scattering startled shoppers and alarmed camera-hung tourists. Garrett made an angry sound.

'Charles,' Jessica said, touching his arm again. 'You do what you do. You can't do this as well.'

'You're right,' Garrett said. 'Let's get the hell out of here.'

They went back to where he had parked the car, and got in without speaking. He put the key in the ignition, but did not start the engine.

'I'm sorry, Jess,' he said. 'Was it an awful letdown?'

'One ugly part doesn't spoil all the beautiful parts,' she said softly.

He started the engine again and they moved off, taking the A34 towards Woodstock. He shook his head sadly.

'This used to be a hell of a good country, Jess,' he said. 'What's happened to us?'

'You sound like 'Disgusted of Tunbridge Wells',' she laughed.

'I can't help it. It makes me angry.'

'You mean, like people who say 'at this moment in time' when they mean 'now'?'

He looked at her, puzzled for a moment. Then he remembered. Jessica had invented a de-stressing game which she called TWIGTHIAH — The World Is Going to Hell in a Handbasket. The idea was to play it when you got angry or frustrated by things you couldn't change.

'Ah, yes,' he said, smiling now. 'And people who say 'at the end of the day'.'

'Them, too,' she said. 'And motorbike dispatch riders who leave on their two-way radios while they deliver.'

'Theme parks.'

'Kissograms.'

'People who turn right on roundabouts without signalling.'

'Radio phone-in programmes.'

'T-shirts with jokes on.'

'Banks where a light comes on to show which teller is available.'

'All right,' he said. 'Better now.'

'Good,' Jessica said. 'You are definitely not lovely when you're angry.'

'Don't get shmart, shister,' he said with a Bogartian lisp. 'I never met a dame yet dat couldn't be improved by a shmack in da mouth.'

Jessica laughed out loud. 'Charlton Heston, right?'

Ten miles outside Oxford he turned down the unmarked road that led to Great Oxenham. They drove through the village, English-pretty with its pond and ducking stool and old wooden stocks, the stout square tower of its Norman church poking its head above the red-tiled roofs of the Cotswold stone houses. A little further on was the entrance to Homefield Hall. From the road a wide drive swept in a long curve up the hill, passing between mature beechwoods and fields until it reached the gravel courtyard fronting the building.

The Hall stood on a bluff overlooking the valley in which Great Oxenham nestled. Of extended E-shape, with its façade of warm sandstone and Georgian windows fronting and uniting much older buildings, it was at once unpretentious and grand. The house had belonged to the Heathcoats — Lady Garrett's family — since the time of Charles II; the first of them, also a Charles, had been a young Scots soldier of fortune who marched south from Coldstream with George Monk, Duke of Albemarle, and helped make the Restoration possible.

'Something smells good,' Garrett observed as they entered the house. 'Let's go and see if Anna has any tea.'

Anna was the cook-housekeeper, a buxom, ruddy-cheeked, German-born woman whose husband, John Grimes, looked after the gardens and the 150-acre estate. She was busy at the kitchen table, but got up, her face wreathed in smiles, wiping her hands on her apron as Garrett and Jessica came in.

'Mr Charles, sir,' she beamed, 'you're back early.'

'Town was a bit crowded,' Garrett said. 'Can we have some tea?'

'I'll put the kettle on,' she said. 'Oh, and by the way, there was a call for you. Your office.'

'I'll call them,' Garrett said. He went over to the cooker and lifted lids. 'What are you cooking?'

'Roast duck,' she said. 'New potatoes and beans picked fresh today by Mr Grimes.'

'Yum yum,' Jessica said, as Anna filled the kettle, then put some china cups and saucers, a jug of milk and a pewter sugar-bowl on a silver tray.

'Where are my parents, by the way?' Garrett asked.

'Sir George has taken the dogs for a walk,' Anna told him. 'Lady Garrett is upstairs.'

The Garretts lived in a comfortable suite in the east wing. The billiards room, the library and the big dining-room were kept open for entertaining, but a good half of the twenty-eight rooms were shut except during the season, when there were house parties most weekends.

'There you are, now,' Anna announced. 'Tea's ready.'

'You have yours,' Garrett said to Jessica. 'I'll be right back.'

He went into the hall and dialled Liz James's direct number. Her familiar cool voice replied almost at once.

'Out here in the country it's lovely and sunny,' Garrett announced. 'We're just having tea. A little later we're having roast duck and I'm going to see if I can't persuade my father to open one of those rather fine bottles of Château Margaux he laid down about six years ago. How are things in the big city?'

'Don't ask,' she said, with a theatrical groan. 'He wants to speak to you.'

'Charles?' Nicholas Bleke's voice came on the line. 'When are you coming back to London?'

'I thought I'd stay down here for the weekend,' Garrett said. 'Unless there's something — '

'No, no,' Bleke said, as if the words were being squeezed out of him against his will. 'Just . . . I've been reading your report.'

Garrett waited.

'I see they picked up the woman, Devieux.'

'They had a prearranged rendezvous,' Garrett said. 'Devieux took a ferry from Fleetwood to the Isle of Man, and then another to Dublin. When she got there she rented an eight-seater minibus. She was carrying false passports and money when they picked her up. André Dur was going to sail the trawler into Dundalk Bay and abandon it. Devieux would pick them up off the beach and drive them to Dublin. Then they'd all take planes.'

'Gathered all that from the report,' Bleke said. 'You took a hell of a chance, boarding that boat on your own.'

'I'd considered the alternatives, sir,' Garrett reminded him. 'Any other way and Dur would have killed the hostages.'

'I know that. All the same, it was lucky for you that American decided to join in. How is he, by the way?'

'McCubbin? He's fine. I talked to him on Friday. He'll be out of hospital by now.'

'And Dur? The Navy never found his body?'

'I never thought they would. There were nearly three pounds of C4 on that paravane. He was right above it when it exploded.'

'That reminds me, the ministry is not best pleased at your sending their secret weapon to the bottom of the Beaufort Dyke,' Bleke told him. 'They have made their displeasure known in no uncertain manner.'

There was no point in rising to that one. The ministry would have been even less pleased if he'd brought the damned thing back on Harry Jackson's boat so the local press could take photographs of it.

'Is there anything else?' he asked Bleke.

'As a matter of fact, there is,' Bleke said briskly. 'I've had word from Six that they've located Bletchlock's secretary. She's in Zurich.'

'Surprise, surprise,' Garrett said. Elaine the fair, Elaine the lovable. Where else would she have gone? 'Will any action be taken against her?'

'It's not likely,' Bleke said. 'The woman hasn't broken any laws.'

'Does Six know if she got hold of Halford's money?'

'They're trying to find out. You know what those Swiss banks are like.'

'I thought they had a new policy. Sort of bankers' *glasnost*.'

'If they have, it doesn't work any better than Gorbachev's,' was Bleke's response to that. 'I gather Six are sending someone out to interview her anyway. Just for the record.'

They'd be wasting their time, Garrett thought; Elaine Harding would lie and lie, and in the end, because they had no leverage, they'd give up in disgust. Whereupon Elaine the fair, Elaine the sweet, Elaine the stainless steel of

Amersham would be what the Americans called home free. For women with the kind of money she had, there was always a Prince Charming waiting somewhere. And if one didn't come looking for her, she could always go out and buy one.

'Well,' Bleke said reluctantly. 'Good to talk to you, Charles.'

'Thank you, sir,' Garrett said. He turned to see Jessica standing in the doorway, a teacup in her hand. She pointed at him and then at it. 'I'm being called for tea.'

'Your mother?'

'No, sir, Dr Goldman.'

'Ah,' Bleke said thoughtfully. 'Jessica is with you?'

'Indeed she is.'

'Down there for the weekend? Meeting your parents?'

'That's right.'

'I see . . . ' Bleke said. There was a pregnant pause. 'Anything . . . significant about that, Charles?'

Jessica put the teacup down on the table next to the telephone. She picked up the notepad, wrote something, laid it down where he could see it, and then started up the stairs. When she got to the top she fluttered her eyelids, did an exaggerated bump and grind, then disappeared along the landing towards her room. Garrett picked up the pad. It said:

VOUCHER:
GOOD FOR THE USE OF MY BODY
IF PRESENTED WITHIN THE NEXT
TEN MINUTES.

'I was just wondering, Charles,' Bleke was saying. 'I mean, you haven't got anything . . . rash in mind, have you?'

Garrett grinned. 'Who?' he said. 'Me?'

THE END

We do hope that you have enjoyed reading this large print book.

Did you know that all of our titles are available for purchase?

We publish a wide range of high quality large print books including:
Romances, Mysteries, Classics
General Fiction
Non Fiction and Westerns

Special interest titles available in large print are:
The Little Oxford Dictionary
Music Book, Song Book
Hymn Book, Service Book

Also available from us courtesy of Oxford University Press:
Young Readers' Dictionary
(large print edition)
Young Readers' Thesaurus
(large print edition)

For further information or a free brochure, please contact us at:
Ulverscroft Large Print Books Ltd.,
The Green, Bradgate Road, Anstey,
Leicester, LE7 7FU, England.
Tel: (00 44) **0116 236 4325**
Fax: (00 44) **0116 234 0205**

Other titles in the
Linford Mystery Library:

DR. MORELLE AND THE DOLL

Ernest Dudley

In a wild, bleak corner of the Kent Coast, a derelict harbour rots beneath the tides. There the Doll, a film-struck waif, and her lover, ex-film star Tod Hafferty, play their tragic, fated real-life roles. And sudden death strikes more than once — involving a local policeman ... Then, as Dr. Morelle finds himself enmeshed in a net of sex and murder, Miss Frayle's anticipated quiet week-end results in her being involved in the climactic twist, which unmasks the real killer.

THE THIRTY-FIRST OF JUNE

John Russell Fearn

There were six people in millionaire Nick Clayton's limousine when it left a country house party to return to London: Clayton himself, and his girlfriend Bernice Forbes; Horace Dawlish, his imperturbable servant and driver; the unhappily married financier Harvey Brand and Lucy Brand; and the tragic socialite Betty Danvers. But neither the car, nor its six occupants, would ever arrive in London. Instead, just after midnight, the car travelled some thirty miles along the country road — and disappeared . . .